Dark White

Neil Christiansen

Weathered Press

ISBN: 979-8-9899158-0-4

This book is a work of fiction. Names, characters, places, and incidents either are the product of the author's imagination or are used factiously, and any resemblance to actual persons, living or dead, businesses, companies, events, or locales is entirely coincidental.

Weathered Press
205 E Butterfied Rd
PBM 447
Elmhurst, IL 60126

Cover art by Neil Christiansen

To my father, Dr. James Christiansen,
for always supporting my dreams
no matter how unlikely they seemed.
You're the smartest man I've ever known
and my only real hero.

For Gayle,
Thank you for being the inspiration of this book
with your dry wit, and deep loving nature.
I love you.

Prologue

October 5, 2019 5:38 P.M.

He was asleep. A post coitus nap after an hour of afternoon lovemaking. So typically male. She had held him afterwards, pressing her body against his, stroking his salt and pepper hair, whispering sweet nothings as he drifted off. It was sweet, she thought. It was vulnerable.

Sweetness wasn't something she normally found attractive in a man and she wondered why she found it so charming now. In truth he wasn't really that sweet. If he had been, she wouldn't be here now. He had to be a little bad for them to end up together. Their relationship, after all, was wrong. The circumstances of their meeting and the conflict of interest that lay between them; they should never have slept together in the first place.

She gently pulled her arm from under his pillow and sat up in bed. Her long hair fell softly on her neck and tickled the tops of her shoulders. On the nightstand was a crumpled, almost empty pack of Parliaments. She grabbed it and withdrew one, straightening it slightly before placing it between her lips and lighting it.

She stood, naked, and walked across the apartment to a cozy armchair and sat down. She cozied up, smoking and gazing out the huge window at the cold October waters of Lake Michigan thirty stories below. The choppy waves were gray and silent from the warm apartment and she reflected on how that made her feel.

Her life had been like those waves; cold and hard, driven by tidal forces she couldn't control. Now she felt something different. Contentment? Was that what it was? Was that all it was?

No.

What she felt now was something more. It was something she hadn't felt in a very long time. So long that she almost didn't recognize it. Love. She was in love. The revelation startled her.

She looked back at the bed. The man, her man, lay sleeping peacefully. Dreaming perhaps. Dreaming of her. It had been so long since she felt this way that she wasn't sure what to do next. Tell him she supposed, but that seemed so childish.

When she had felt it before, all those many years ago, she had said it. She had said it so often. Declaring it, insisting it, and demonstrating it. What had it gotten her? He had been taken from her. Torn from her. Stolen away by powers beyond her control.

She had lost that love, and with it her capacity for love. Or so she thought, but now, here she was feeling it all over again. It had never occurred to her that it would happen again and one thing she was sure of- she wasn't going to let it slip away this time.

The clock on the nightstand said quarter to five in the afternoon. She wanted to remember. She wanted this moment to freeze in her mind's eye forever. She was happy again, and this was going to be the moment she grabbed that happiness and held on to it for good.

She pounced from the chair and ran to the bed. She dropped the cigarette butt into a half full glass of leggy chardonnay and leaped onto her sleeping love.

He jerked, surprised at the waking.

"Boo!" she exclaimed with a mischievous twinkle in her eye.

"Oh Jesus, you scared the shit out of me," he said, breathing heavily.

She laughed and dropped down pressing her slender naked body against his and kissed him softly on the mouth.

"Mmm, you taste like smoke," he said.

She sat up and straddled him.

"I know," she said. "So, I was just thinking."

He wiped sleep from his eyes, then put his hands behind his head and stared at her.

"Oh yeah? About what?" he asked with a yawn.

"I was thinking," she said again and cracked a huge smile, "that we should get married."

His phone rang.

Part One

Gavin

Chapter One

October 5, 2019 6:29 P.M.

The rain fell in sheets, straight as pinstripes through the narrow canyons of glass and steel. It battered the pavement making blisters on the cracked asphalt, turning it dark and heavy. Small puddles formed in the cracks and ragged uneven surfaces reflecting the hazy streetlights and glowing windows of the high-rises. It was a cold rain with October winds driving it down like spikes from the ever-blackening slate gray sky.

I burst out the flimsy alley door of the warehouse and stumbled before tripping sideways into the stone wall of the next building. A pain like hot needles shot through my shoulder and down my arm forcing my fingers into a tight uncomfortable fist. I bent over wheezing and forced them open again, one at a time, then pressed them against my ribs taking short sharp breaths. The rain ignored me and continued, hammering against my, now heavy, felt fedora and charcoal wool overcoat.

I looked up bleary eyed, squinting through the deluge, gauging the distance out of the alley to the main road, and then on to my car. I wasn't sure I was in any condition to drive, but I knew I had to get away from that place and out of the rain. Holding the wall of the building I hobbled down the rough gravelly ground towards the clean smooth concrete sidewalk and the lights of the traffic.

Out in the weather I couldn't differentiate between the wet of the rain and the wet of the blood, but the pain in my side told me that both were present. The wound wasn't too deep, not life threatening, but it hurt and more than just physically. It hurt my pride.

Look, I hated my job, but I was usually pretty damn good at it. It had been years since I'd let something go that wrong and it bothered me.

It was done. I hadn't failed, but I'd fucked up and I had a concussion and a bone deep gash in my ribs to prove it. I needed a break; some time to get my head back in the game and to stop feeling sorry for myself. Everyone hates their job, I thought. Why should I be any different?

At the mouth of the alley I leaned upright against the corner stone and surveyed the scene. Traffic was heavy, headlights and taillights smeared together in wide bands of scarlet and violet-white between fuzzy dots of red and green that punctuated the intersections. Foot traffic was light, almost non-existent in the downpour which was good. It meant I could move slowly without the questioning stares of other pedestrians on the three-block exodus to my car.

After about a block the anchor of anxiety from the nearly botched job fell away and disappeared in the runoff, down the sidewalk in narrow streams and off the curb joining the greasy gutter water at the edge of the road. All I had left was the weight of my bloodied ribs, waterlogged hat, jacket and shoes, but that was enough. It took me twenty minutes to cross the next two blocks. I had to stop and rest from time to time, leaning against buildings, trying my best not to look drunk or deranged. The last thing I needed was a concerned law enforcement officer coming over to check on me. I wasn't worried about being arrested, not in this town, but I really didn't need the hell she would put me through if I ended up featured in another official report. That would be worse than a night in jail.

"Jesus Gavin, why are you doing this? Why am I still doing this shit?" I mumbled to myself.

It wasn't getting easier anymore. I'd crested that hill seven years ago. No, now it was starting to get harder again. Harder and more tiresome.

Finally, soaked to the bone and beginning to prune, I crept up on my car. It was parked near the corner on a side street in front of a yellow fire hydrant. A restored 2005 Chrysler 300; black with custom deep brown leather seats, it had been a gift of sorts; donated after I put the previous owner out of someone else's misery. It was right where I had left it and as always, free of tickets.

I opened the driver's door and dropped myself in the seat. Water ran off my face and hands and squeezed out of the dense wool of my overcoat, pooling in the seat and running down the leather into the black carpet on the floor. I wheezed and coughed and pulled my legs into the car slamming the door behind them. The rain continued to pound on the roof and windshield creating a rattle like a broken garbage disposal.

It was ten minutes before I found the energy to put the keys in the ignition. Another three before I could turn them. Then, summoning all my effort, I dropped the transmission into gear, spun the tires, and headed towards Lake Shore Drive. I was going home.

* * *

6:04 P.M.

It was the sound that woke her. The explosive crash that pulled her out of unconsciousness and slammed her into reality like a raw egg hitting a tile floor. Her mind was blurry, and she couldn't remember where she was. She tried to open her eyes but they were sealed, sticky and dry. She tried turning her head, but her neck ached and cracked with the effort. Her whole body felt sore and worn. Her lips were dry and cracked. She licked them, but her tongue was leather, and it stung while the taste of copper filled her mouth.

Where the hell was she? She strained to remember, but her focus drifted back to the pain in her body. She tried again to open her eyes, but they still would not comply. They felt swollen and damp, and they stung at the corners. She concentrated on her surroundings. She was on her back, but not in bed. The surface was hard and sturdy; the floor. She felt a sickly anxiety crawl over her.

Why was she on the floor, what kind of floor? Not carpet, it was hard and smooth. Tile? The bathroom maybe? Had she fallen in the bathroom? Time felt like it was moving very slowly, maybe she'd knocked her head on the sink? She closed and opened her hand letting her fingertips and nails feel the surface below her. It was hard wood, smooth with tiny seams between the narrow planks. It was warm.

It was wet.

A chill ran down her aching spine. Her body jerked painfully with an involuntary surge of panic. Her lungs gasped air that felt like broken glass in her throat. Her heart began to race. Adrenaline filled her veins and almost instantly the fog in her mind lifted. Panicking, she tried to stand up, but her body felt like it was made of clay and she found her head too heavy to lift. With effort she managed to pull her knees up towards her chest and lay her feet flat on the floor. She felt wetness between her toes.

She was barefoot!

She pushed hard with her legs and slid backward half a foot before she lost traction on the slick floor. She tried again, and again, slowly creeping backwards until her head slammed sharply on the wall behind her. She winced at the pain from the impact, but kept pushing, pressing the palms of her hands on the floor for assistance. Gradually she managed to upright herself to a sitting position. She paused for a moment and listened to herself breathing. She wiped her eyes with the side of her hand. Pain shot through her skull, but she pressed hard to clear away the dry flakes and forced her eyes open.

Her blood ran cold, and her breath vanished.

The room was vast. It looked like it took up the entire floor of the building. It was, at the moment, dimly lit by nothing but city lights streaming in through the floor to ceiling windows that made up the outside walls. In front of her everything was open, no walls separating the living spaces. She could see into the bedroom and the kitchen. A huge fireplace in the living room and a long table in the dining room she was in. The floor was mahogany covered in spots by expensive looking oriental rugs. There was a large sofa that looked like it was upholstered in Italian tapestry next to a large high-backed leather chair. In the far corner was a huge king-size four-poster bed with the sheets and blanket half on the floor next to...

The room began to spin. On the floor next to the sheets and blankets and pillows were her clothes.

She looked down at herself in horror and found that she was naked except for her underwear. She was covered in crimson and sitting in a smear of blood that she had apparently made while pushing herself back to the wall. In front of her was a large pool of scarlet and the body of a naked man with a cell phone in one hand and a small pistol in the other. He was lying face down in the wide puddle of blood. In front of him, right next to where her smear print began, lay a heavy looking black handgun. Then the sound again.

CRACK!

The doorjamb splintering was like dynamite. The girl lost her balance and fell back to the floor, catching the back of her head on the baseboard as she went down. Pain shot like daggers through her scalp and into her eyes. There was commotion all around her now and blinding bright lights. She jerked her head, which only served to reopen the wounds over her nose and eye. Blood streamed down her face again and she squinted through the warm liquid.

There were a dozen figures in black surrounding her and moving around the room. Then there were hands on her, touching her body, her neck and arms and waist. She squirmed to free herself, but it was useless.

"She's alive." She heard.

"He's not." Came from someone else.

"Look at this." From right next to her. She felt her arm being pulled and her fingers pried open. "The pattern matches the grip."

There was a flash and the distinct sound of a camera shutter. She tried to scream, but she couldn't make a sound. Now the hands were pushing her, rolling her, flipping her on her chest. They pulled her arms behind her. There were bright flashes and more sounds of camera shutters, then the feeling of cold metal on her wrists and she couldn't move.

"Miss...Miss?" She heard the voices but couldn't speak to answer.

"Lady, what's your name?"

She tried to struggle free of the handcuffs, but something heavy and solid came down on her back and held her still.

"Lady, your name?"

"Found a purse." Another voice said. "I.D. says her name is Rose. Weather Rose."

"Miss Rose, you are under arrest for the murder of Special Counsel Brandon Grayson. You have the right to remain..."

And again, everything went black.

* * *

6:41 P.M.

State's Attorney Maureen Adalet was stalling. She was grateful that her job gave her a legitimate excuse for long hours and late nights. There was always a set of briefs that had to be filed last minute, a witness that needed to be interviewed, or a judge that needed a conference after court. When one of those things didn't exist, she could always say they did. There was no way to prove otherwise, least of all by her family.

She wasn't proud of her behavior. There was a shame in avoiding your family, staying away because you couldn't look your daughter in the eyes or tell your husband the truth. Her life weighed on her and no amount of work, no rate of conviction, no balance of blind justice's scales could make her forget what she had failed to do and what she had done to atone for that failure.

Justice wasn't blind. Justice had twenty-twenty vision and she stared down at Maureen day after day holding that goddamn sword and threatening her with the scales that would judge her in the hereafter. She knew she was damned and every day that she pushed the weak little pawns around the chess-board of the city she felt the albatross of her fate hang heavier and heavier around her neck.

It wasn't always like this. She was a different person before. A different lawyer, a different mother, a different wife. She was kind and loving and determined and fearless, but that was before this job and before... before it happened. It was before Gavin, before she realized that only the foolish are fearless and the one thing everyone should fear is what they have inside themselves.

She was thinking about all this, thinking about where it all went wrong and how any of it could ever be fixed when her door opened, and her assistant walked into her office. The intrusion startled her, and she spun around from the wide window behind her desk. Her assistant was a mousy little thing, rail thin and auburn with bare shoulders and a stupid fucking crystal hanging in a wire basket around her neck. She annoyed Maureen and would have been fired a dozen times over if she wasn't so fucking good at her job.

"Oh, Ms. Adalet," Lauren said, seeing her turn around behind her desk. "I'm so sorry, I thought you had stepped out."

Well, usually good at her job anyway.

"I was just coming to drop a message on your desk. Detective Megan Hinde called and wanted you to get back to her as soon as possible. She said there's been an incident involving a..." she glanced at the handwritten note she was holding. "Weather Rose. She sounded pretty alarmed. Apparently," she looked down at the handwriting again. "Brandon Grayson has been shot. I think he's the-"

"Yes Lauren," Maureen snipped, feeling all the blood rush out of her face. "I know who Brandon Grayson is. You're sure she said Weather Rose?"

Lauren nodded a firm affirmative.

"Oh yes ma'am. Quite sure. That's a very unusual name and I wouldn't mix it up."

Maureen was breathing heavily now and felt a light layer of sweat form between her skin and her clothes.

"Okay Lauren," she said dismissively. "I've got it, you're dismissed. Go home and get some rest."

"Alright Ms. Adalet. I've just got to finish up-"

"It can wait, Lauren. Go home. You're done here for tonight."

Lauren looked at her skeptically, then with a shrug of her bare shoulders turned and walked out of the office. Maureen heard her close her laptop and put on her coat. A moment later the sound of the elevator opening and closing again left her finally and completely alone. She picked up the phone on her desk and dialed.

* * *

6:55 P.M.

Detective Megan Hinde screamed down Lake Shore Drive at eighty miles per hour, her lights and siren filled the darkness of the October night and made the rest of the traffic part in front of her like the Red Sea. She was in a panic, furious with intention and worried that she might be, already, too late.

Her phone rang with the ominous melody of the Star Wars Imperial March. It was a special ring that she used as the signature tone for her boss. Not the Lieutenant at the precinct, her other boss. She glanced at the screen of the phone in its cradle on the dashboard and read the caller ID.

SA Maureen Adalet

A sense of dread churned in her stomach as she punched the large green button that accepted the call.

"Meg-"

"You've got to be fucking kidding me, right?" the voice on the other end bellowed.

Detective Hinde winced and looked at the phone as if it were the actual person.

"Afraid not," she said. "Vic is Brandon Grayson. He's the Special Pros-"

"I know who the fuck Grayson is," the woman on the phone said. "And the perp?"

"Yeah, looks like it's her," the detective followed.

"Are we sure?"

Detective Hinde took a long breath and let out a sigh.

"Yeah, we're sure. It's Weather."

There was a long silence then. Detective Hinde stared at the phone waiting for the tirade she had been expecting since she had arrived at the crime scene. It didn't come. Eventually she broke the quiet.

"Mrs. Adalet?"

"Does he know yet?"

It took the detective a minute to catch up.

"I'm sorry?"

"Gavin," the voice was sharp. "Fucking Gavin Gayle, does he know about it yet?"

"I don't know ma'am. I- I don't think so. I don't know how he could."

"But you're on your way there now?"

Detective Hinde hit the lever next to the steering wheel activating the left turn signal and swung the wheel flinging the old Crown Vic off of LSD and onto the side streets of Chicago's South Side.

"Yes ma'am, I'm on my way to The Club right now."

"Okay."

Silence.

"Okay, I'm heading down to the precinct station now. You just make sure he understands that this is off limits. It's going to be enough dealing with the Feds, I don't need to play triage nurse to his bull shit too."

The detective bit her lower lip.

"Ma'am, all due respect, that might not be the best idea."

"Excuse me," came the belligerent voice on the other end of the call.

"I'm just saying, having the Cook County State's Attorney show up for a routine interrogation, it could draw extra attention. Someone might start wondering why this girl is so important."

There was a pause and Detective Hinde wondered if her boss was actually considering her advice.

"The victim is a Special Prosecutor for the Justice Department of the United States. The case and the questioning are anything but routine. How about you stick to the responsibilities I assign to you and let me make the decisions about where my time is best spent?"

Hinde nodded to herself in the car.

"Understood ma'am," she said.

"Good. Text me when you're done with our associate."

"Will do ma'am," she said.

"And Megan," the State's Attorney added, "Don't use your personal phone."

Hinde sighed.

"Of course, ma'am."

Hinde wound herself through the smallish squat brick homes of Calumet Heights. She had killed the lights and sirens so as to not attract too much attention, but she was still traveling at a clip well above the posted speed limit. Once she rounded the curve where Colfax turned into Torrence though, she slowed down. She was getting close to Gavin's neighborhood and she didn't want him getting wind that she was coming.

In this part of the city everyone loved Gavin and with good reason. As far as they were concerned, he kept them safe. No one messed with the locals down here. No one wanted to end up on Gavin's list. Megan chuckled to herself at the thought.

What they didn't know, of course, was that Gavin didn't have a list. He didn't even have a say. He took care of business, sure, but not of his own choosing. He took care of what SA Adalet told him to, and it was Megan that delivered those instructions. It wasn't Gavin that kept things clean and tidy, it was the State's Attorney.

Still, everyone assumed it was Gavin and if they saw a cop car heading down his street looking anything other than lost, he'd almost certainly get a phone call. For this news it was better that he did not have advanced warning.

She pulled over a few blocks from The Club in front of Saint Kevin's Parish Church on Torrence. She didn't want to tip anyone off that she was there by parking her unmarked in front of The Club directly. She hopped out and spanned the last couple blocks on foot.

The street level face of The Club was an abandoned storefront. It had a faded red awning and red wood facade with a small wide window papered over in old yellowing newsprint and wrought iron next to a heavy green wooden door. She stared at the door, not wanting to touch it, knowing that this was not going to go well. She looked at her phone and thought about everything that was about to happen, sighed and raised her hand to knock.

Chapter Two

December 31, 2006 9:41 P.M.

It was brisk I remember. Chicago has cold winters, but I don't remember it being frigid, just brisk. Weather and I held hands and walked across the quad at the University of Chicago. It was chilly enough that we could see our breath in the dim yellow light of the streetlamps. It hovered around us, wisping past our faces and trailing behind like the thin tail of a comet.

Weather, as usual, was overdressed and under bundled for the winter climate of the city. Only a light knit sweater separated the freckled snowy skin of her shoulders from the, nearly, January breeze. Her fine auburn hair danced along the tops of her shoulders and her thin delicate legs stood bare below her light black dress. It was absurd to dress like that at that time of year, but it was also charming, and probably intentional. She was giving me the opportunity to be chivalrous. I took it and offered her my coat.

It was New Year's Eve and we were on our way to a party at Snell-Hitchcock, a dormitory on campus. It was the end of my first semester at college and being away from home was a relief. Life after my parents split had been chaotic and emotionally exhausting. I was glad to be on my own, taking control of my life and leaving the baggage of my broken childhood behind.

It had been a smooth four and a half months. My grades were good. Not top of my class, but perfectly respectable. My professors, well mostly P.A.s, seemed to like and respect me. I had a couple good friends, which was all I needed. More than one or two people in a room at a time tended to make me anxious.

Weather was a year younger than me, but infinitely smarter. She was that kind of person, the kind I can never seem to understand. She could become an expert on any topic in about three hours given a spiral notebook and a library card. She was beautiful and kind, outgoing and self-aware, she was the perfect balance to my fragile and unstable ego.

She was my New Year Eve date, my midnight kiss, but also more than that. We were also celebrating her early admittance. She was top of her senior class and had graduated Plainfield South high school a semester early, so she was here at U of C to start classes after the winter break.

It was a reunion of sorts. We had dated on and off, but mostly on, throughout high school, and if honesty is to be employed, since pre-school. Our Moms were friends, so we had been forcibly attached at the hip since toddlerhood.

So, there we were, two childhood sweethearts reconnecting in maturity and walking hand in hand to a party in a Gothic University dorm, unencumbered by curfews or parental supervision. We didn't have to hide affection publicly or keep the door open when we were alone in a room. Finally, we were free to just be ourselves and be together. It was the most romantic feeling I'd ever experienced.

The party was a huge affair, taking up the entire Snell Hall portion of the combined buildings and attracting attendees from all over campus even though it was officially a residents' only event. We went in through a side door that had been propped open for the occasion by some of the residents so that non-house-members could sneak in without going through the front door where IDs were checked.

The building was beautiful. It felt the way college is supposed to feel. White limestone tiles covered the outside peeking through dense vines of ivy. The window panes were green with oxidation and the windows fogged ever so slightly at the edges. Inside, the walls were paneled wood and intimidating staircases that wound up the four floors of dorm rooms. The combined houses only held about a hundred and ten students, give or take, and of that Snell was somewhere in the area of fifty, but that night the place was packed. There had to have been four hundred students shouting and dancing and drinking and playing. It was chaos riding the thin edge of bedlam.

Weather and I pushed our way, slowly, through the swarms of party goers, down the hall to the Tea Room where the heart of the event was located. It was loud and sticky and smelled like a locker room after a basketball game. It was just the kind of environment I usually tried to avoid, and I could feel my anxiety starting to build from the noise and the bodies pressing against me from every direction. Then I felt a squeeze. The gentle grip of Weather's hand around mine, calming me and focusing my energy and attention on her.

In the Tea Room, Weather let go of my hand and looked around.

"Introduce me," she said eagerly. "I want to meet people."

I darted my head around looking for anyone familiar. I didn't go to parties much, and the faces in the room may as well have been pictures on milk cartons.

"I don't know any of these people," I said leaning into her ear to be heard over the cacophony.

Weather smiled and kissed me on the cheek.

"We should do something about that," she said. "Come on, introduce me."

She grabbed me by the wrist and pulled me over to a corner where a small group of girls was chatting with light, but serious faces. They were carbon copies of each other, just with different hair. Thin and fashionable with eyeglasses and earrings. Weather walked right up to them and cleared her throat for their attention. It worked, they all looked at us with curious expectation. There was a moment of silence, then Weather jabbed me in the ribs with her elbow.

"Oh, um, ladies," I said in an awkward attempt to be charming. "I'd like you to meet Ms. Weather Rose. She is my beautiful and brilliant girlfriend who will be joining us as an English major here at this prestigious institution of learning."

The group of girls stared at me blankly with slack jaws and thousand-yard stares. Weather grimaced.

"Sorry for my boyfriend," she said meekly. "He's an engineering student."

There was a mild chuckle from the group and one of the girls put out her hand for Weather to shake.

"Welcome Weather," she said, "to our prestigious institution."

Weather smiled. "Of learning," she added, and the group all laughed.

The girls introduced themselves with names right out of an Archie comic. Betty and Veronica. Chloe and Delilah, and all announced their majors. English was the prevailing area of study unsurprisingly.

"We were just talking about our favorite instances of Chekhov's Gun." One of the girls said. "Any thoughts?"

"Oh, we're not really gun people," I said.

The group of girls burst out laughing. Weather too. I had no idea what the joke was, but I felt foolish and tasted stomach acid in my mouth.

Weather put her hand on my back and rubbed it in small slow circles. She stretched up on her tip toes and kissed me on the side of my forehead.

"Why don't you go find us some drinks Hun," she whispered.

I looked at her for a moment, unsure of what I should do.

"It's okay Gavin, I'll be fine, and you look like you could use a cocktail."

I shrugged.

"I guess. I guess I'll be right back then."

She smiled at me so sweetly then. She smiled at me and took my hands in hers and said, "Thanks hon, love you."

It was the first time. The first time she had said that, and she said it so casually. Not a big thing. She just said it. She didn't even wait for me to return it, she just turned back to the girls she'd just met and continued giggling and talking and having a great time. She was at a huge party with people she didn't know, and she was simply at ease and fitting in. I had known it before, but at that moment it really hit me how much I loved her too.

The bar wasn't in the Tea Room. The party, while over-flowing with uninvited guests that were being intentionally overlooked, was still a sanctioned University event for minors, and as such, did not have alcohol available officially. There were, however, numerous collections of beer and liquor arranged in bar-like setups in the dorm rooms throughout the building. I made my way out of the Tea Room and started strolling down the hall to find an open door with just such a setup, and something I could drink.

It was a failure of my upbringing that I have tastes incompatible with the poverty of college life. Most kids that age live on Old Milwaukee, Busch, or if they really want to splurge Coors Lite. I myself, even then, could not stomach the stuff. I drank beer rarely and only if it was lovingly crafted in small batches. Mostly I preferred Spanish Tempranillo, Rye Whiskey, or Gin that was at least three shelves up from the floor at the liquor store. Needless to say, finding these items was going to be impossible here. My best bet was to find someone with a bottle of Old Fitzgerald and add a lot of ice.

I was approaching the end of the hall when a wave of red hair appeared in the crowd. Not red like you're thinking either. This was fire engine red, Stacy red. It's amazing how fast panic can set in. Stacy DeBruin was my ex, sort of. She was a girl I had met the first week of school, during orientation. She was of average height, slim, athletic and well designed. She was beautiful, but not more so than the copious number of other well-designed undergrads that roamed the campus. The one thing she did have that made her stand out from the crowd was that hair. That long glorious red hair, when you added that to the picture she transformed into a vixen.

I had been smitten with her from the moment I met her, and much to my surprise, she had been smitten too. We had known each other for exactly four hours when we fell into bed together. It was wild and unbridled sex unlike anything I had ever experienced. We had sex like I'd seen on the internet, hot and loud and rambunctious and long and when it was over, I felt like overcooked pasta and fell sound asleep in her arms.

We did that a lot, had sex. It had to have been a dozen times or more, each one better than the last. We didn't talk much, didn't go into the stories of our lives or dreams for the future. We met up after classes, ate crappy delivery pizza, drank and fucked like rabbits until we passed out. It was everything I thought I'd ever wanted.

I did feel guilty though. I felt like I was cheating on Weather even though we had agreed, and by agreed, I mean Weather had told me it was okay to see other people while we were apart. Still, this didn't feel like seeing someone else. This was more. There was a craving that I had never experienced before. A need for her, for her body. I was eighteen years old and my hormones made sure that all I could think of was her. It wasn't the same as Weather, it wasn't love. It was desire on a primal level.

Stacy, however, saw it differently.

Two or three weeks into classes, when the workload had built up to the point that we hadn't had time to hook up for a few days I took some shit from this kid Josh in my CAD class. He was a bit of a prick, one of those health-conscious metrosexual types that probably spent more time in the gym than he did in class.

"So, you're giving up already," he said.

I remember being confused.

"Giving up on what?"

"School. I hear you're dropping out."

I let out a burst of laughter.

"What? No way, it hasn't even gotten hard yet."

"Mmm hmm," he mocked. "That's not what she said."

I stopped clicking at the computer and turned to face him.

"What are you talking about?" I asked, feeling that uneasy lump starting to form in my throat.

My classmate glanced at me with a smirk, then, when he saw my expression let his own draw serious.

"Dude, Stacy is telling everyone that you're dropping out."

My throat closed up and there was ringing in my ears.

"What?" I nearly shouted, then caught myself. "What?" whispering now. "What the hell are you talking about?"

"Dude, your girlfriend is under the impression that you are leaving school to go work for her dad."

It felt like someone pumped a pitcher of ice water into my blood and the familiar sensation of a panic attack started to swell in my chest and creep up my back like a million tiny spiders.

"Wha- Her what? Her dad? Why would- Dude, I don't even know what her dad does. Why would I do that? Why would she say that?"

"How the fuck would I know," he shrugged. "But I don't know what you're getting worked up about. Stacy is hot and she's loaded. Man, I'd kill to trade places with you. She says you two are in l-o-v-e and that you are going to go sell cars or some shit so that you guys can get married."

I jumped out of my chair.

"The fuck!" I yelled.

"Mr. Gayle," the instructor boomed. "Is there a problem?"

I looked up at him, my eyes wide and glossy. My fingers were numb and I was moments away from breaking out in tears.

"Well?" the prof said again.

I shook. I looked down at my classmate who had turned back to his computer and was clicking away at his drawing of a rustic farmhouse being converted to a huge single-family home. I looked back at the professor and then grabbed my backpack and stormed out of the classroom.

The ensuing fight was long, loud and very public. I screamed at her and called her awful names, something I regretted later. I hated being that guy, letting my anger take over, but I couldn't believe what she had done. She cried and apologized, but ultimately stuck to her guns. She was sorry she hadn't talked to me first. Sorry that she told other people her plans before me, but she insisted it was what was best for us. She said we were meant to be and that I just couldn't see it yet.

I spent the rest of the semester avoiding her and dodging her phone calls. I talked to the administration and tried filing a sexual harassment case, but no one took an eighteen year old boy seriously when he said that the hot girl wouldn't leave him alone, and unless I could show that I was concerned for my physical safety, there was nothing they could do.

I got creative at finding ways to stay away from her and avoiding interaction. It mostly involved not going to my dorm room and being late for classes. My reputation suffered a bit, but I was able to square it with the people that mattered.

Now I was trapped shoulder to shoulder in a crowded hall, unable to make evasive maneuvers and closing in on her for the first time in months. I tried to move away, pretending I hadn't seen her, but she was already calling my name.

"Fuck," I muttered as I felt her hand grab me by the shirt.

I turned and looked her dead in the eyes.

"Gavin," she said in a sweet sing-song voice. "God, I've missed you. Glad you got my message."

I frowned.

"Stacy," I said as coldly as I could. "I don't know what you're talking about. I don't listen to your messages."

She raised her eyebrows quizzically.

"But you're here," she said. "You must have gotten my invitation."

I had forgotten that Stacy lived in Snell. Her tiny twin bed on the third floor had been my introduction to the famous building. I winced and shook my head.

"No Stacy. Everyone knows about this party, you had nothing to do with me being here. I didn't come to see you, I'm here with my girlfriend. In fact, if I had known you were going to be here, I probably wouldn't have come."

A big smile spread across her face.

"Oh, you're so cute," she said. "Gavin, I live here, of course

I'd be at the party. I like the routine though. Playing hard to get? Very sexy. Girlfriend's a nice touch too."

She mocked looking around the crowd.

"I don't see anyone, should we be naughty on the sly?"

She put her hand on my shoulder and I jerked away.

"Oh my fucking God, you're a lunatic," I shouted.

People turned and looked.

"Gavin, you're making a scene," she whispered.

I backed up and turned away. People watching the two of us spread apart, giving me room to move. I headed back down the hall, almost running and the crowd seemed to give up on the show and went back to their previous revelries. Stacy disappeared into the mass of strangers.

Back in the Tea Room I maneuvered back to the corner where the group of girls had been, but there were just a couple of guys sipping Miller Lite and talking about the Cubs' shitty season. I spun around, frantically looking for Weather. She was nowhere to be seen, but I did spy one of the girls that had been in the group and made my way over to where she was sitting.

It was Veronica, the girl that had shaken Weather's hand. She was on a plush red sofa sipping a clear plastic cup full of some kind of pink wine and laughing with a new group of girls, all decked out like they were going to be peeling their dresses off on stage later that night.

"Excuse me," I blurted out half wheezing and interrupting the girl mid-sentence.

She looked up annoyed then recognized me and smiled.

"Hey," she said. "Engineering dude, right?"

I frowned, rolled my eyes then nodded.

"Yeah, where's-"

"Yeah," she interrupted. "Your girlfriend was looking for you."

"What?"

"Yeah, Weather, right? She was wondering what was taking you so long. She went off to find you. Did she? Find you?"

I shook my head.

"No," I said in an irritated voice. "No, she didn't. Do you know where she went?"

The girl shrugged.

"I dunno," she said, already turning back to her friends. "Some guy was taking her to find you."

I straightened up. My antisocial personality was starting to fight back against my best efforts to be friendly. If Weather were here, she would touch my neck or stroke my arm. She'd do what she does, and I'd be able to turn off the faucet of my frustration, but she wasn't here.

"Some guy? Who? Who was it?"

She looked back, now fully annoyed.

"If I knew who it was, I wouldn't have said some guy."

I stared back at her, incredulous.

"Do you know which way they went?"

She looked back at me again, then just went on with her conversation.

I sighed. The last thing I wanted was to go back out into the hall and risk running into Stacy again, but I also wasn't going to let my seventeen year old girlfriend wander around alone in a drunken college crowd, or worse yet, with some drunken college guy. I pressed my way through the swelling crowd and made it out into the corridor.

I'm not an especially tall man. I come in at a totally respectable (in my opinion) five foot ten inches. Still, in a crowd, I'm looking at the backs of peoples' heads. On my tip toes I could roughly see over the swarm of people packed wall to wall and to my best judgment I didn't think Weather was one of them.

Around the corner from the Tea Room was the main

stairway and I fought my way through the kids like a salmon until I made it there. The stairs were less congested, and I was able to move up them without a hassle.

I continued my search, growing more and more frantic, up and down the hall of the second floor and then the third, panic surging with each empty room. The fourth floor was suites and the party hadn't moved that far. There were a few people scattered about, but it was quiet and easy to see Weather wasn't there. I retraced my steps back down the floors checking each room again and asking anyone I knew, which wasn't many, if they had seen Weather.

It was my fourth pass down the hallway of the second floor when I noticed a closed door and felt a greasy chill. Every other dorm room in the building had been open. Partiers moving in and out, bar service in some, movies or football games in others. Everything was open but this room.

I pushed through the people between myself and the door and pressed my ear against it. It was quiet. I listened hard, leaning into the door and holding my breath.

Nothing.

I started to move away, and I heard... something. I couldn't identify it exactly, but it made the hairs on the back of my neck stand up. I leaned in again and listened and there it was again. Soft. Like a whimper.

Turning the doorknob gently I cracked the door to peak in. I saw bare skin, muscles pulled taught along a wide back and a thick neck bulging with wide veins. There were thin twiggy legs bare and squirming and sounds that sent chills down my neck.

The door flew open at my insistence and nearly knocked over another boy. He was standing just inside, staring gap jawed at the fold out screen on a small camcorder, pointed at the two on the bed. He had oily skin covered in zits and dead eyes that made me queasy. The door creaked as it met the end of its hinges and banged against the wall. Both of them turned to look at me.

The boy on the bed had a red blotch on his face in the shape of a hand and a bloody nose. There were scratches on his chest and neck, and he was glistening with a light coating of sweat. I vaguely recognized him but couldn't put a name to the face.

"Close the door ass ho- oh," he said, and as he moved, I caught sight of who he was kneeling over.

It was Weather.

"Oops honey, looks like we got caught."

She was almost naked. Her legs bare, her shirt torn open and one breast hanging out of her bra. Her face was swollen and red and there were tears streaming down her cheeks. She was gasping, trying to scream, trying to talk, trying to get away.

The boy turned back to her and pressed his hand hard over her mouth.

"Shut up bitch!" he said, then added, "get the fuck out of here Gayle, we're trying to make a movie."

My rage took over without my even noticing. I didn't feel the flush of heat as my face went red and I can't pinpoint exactly when my vision got blurry. I do remember hearing a pop, a kind of snap and then blood rush through my ears silencing the sounds of the party behind me, but I didn't feel anything, I just moved.

With one step I put my fist through the nose of the boy holding the camera. The cartilage crumpled under my knuckles like corrugated cardboard and I felt the small top bone of my pinky finger snap.

Blood sprayed across the wall and on my face and shirt. The camera clattered to the floor and the boy collapsed in a heap.

I stepped over him and wrapped both of my hands around the other guy's neck. I jerked hard and he tumbled off the mattress and onto the ground, his throat still between my fingers. Pain from my broken pinky was shooting up my hand and arm and causing brief flashes of clarity, but they were quickly extinguished by the yellow fog of rage that had taken over my body.

I dragged the stunned student across the small room and slammed his head into the cinderblock wall. He fell onto the tile floor spilling blood from a gash in his scalp. I dropped down over him in the same position he had just been over Weather.

Then the beating began.

I didn't really see any of it. Nothing registered at a sensory level, I just started hitting him. Over and over I pushed my fists into his ever-reddening face. I felt another finger break, then another, but I didn't stop.

The boy didn't move, he didn't struggle, not once. He didn't scream or cry for help. The truth is he was probably unconscious before he even knew what was going on. By the time I had him on the floor he just laid there as I beat him into hamburger meat.

I don't know how long it went on. It could have been thirty seconds or thirty minutes. Eventually I felt hands on my shoulders, then tugging, then pulling. Finally, thick arms like tree trunks wrapped around my chest and pulled me off the clearly dead body of the boy. They dropped me on the floor across the room and finally, uncontrollably, I started to cry.

Chapter Three

April 15, 2007 2:27 P.M.

I stood silently in the ornate walnut accented room on South California Avenue. I couldn't move. I felt like a block of cold stone. A statue being looked upon by twelve strangers as if I was some offensive piece of modern art. Every muscle in my body was locked in place, held rigid by fear and yet, still, I was transported. The journey out of one life and into the next was accomplished through nineteen simple words.

"We, the jury, do hereby find the defendant, Gavin Gayle, guilty of the second-degree murder of Joshua Miller."

Just under twenty words and I was transported to a world where I was a monster. I was a criminal, a killer. I was a murderer and there was nothing I could do to ever find my way back.

Weather was a wreck after the party. She was dealing with the trauma of watching me beat a man to death with my bare hands, but more importantly the trauma of being brutally assaulted, beaten, and violated. She was a shell of herself. Pale freckled skin stretched over an empty bubble of rotten air. She was broken.

She came to see me once, in county lockup, the day after the indictment. She looked okay, no visible bruises or scars, but she was shattered, not the woman, the girl, I loved. She said only one thing the whole time she sat across from me. A question.

"Was there someone else? Before. Before I graduated, did you have another girlfriend?"

I was shocked by it. I had never told her about Stacy. It had been a mistake and I didn't want it to influence our relationship going forward. Somehow, she'd found out though, somehow someone had told her. I felt my heart clench up in my chest and a sob catch in my throat. I nodded.

She just cried. She just stared at her lap and cried and cried. That was the last time I saw her. She never testified in court. She never even gave a statement to the police. They told me that when she tried to talk about it she just broke down. Eventually a state appointed psychologist exempted her from having to speak to anyone and that was the last of Weather's involvement.

After that it was just the police, the prosecutor, and the history of my short temper versus my own word. They never found the camera, the tape, or the boy who had been recording the attack and without any evidence backing up my side of the story the public defender that was representing me had nothing compelling to present during my defense.

The prosecutor, A.SA Maureen Adalet, on the other hand had a very compelling story. A story about a beautiful young woman who had been abandoned by her on again off again boyfriend at a college party; had met another boy, gone off to make out in the privacy of his dorm room and been discovered. The boyfriend, with a history of rage issues, had lost it, slapped the girl around and beaten the boy to death. The jury ate it up.

I was taken out of the courtroom in handcuffs, put in a

school bus that had been painted white and labeled Cook County Department of Corrections. They drove me thirty-two miles south to Statesville Prison in Lockport IL. They locked me up less than ten miles from the house I grew up in and I never saw my family again.

My mother was humiliated. She wrote me one letter right after I was sentenced. She told me that my actions were an embarrassment to the family and that she had enough to worry about without a son in prison. I'm sure they weren't her words. My mother had always been a loving and positive presence in my life, but my stepfather had a way of making his feelings hers. Still, she never came to see me and never wrote again.

My father died. It literally killed him. He walked out of the courtroom, down the steps of the building, raised a hand to hail a cab and had a stroke. He was dead before I was on the bus. I don't know if he even had a funeral, no one ever told me.

I was alone. I never minded being alone, being away from other people. I was naturally introverted, and crowds made me anxious, but this was different. I was surrounded by people most of the time, but there was no one left in the world who cared who I was or if I was even alive. It's a kind of loneliness that takes over, devours you, and becomes who you are. If no one knows you exist, do you?

* * *

Prison wasn't so bad. That's a lie. Prison was the worst place imaginable. That's not hyperbole, I've had a lot of time to imagine things and nothing I've been able to come up with is worse than prison. It was always cold, not frigid, but the kind of cold that makes your toes hurt. It was crowded and angry and smelled like piss and BO. It was a dangerous terrifying night-mare that rebooted itself every day when the hellish sodium vapor lights flickered on and your cell door unlocked with a hollow clank. The thing is, a person can get used to anything, and I got used to prison.

The structure helped, but that didn't come right away. That's the first thing you have to do in prison, find that structure. Of course, prison is all about structure, but there was a surprising amount of variability in it. The first thing you have to do is find a job and my job for the first two weeks was getting my ass kicked on a regular basis. I spent a lot of time in the infirmary.

It was an irony, I felt, that I was in that place to begin with for beating someone to death, and now I was getting beaten to near death, for no apparent reason, all the time. It was an irony, but a fair one. I deserved it I thought, so I kept letting it happen.

The first time I got hit was for sitting at the wrong table. Prison is a terrible place, the worst place maybe, but the mess hall; that was the worst place inside the worst place, the seventh circle of Hell. Nobody wanted to spend any time there. No one with two brain cells to rub together anyway. The mess was where the gangs made base and made war; on each other and on the prison itself. It was where they beat their chests and showed their strength to each other and the guards. There were maybe half a dozen gangs at any one time operating inside the prison and they carved up the mess into their own bloody little nation states.

The second day inside I grabbed my tray of chicken, rice mush and stringy asparagus and found an empty spot at one of the tables. I took a seat and started forking food into my mouth. It wasn't good, the asparagus especially was limp and bitter, but it was edible in so far as there was nothing else to eat. Less than a minute after sitting down there was a tap on my shoulder. I turned to see who it was and a fist the size of a softball collided with my right eye and split my eyebrow open.

I felt it again, explode inside me. My anger. My rage. That which I had let become me and define me. I felt myself swelling, filling up with hate and ready to do whatever I had to to extinguish my anger. I jumped to my feet, puffed up my chest and leveled my remaining eye with a gnarled looking man in his mid-forties. I was heaving, breathing through my mouth and balling my hands into fists so tight my nails left marks in my palms. Blood dripped down my cheek and fell onto my orange prison jumpsuit.

The man looked at me with indignation.

"You don't belong here kid," he said.

I stared at him, simmering. I could take him, he was old. Maybe in his forties. He might have been stronger than me, maybe. He was tall and lanky with muscles bulging out of his rolled-up sleeves, but his skin was soft, loose, like there used to be more muscle that had since melted away. I was younger. I could move faster. I knew I could beat him. I felt myself getting ready to take a swing, then I heard Weather's voice. In my head I heard her clear as day, as if she was standing right next to me.

"Gavin, don't."

That's all she seemed to say. Her soft comforting voice, almost musical.

"Please Gavin, don't do this."

My heart slowed down. I felt my fists unclench and my breathing returned to normal. I wiped the blood from my face and looked into the man's eyes, squinted and turned away to sit back down.

The second shot hit my ear. The room rang and I went down on my knees. Then a foot in my gut with the crack of a breaking rib and another shot in the eye. After that I was on the floor. More men gathered around me. They began kicking me in the face, the chest and the back. I felt pain fill every corner of my body before I choked and spat blood on the ground. Then I blacked out.

When I woke up, I was in the infirmary. I had a broken rib wrist and finger, two missing teeth and seventeen stitches in my face. I laid there staring at the speckled white ceiling tiles feeling lost and alone and wondering why I hadn't fought back. But I knew why. I knew that Weather was with me, in my head telling me the kind of man I needed to be. Telling me to be better than them. She was gone from my life, but she remained in my heart and I was going to live up to her expectations. I was going to become the man I should have been before. A man in control of himself.

That's how I lived. I never fought back. When I'd get out of the infirmary I'd go about my business and eventually, sometimes within mere hours, I'd set someone off and they would bang me up and back I'd go. I let it happen because I deserved it and because letting my rage win over my humanity was something I would never let happen again.

After a few months, when my finger was out of the splint and I could walk on my ankle again, I got a job in the laundry facility. I had been an engineering student and they needed someone to fix the machines when they broke down as they invariably did. The Laundry didn't just service the prison, it took care of the linen for all the local hospitals, colleges, and a few hotels. We processed over a million pounds of laundry a month and that meant lots of machines that needed to be working all the time.

The job meant that I was busy during the day and out of the way of the gangs and brutes. It also meant I had some money. I made about ninety-four cents an hour. Roughly one hundred and fifty dollars a month. In prison terms I was in the one percent. Money meant I could eat better, live more comfortably, and when necessary, pay people not to break parts of me.

It also meant making friends. There was only one guy inside that was as good with machines as me: Jeremy. We worked together rebuilding washers and dryers. We chatted about life and we watched each other's backs. We found a safe place to eat, away from the mess, and we shared our secrets. I don't know if you can really have friends in prison, but if you can he was mine.

Jeremy was in Statesville for DUI related vehicular manslaughter. One night his girlfriend left him, moving out of state with their four-year-old daughter. He got drunk on cheap beer and when he ran out, he got in his car to drive to the liquor store. On the way he swerved to miss a dog that ran out into the street. His car hopped the curb and he hit a nineteen-year-old girl walking home from her job at a grocery store.

He never fought it. He pleaded guilty without a lawyer and never asked the judge for any kind of leniency. He was a good guy that made a bad choice and took the consequences without an ounce of bitterness. He knew what he did, and he believed he belonged where he was.

He was my spiritual mentor inside and he replaced Weather as the voice of reason in my life. I came to depend on him and his presence to remind me that this was all happening for a reason. We were there because of our choices and if we learned to control those choices we had a shot at a real life, at real happiness when we got out.

Jeremy was murdered one year three months and eleven days into his sentence. It doesn't matter why. In prison there really aren't any reasons that things happen, they just happen. When he died, I cried for the first time since the night of the party. It wasn't fair, and it wasn't right, and I just couldn't take it anymore. The rage in me crackled like a wildfire and it finally succeeded at drowning out Weather's voice in my head.

I found the man who killed Jeremy, a pale tattooed hulk

called Benson, in the dusty yard where we went to work out. There were free weights and welded bars for chin-ups. There was a path worn into the dry ground for running laps and a small patch of dry grass where groups sometimes gathered to play touch football. The man responsible was on his back, bench-pressing barbells.

He was big. Bigger than me, but that didn't matter. He was essentially pinned down and I was free. I walked over to where he was pressing and picked up a twenty-five-pound steel weight. It was cold and hard and rough in my hands. I stared at it in my fingers for just a moment, then with one swing smashed him with it in the side of the face. He dropped the bar he was holding, and it fell on his throat. They didn't even take him to the infirmary, just the morgue.

I got another twenty-five years added to my eighteen-year sentence for that, but I didn't care. As far as I was concerned, I was going to die in that hole. I wanted to die there. I had been kidding myself. There was nothing waiting for me on the outside. There was no hope for a life, no chance at happiness and no one to miss me when I was gone.

Chapter Four

_____

March 18, 2011 11:38 P.M.

State's Attorney Maureen Adalet couldn't sleep. She should have been content in her king size sleep number bed between seven-hundred thread count Egyptian cotton sheets. As the newly elected State's Attorney for Cook County she was making a good living, was well respected, and had a loving family. She worked hard to bring order to her corner of society. But her life wasn't what brought her discontent. Anxiety sweat through her pores because Maureen had a teen aged daughter, and she was late getting home.

Samantha was smart, she was responsible and respectful, but she was also sixteen and beautiful and she had recently earned her driver's license. Tonight, she had used it to drive herself to a party at a friend's house with a promise that the parents would be home and that there wouldn't be any drinking. But there was also a promise to be home by eleven-thirty and it was now eleven-thirty-eight.

Maureen didn't want to be one of those parents that got all bent out of shape over eight minutes, but Samantha wasn't one of those kids that tried to stretch out curfew for eight extra minutes. The reason Maureen trusted her to drive to a party at sixteen was that Samantha had always given her reason to.

Two more minutes. Two more minutes and she would call Sam's cell and see what was going on. She stared at the digital clock on her bed stand and suddenly wished it was an analogue clock with a third hand. Minutes seemed very long when you didn't have a second hand to follow.

Eleven thirty-nine

Eleven thirty-nine

Eleven thirty-nine

Eleven forty. Maureen reached over to the bed stand and lifted the house phone out of the charger.

It rang in her hand.

She felt a moment of relief and glanced at the small glowing green screen above the number pad. The caller ID read 'Adv Il Med Cntr'.

Maureen's heart stopped. She stared at it for a long time. On the fourth ring she pressed the green button and put the phone to her ear.

The voice on the other end of the line had been calm and business like.

"May I please speak with the parent or guardian of Samantha Adalet?"

Just hearing her baby's name come out of the phone made her start to sob. She let out a wail and tears poured down her cheeks. Her husband sat up next to her, woken by her cry. She was shaking and dropped the phone in the comforter on her lap.

"What's wrong sweetheart?" He said.

He picked up the phone and looked at the screen. His face went white and he put the speaker to his ear.

"Hello, this is Jason Adalet."

"Mr. Adalet, this is Rosemary Gile at Advocate Illinois

Masonic Medical Center. Are you the parent or guardian of Samantha Adalet?"

"Yes, I'm her father."

"Mr. Adalet, I have Samantha in our Emergency Room. She has suffered some injuries. I think it would be best if you came in to see her."

"What kind of injuries? Is she okay? Was it a car accident?"

"Mr. Adalet, I really can't give that information over the phone. If you could please come into the hospital, we can discuss it in person."

"But is she okay?" He was beginning to sound angry.

"I'm sorry sir, I know you are concerned, but I really must insist you come in and discuss it in person."

Maureen didn't remember much until the hospital. Jason got her out of bed, and dressed, and into the car. They drove the ten blocks to the hospital in less than fifteen minutes. The admitting nurse at the front desk checked their IDs and called another nurse who led them back to a small curtained off area where their daughter laid like a ragdoll in a hospital bed.

Samantha was awake, but something was wrong. She was out of it, spacey. She recognized her parents, but she couldn't maintain focus. Her hair was messed up, her makeup smeared across her face. She had a good-sized cut on her lower lip, and dried blood under her nose. Her t-shirt was torn almost completely in half, down the front, her bra was broken in the middle and hanging off her shoulders, and she didn't have any pants on.

The hospital staff explained that she had been found by a passerby, slumped over on the bench at the bus stop at Halsted and Wellington. The police, who were waiting in the lobby to talk to Maureen and her husband, and to collect Samantha's clothes for evidence, had been called and they transported her to the hospital in their squad car. It was not proper procedure, and technically could have been grounds for reprimand, but they had felt that given the situation, speed trumped procedure, and the hospital staff backed them up on their assessment.

A rape kit had been performed, but no semen or vaginal tearing was found. A blood sample had been taken to screen for drugs and alcohol. Her wounds had been treated and she had been given an IV to get her fluids up as well as a broad-spectrum antibiotic just to be on the safe side.

Maureen and her husband tried to question Sam about what had happened. Did she know who had done this to her? Was this at the party? How had she gotten to the bus stop? But she was incoherent and sliding in and out of consciousness. Finally, she closed her eyes and went to sleep and Maureen and Jason went to the lobby to talk to the police.

The cops took some information and shared what they knew so far. They got Maureen and Jason's contact information and promised to stay in touch.

The next few days were rough. Maureen spent most of the time in the hospital with her daughter. Samantha didn't remember much of what had happened, but she swore that she didn't have a drink the whole night. She had been at Marci's house for the party. There were boys there, but so were Marci's parents, and there was no alcohol at all. This was backed up by the tox screening that came back from the hospital. No alcohol was found in Samantha's blood, but they did find traces of Flunitrazepam.

Flunitrazepam, Maureen knew from her job as a prosecutor, was more commonly referred to as Rohypnol, and was often used in drug-facilitated sexual assault, or 'date rape'. There had been no conclusive outward signs that Samantha had been raped. No vaginal tearing or semen found, but the thought that someone had given her Rohypnol in the first place made Maureen sick to her stomach. The worst part was that she had nothing to go on. Everyone at the party had been questioned and everyone claimed to know nothing. All she could get from Samantha was that she had been spending time with a boy named Kevin Dobson.

All of this added up to a slim likelihood of finding out what had happened to her daughter. Maureen was a wreck. She spent her life putting the bad guys behind bars, and now, when her daughter was drugged and turned up battered and beaten, she couldn't do anything to protect her. She felt helpless and with that came a sense of hopelessness.

After a couple weeks, Samantha returned to school. There was a distinct sense of being out of place for her. She told her mom that she felt like an animal in a zoo. Everyone was staring at her, whispering behind her back. A rumor started floating around that she liked rough sex. She was branded a slut by the kids at school and harassed and tormented daily. After a couple weeks of that Maureen pulled her daughter out and enrolled her in a private academy near their house.

Almost a year later, Samantha was starting to piece her life back together. The nightmares had stopped for the most part and she was starting to spend time with friends again. A boy named Trenton, from her old school, had started to come by and check on her from time to time. Eventually they started hanging out and the word boyfriend started coming up in conversation.

Maureen was concerned, but against all statistical probability, he wasn't trying to get her undressed, at least as far as she could tell. They spent afternoons sitting on the couch in the living room watching TV or playing cards, and he never asked her to be alone with him.

It was about three weeks from the first mention of the word boyfriend when it happened. Trenton played basketball at the public school. He was good enough to make the team, but far from a star player which meant he wasn't one of the popular kids. He knew his teammates, but they weren't exactly friends. When practice ended that late February afternoon Trenton stayed on the court to practice free throws before the weekend game. When his arm got too sore to throw another, he headed to the locker room to hit the showers.

"Oh shit!"

"No way!"

"Holy fuck, no fucking way!"

The voices were hushed but full of energy and laughter. Normally Trenton ignored this kind of testosterone fueled male bravado. He loved sports, but he hated the machismo that generally went along with them. He was happy to just get the exercise and call it a day, but something about the way the voices carried gave him a bad feeling.

Trenton walked over to the crowd gathered around one guy. It was Kevin Dobson, the captain of the team and a real fucking asshole. They were all watching a video on his phone and laughing. It was a poorly shot video taken with the camera on the phone, dark and shaky, and it was hard for Trenton to see what was going on in it.

Then suddenly, everything came into focus. In the middle of the frame was Samantha. She was lying on the grass under a streetlamp. A grade school playground was visible behind her. Her pants were around her knees and her t-shirt was ripped down the middle. This was a video of her assault. This was a video of her, barely conscious, being touched and grabbed and handled and these guys were standing around and laughing at it.

Trenton exploded.

"What the fuck!" He yelled at the top of his lungs.

The laughing stopped. Everything went quiet. Everyone turned and looked at Trenton for a long moment. He could hear the blood pumping behind his ears and the tinny sound coming from the phone.

He didn't move, he didn't step, he didn't crouch or lean, he just swung. He swung his right fist hard and wide and made contact with the kid's cheekbone. He felt the boy's face crack under his fist, and he felt the small bones in his hand snap against his chiseled jaw. The boy fell backwards and sideways into the bank of lockers behind him. The phone fell out of his hand and landed face first on the cement floor. Trenton heard the glass shatter on impact.

He leaned over and picked up the phone, and without looking back, without changing out of his gym uniform, bolted out of the locker room and straight to his car. He drove a steady nine miles over the speed limit all the way to Maureen's office, walked past her receptionist and into her afternoon status meeting with the Consumer Fraud Division. Shaking with rage and fear he walked up to her desk, leaned against it with his left hand, and with his now swollen broken right hand placed the phone directly in the center of her desk.

In the weeks after that day Maureen often wished that he had never brought her that phone. She wished that she had never known it existed. The phone confirmed all the worst things that she had feared about that night. That Samantha's trusted friends had betrayed her in unimaginable ways. It proved who the boys involved had been, and in the end, it was completely unusable.

The boys on the video were all arrested. Several of them, including the owner of the phone, Kevin Dobson, made confessions before their lawyers showed up, but in the end, Kevin's lawyer argued that the phone was illegally obtained when Trenton assaulted him and stole it. The phone was deemed inadmissible and since the confessions were given under duress, they were deemed 'fruit of the poisonous tree' and were thrown out. Ultimately, because of that phone, all the boys that drugged and tortured her daughter were able to look her in the eyes and walk away.

Maureen was crippled with guilt. She grew distant from her family and spent long nights sitting in her office crying. She had failed her family, failed her daughter, failed her job, and failed herself. Eventually her depression pushed her towards drastic measures.

On a cold October evening Maureen sat in her office on the thirty second floor of her building. Most of her staff had gone home for the evening and Maureen had been listening to the quiet for some time. She was lost in the silence around her and it was soothing. It was calming and reassuring. All she wanted was to have this silence forever, to not feel the pain anymore, to not hear the judgment in her family's voices and ridicule in her colleagues' tone. All she wanted was what she had been unable to give her daughter. She wanted peace.

She was slowly spinning the cylinder of a gleaming nickel-plated Smith and Wesson .357 magnum between her thumb and forefinger. The steady click, click, click seemed thunderous in the silence of her office. It gave her conviction, and it gave her courage. She released the cylinder and it folded out from the weapon. She slid her hand into the shallow pocket of her jacket and pulled out six dull brass rounds and one by one dropped them into the six chambers of the cylinder. She rotated the cylinder back into position and her thumb eased back and found the crook of the revolver's hammer. It was harder than she expected to pull it back into position. The gun was heavy, and the spring was tight, but with just a little effort she heard the hammer click and lock into place.

Maureen took a deep breath, closed her eyes and thought of her life before all of this. She remembered being in law school, drinking after big exams with her friends. She remembered meeting her husband and going on long walks and talking about their future. She remembered getting the job in the SA's office. Starting a real career in the law. She remembered the case that made her famous, that got her elected State's Attorney. She remembered-

She remembered Gavin Gayle.

He had been a punk. A ruthless kid who showed no remorse for his actions. She had hated him from the moment she met him. Slightly under average height, but solid; strong. He was built like a brick shithouse and wore a permanent scowl under his soft sandy curls. He had caught his girlfriend cheating and beat her up and then killed the kid she was with.

Of course, he swore that's not what happened. He swore that he walked in on her being attacked. He came to her defense. They all say shit like that, but if it were true, she would have said so. She would have jumped to his defense. Of course, she hadn't. She hadn't said anything. It was a slam dunk case, even for an Assistant State's Attorney like her.

That was until the tape showed up. He had always said there was a video. One of those small handheld camcorders with the fold out screens. He said someone was recording the whole thing, but of course there was no such evidence. Then, the day of her closing statement, after spoon feeding the jury her compelling and airtight case, she came back to her office; and there it was.

It was in an envelope, delivered by U.S. Mail. No note, no information on the sender. Just a brown envelope with the tape inside, and on the tape, the video of Weather Rose being attacked and Gavin coming in and saving her.

Maureen thought a lot about the tape that night. She thought about where it could have come from, why it just showed up, what it meant for the defense, and what it meant for her. For her, for her it meant that the most high-profile case she'd ever worked on was over. She wouldn't win it. It would crumble around her and be forgotten. Her name would stop showing up on TV and in the papers. The Tribune had called her a shoo-in for the next SA. For her it meant hitting a brick wall at a thousand miles an hour. For him, well, he was still the kind of kid that could beat someone to death with his bare hands. If he didn't go down now, he would eventually. Eventually after someone else got hurt.

She took the tape and slid it in her purse and zipped the pocket shut. That was that. She didn't think about it again; until now.

She jumped and her heart skipped. She very nearly let the gun she was holding in her lap go off. She was shaking a little and almost started to cry. She looked up and shook her body to regain composure.

Maureen closed her eyes again and began to cry. She felt the heavy steel in her hands and thought about her life and her family. She slid her thumb back to the hammer and pulled back just slightly, eased the trigger back just a hair and slowly guided the hammer softly back to a resting position, then set the gun down on her desk and leaned back in her chair and sobbed.

She cried until she slept. When she woke up it was dark. The clock on her wall, barely visible in the dim light cast by her desk lamp, read one thirty-eight. She looked at her cell phone and saw nine missed calls, twelve text messages, and seven voicemail messages. She decided that it was too late to call home, but she sent her husband a text saying she was sorry, and she had fallen asleep at the office. She would be home soon and would take the day off.

She swiveled in her chair to face her desk and drew a set of keys from her purse. A small brass key in the middle slid neatly into the lock on the top right-hand drawer of her desk. She twisted it and pulled the drawer open.

Deep inside she retrieved the small black plastic square. She turned it in her hands and remembered how she felt when she put Gavin away. She felt proud, she felt strong, she felt powerful. She gently set the evidence back in the desk, picked the gun up and slid it in the same drawer, then locked it again. She grabbed her phone, jacket and hat and pushed her chair back in, under her desk. Everything was going to be okay now. Now she knew what she had to do.

Chapter Five

June 12, 2012 12:16 P.M.

The tables in the prison mess were laid out in a grid system. Each of the collapsible tables held sixteen men, eight per side. There were ten rows and four columns. Forty tables. Six hundred forty men total, plus ten or so men working in the kitchen and slop line. Call it six hundred fifty. For that, they had eight guards in the hall during all meals. Eight. Two at each of the two entrances and four strolling through the grid.

After Jeremy died and I took care of that asshat Benson I started eating in the mess again. People didn't fuck with me anymore; I had a reputation. A new reputation. I was the guy that would drop a fucking free weight on your head, and I sort of liked it.

I always sat in the same seat, north end, last row, last seat. I don't like being boxed in. I wanted to be able to move, to escape quickly if the situation demanded it. Being at the far corner meant that if there was a situation, something that escalated, I was already out of the crowd. I wouldn't have to move through a sea of men bleeding testosterone and resentment. Riots were vanishingly rare, and mass brawls only slightly less so, partly because of the institutional consequences, but also because I made sure of it.

The extra quarter decade added to my sentence spoke volumes to the other inmates. It let them know that I didn't give a shit. I did my best to back that up. I knew I wasn't getting out, and the satisfaction my revenge had given me all but silenced the nagging voice of Weather in my head.

After that I had taken it upon myself to make sure that the well-behaved inmates were protected from the less courteous. I didn't care about drugs or gangs, but I did care about violence. I made it my job to bulk up, muscle up and get into other people's business. I put myself between those trying to do their time in peace and those out to make a name for themselves. The guards noticed and all but endorsed my efforts. Life got better, not just for me but everyone, but in prison you just never know what can happen and I found it best to stay at the fringes, just in case.

The truth is most guys had a specific place where they sat. Mostly it was the same guys sitting around me every day and mostly I was okay with that. I liked routine, it's what made the whole situation tolerable. Predictability and routine were your best friends inside, they're what kept you safe.

I wouldn't go so far as to say I trusted the guys I sat with, that would be a bridge too far. I didn't really trust anyone in there, but I did know them and in prison as in the world at large, the devil you know is better than the devil you don't. So, I had my spot and they all had theirs and that's the way it was.

Mostly.

That day we were eating asparagus again. As usual it wasn't good. It was cold and overcooked. Mushy and bland and enough to make you gag if you looked at it when you ate it, but it was on the line, so it was what we ate. In retrospect I'm pretty sure the reason there was so much asparagus in our diet was to reduce the sexual proclivities of some of the inmates. Even cold, over-cooked, mushy, bland asparagus was effective at making your piss smell foul.

Across from me sat Marco. Marco was of some kind of Mediterranean descent. He was in for shooting his business partner after their startup went belly up. He suspected his partner of embezzling profits and causing the company to fail. I suspected that there were no profits and he was just a douchebag that didn't know how to manage his anger. I suppose I was the pot, and he was the kettle.

Marco was chatting with the guy next to him, rambling on about something that I was trying hard to ignore. I mostly tried to ignore as much as I could, but my attention was caught when Marco suddenly stood up. I glanced up and saw a big guy I didn't recognize. He was tall, with a big frame, sandy blond hair cut short and starting to gray. He wore a five o'clock shadow even though it was only just after twelve in the afternoon and had deep lines around his eyes and across his forehead like a farmer after a grueling summer in the fields. He whispered something to Marco who leaned back to look the guy over. Another whisper and Marco stepped over the bench, grabbed his tray and left. The new guy took his seat.

I looked at him with deep disapproval. This was the kind of thing that made me nervous and when I got nervous that churning in my guts started up. I felt the hairs on the back of my neck twitch and tingle and a little ringing started up in my ears.

"I'm Jake," he said to me ignoring the others around us. His voice was deep and had a rattle to it like he had a loose stone stuck in his throat. It was unsettling and I tightened up inside.

"Hello Jake," I said without giving way to friendliness.

"You're Gavin, right? Gavin Gayle?"

I paused for a moment then gave him a small nod. He talked

fast, verbal diarrhea. He was trying to get it all out before I stopped him.

"Good. Gavin I'm gonna show you something. I'm gonna show you something and then you and I, we're gonna put on a little show. The two of us. I'm telling you this now, giving you a heads up because I need you to trust me."

I cringed; this was getting worse by the minute.

"I don't know you," I said.

"I know that. I know you don't know me, and you don't trust me. Me or anyone else for that matter, but, and I can't stress this enough. This is really important, and I really need your help."

I didn't have anything to say to that. I didn't mind helping people out when it suited me, but there was something about the way this guy was acting that gave me the heebie-jeebies. There's a difference, albeit small, between not trusting someone and distrusting them. As he had said, I didn't trust anyone in there, but I was beginning to get the slightest instinct to distrust this Jake guy. I just stared at him.

"Right, okay," he said.

Jake pulled out an object and set it on the very edge of the table. He covered it with his arms and hands such that only I could see it. It was a knife, or more specifically a dagger. Not a shiv, a real dagger. It had a shiny chrome blade and a thick black handle. This was not something a person could get in prison; this was real world merch. It had to have been smuggled in intentionally and it had to have been by someone who had power. No way this got shipped in, inside a birthday cake. It was real and dangerous, and it was in the hands of a man I didn't know sitting directly across from me.

"You know who I am, right?" I said in a slightly threatening tone.

"I do."

"What is it you think is going to happen here?" I asked.

Jake nodded and motioned at the blade with his eyes.

"I have a friend. On the outside. Someone pretty important actually. She's got a daughter. Good kid, sweet, good grades, no drugs, no drinking. She ran into some trouble, like what your friend got into, but she didn't have a guy like you to stand up for her. When you get out, I want you to help her."

I gave a tired snort.

"I'm not getting out Jake. Not anytime soon. If you know who I am, then you know I got another twenty-five added on after the thing in the weight yard and nothing I do in here is ever going to constitute good behavior. Sorry man. Plus, not to belabor the point but, I don't know you."

"I know. I have nothing I can do right now, at this moment to make you trust me, but the thing is," he rubbed a palm over his tired face and through his aging hair. He looked exhausted. "The thing is I need you to. I need you to trust me and I need you to trust me right now. Right now, at this moment. This is the moment we have and all I can tell you is," he took a deep breath. "I've been in here a long time."

"And that's supposed to make me trust you?" I laughed.

"I've been in here a long time Gavin, and you don't know me."

I saw where he was going. Since the incident with Benson in the weight yard I knew everyone, everyone that was potential trouble at least. I advertised, by way of word of mouth, what was expected. Guys inside knew, do as you like, just don't piss off Gavin. It was clear I wasn't trying to impress anyone, and I didn't care about getting out. Act up, make my life harder or more unpleasant and I'd simply eliminate you as a problem. I was hopeless and angry and had nothing to lose. If I didn't know this guy it meant he'd been keeping himself clean in there.

"That's something," I said. "But I'm sorry, it's not enough."

"I know," he said with a tone that was tired and genuine. "I told you, I can't make you trust me. I just need you to."

"So, Jake-?"

He looked me in the eyes, picked up the cup of coffee that was sitting between us and dumped it down his own shirt.

"What the fuck?" he yelled. "What the fuck was that? Who the fuck do you think you are?"

My heart stopped and I felt the cold metallic sensation of adrenaline surge through my body. I jumped out of my seat and took two quick steps back, but Jake was up too. I side stepped and he matched me move for move.

"You whiny entitled piece of shit, who the fuck do you think you are?"

The room went quiet. Everyone was looking at us. I side stepped again, but he followed me and stepped closer. In a flash he moved his hand past his shirt and produced the knife. He started swinging it at me, wide arcing swings coming nowhere near me, but showing off the blade to everyone around. The fluorescent lighting in the mess hall gleamed on the chrome blade and caught everyone's attention. The four guards who had been strolling the room started moving in quickly towards the commotion.

"No. Jake, don't do this," I pleaded.

"Now!" he whispered.

I looked around trying to find a way out. The room was packed, and everyone was starting to gather around us. I stepped back onto my left foot, faked right then stormed forward trying to get past Jake. He spun backwards and caught me in the chest with the back of his right forearm. It knocked the wind out of me, and he grabbed my shirt and spun me to face him. Then, quick and simple, he slid the blade into my side, right between my ribs.

I was shocked. There was no pain. Jake looked into my eyes

and we stood there for what felt like an eternity, holding on to each other, not moving, not speaking.

Then the pain set in and I felt the knife slide out. I felt my knees buckle and I fell to the floor at his feet. He came down with me, holding me, lowering me gently. There was blood everywhere now. It was on me, on Jake, on the knife and the floor. I felt a sense of quiet and peace. I laid my head on the floor, closed my eyes and heard that same breathless voice say, 'thank you'.

There was commotion around me, and I felt Jake get pulled away. There were hands on my body, touching me, feeling me, looking for the wound, but almost immediately I heard the voice of the managing physician of the infirmary clearing people away. I was lifted off the ground and placed gently onto a stretcher. My wrists and ankles were strapped down and we started moving. There was a long and rushed journey down the corridors of the prison and through the double swing doors of the infirmary, then silence.

Blood was everywhere now. It was on my face and in my hair and all over my clothes. It ran between my fingers, oily and sticky. I felt cold and the room swam around me. I remember wondering how I was still alive. How much blood do you have to lose to die?

I saw the doctor, in a prison guard uniform with a white lab coat over it. He approached me and looked me up and down. He bent over and looked into my eyes. He whispered something to me, but I couldn't understand it, then he picked up a syringe off the steel tray next to the gurney and gave me a shot of something. Almost immediely the room went gray and foggy and suddenly black.

Chapter Six

June 12, 2012 4:07 P.M.

The room was different when my lights came back on. It was larger and brighter. The bed was wider and more comfortable with sheets on it and a dense heavy blanket over me. There was a sound, familiar but out of place. I looked around and found the source, a television. I wasn't in the infirmary anymore; this was a hospital room. I was in a civilian hospital.

You would think that that would have made me elated, but it didn't. It made me nervous. I was never one for change to begin with, and in prison you learn pretty quickly that change is almost never good. I wasn't in prison anymore and that scared me because I didn't know why.

The idea of running did cross my mind. Of course, it did, but it didn't stay there long. Inside you're always being watched even if it doesn't seem like you are. That's a condition that gets inside you. It makes you paranoid and you don't just wake up and let it go. I may have been out of prison for the moment, but I was still under guard. No doubt about it. If I tried to run, I'd get a nightstick in the skull faster than I could check my watch, which I didn't have.

My side ached a little and I moved the blankets to see the wound. It was small. Shockingly small. Four stitches holding it closed and a little redness around the edges. How had a cut that small made so much blood? Why would a cut that small justify taking me out of the prison for treatment at a real hospital? I was feeling the tension building in my chest and shoulders.

Knock knock.

It was two quick raps on the door, and the knocker didn't wait for a response. The wide door swung open and an old black woman in nursing scrubs walked into the room with a smile.

"Good to see you're up young man," she said sweetly.

I coughed and dry swallowed.

"Yeah? Where am I?"

She laughed cheerfully.

"Why can't you tell? You're in The Signature Room on the ninety-fifth floor of the Hancock building. I'm Loretta, I'll be your server tonight. Would you like to start off with an appetizer perhaps? I have raspberry Jell-O in a plastic cup."

I managed a weak smile.

"What hospital is this?" I said.

"Well now, we are back to reality aren't we then. You're in Stroger Hospital young man, and good for you too. We see a lotta stabbin's so you were a piece of vanilla cake."

"Stroger?"

Stroger hospital was in the city. It was downtown. More than thirty miles from the prison. There had to have been four dozen other hospitals between Statesville and there. Why? Why would they take me all the way to the city? It was true that Stroger had a reputation for handling stabbings and shootings. If you got shot in the city, that's where you wanted to go. They just had so much more experience with it there.

But if my wound was so bad that they needed to get me out and to an ER why would they waste the time going all the way to the city. And if it wasn't so bad that time was of the essence why bring me to the experts here. It was paradoxical and it sent a chill down my spine.

"So, uh, where are-"

"The detective is right outside. She's on the phone right now, but I'll let her know you're up and movin'. We'll have you outta here in no time John."

I frowned.

"Gavin."

She raised her eyebrows.

"What's that?"

"My name is Gavin," I said.

She lifted a metal clipboard from a pocket at the end of my bed.

"Gavin? Not John?"

"That's right," I said.

"Gavin Smith?"

"No," I said. "Gavin Gayle"

She bit her lower lip slightly and took a pen out of her breast pocket. She started scribbling.

"G-A-I-L?"

"G-A-Y-L-E," I said.

She nodded.

"All right Gavin, I'll let the detective know you're awake."

Loretta left and I let out a long sigh. Who the fuck was John? Then it hit me, and I felt a cold sweat break out across my body. Smith. She had John Smith down as my name. Not as bad as John Doe, but that's for dead people. If you're living and anonymous you use John Smith. Why was I a secret?

The door opened again and a young woman in a professional looking suit and sensible shoes walked in. She didn't have a purse but clipped to her waist was a holstered handgun and gold five point star with an inset circle and a coat of arms. She was Chicago PD, not State.

"How ya feeling there killer?" she said by way of introduction.

I tried to sit up a bit, straighten myself out. I was in a hospital gown, which always leave you feeling a little exposed and vulnerable, on top of which, I was actually and in fact exposed and vulnerable.

"Hi," I said with the most confused voice I could muster. "What's-"

"No no no. You're not talking now, I am. Got it?"

Her abruptness was startling and stopped me in my tracks.

"Okay, good. Here's how this works. I got no answers for you. Don't ask me things cuz I just don't know. I have two jobs. Get you outta the ambulance and inta the ER, and then outta here and inta the car. Beyond that, I don't know, and I don't wanna know. Got it?"

My head spun. What was going on here?

"Got it?"

I nodded.

She walked over to a flat door next to the entrance to the room and opened it. She pulled out a wad of clothes and walked back to the foot of my bed and threw them at me.

"Good, now get dressed. We got places to be."

This woman scared me. The whole situation scared me. I felt like Alice down the rabbit hole except that I didn't even chase the rabbit. It was like going to bed at night and waking up in another world.

"Chop chop!" she said.

"Am I-" I started.

"I told you, I don't have answers. Just get dressed and get moving. You aint gonna die, I promise."

I climbed slowly out of the hospital bed and put on the clothes she had thrown me. Jeans that were too big with bright patterns on the seat and down one leg, a baggy plain white t-shirt and an oversized Chicago White Sox sweatshirt with a hood. There were High Top sneakers in the closet, but no socks. Once I was dressed, I stood in front of the detective and put out my hands. She stared at me confused.

"What are you doin'?"

I looked at my hands stretched out to her, wrists a few inches apart.

"I, uh…"

She rolled her eyes.

"I'm not cuffing you, you fuckin' moron. How the fuck would that look. Just stay close to me. Don't fuckin' wander. Got it?"

I nodded.

"Uh, yeah. Got it."

"Okay then," she said, and we walked out the door.

It was strange walking through the hospital. I felt like everyone should be watching me. I felt out of place, criminal. I felt like everyone knew who I was and that I didn't belong there. I kept waiting, subconsciously I think, for someone to stand up and point at me. To shout hey you, what are you doing here? I felt like a child trying to sneak into a strip club.

No one was watching though. No one stared. No one even looked. I walked with the detective down the long pale hallway to a bank of old elevators. I stood rigidly as we waited for the elevator car to arrive and the doors to squeal open, then followed her onto the lift and stood silently as she pressed the button for P2. The doors squealed shut again and I got that forgotten sensation of movement without moving.

When the doors opened again, we stepped out into a dark, cold underground parking garage. The concrete ground was wet, and the air had an acrid rusty taste to it. We moved silently down an aisle of cars that felt just slightly futuristic to me. I hadn't seen a car in five years and the designs felt just a little curvier with colors just a little off from what I remembered.

At the end of the aisle we turned and headed down another row of cars. Halfway down was a police squad car with its engine running and headlights on. The detective walked me up to it and opened the rear driver's side door.

"Get in," she said curtly.

I did as I was told.

It had been a while since I'd been in a police car, but it was just as I remembered. There was no legroom, the seats were a kind of plastic made to look like, but not feel like leather. There was a panel of thick bulletproof Plexiglas separating the front and back seats and a wire cage up against that. There was also another person.

Across from me in the back seat was another woman. This one was slightly older and significantly better dressed. She had on a black pencil skirt slit up past her knee, black stockings and red heels. Her blouse was red silk and covered by an expensive looking blazer. She wore gold jewelry around her neck and at her ears. Her makeup was expertly applied, and her long brunette hair was pulled up into an elaborately braided bun. I knew this woman.

"Gavin," she said in what sounded like a rehearsed professional tone.

The driver's door opened, and the detective climbed into the car. She buckled in but didn't put the car in gear. She just sat there, facing forward, silently like a limo driver minding their own business.

I looked at the woman and grimaced. I had a pain in my gut and the first low waves of an anxiety attack washing up into my lungs.

"It's nice to see you again," she said.

I gritted my teeth and fought against the panic that was trying so hard to take hold of me. I let out a long breath and closed my eyes. When I reopened them, she was still there, staring at me with her hazel gaze.

"ASA Adalet," I said. "What is going on?"

She smiled shallowly, then the smile widened and soon she was laughing.

"What's so funny," I asked.

"Oh Gavin. It's okay, you've been away."

She said it like I'd been in the Bahamas for a week.

"It's not ASA anymore. I moved up. State's Attorney Adalet will be just fine."

I felt the nausea hit me like a bucket of water. I had to cover my mouth to keep from throwing up in the car. Maureen Adalet was the State's Attorney now. My shock must have been apparent because she reached out and put her hand on my shoulder.

"It's okay Gavin. Actually, I probably have you to thank for it. Trying your case made me a household name. The election was a landslide."

I leaned back and put out my hands for support.

"Hey, be happy," she said jovially. "You're here with me instead of getting raped in a cell down south. You've got me to thank for that and I'd never have been able to pull that off as an Assistant."

"But why Maureen?" I said with hesitation. "Why am I here?"

She smiled.

"The why's will come Gavin. They exist. Obviously, there's a reason I went through the substantial trouble and risk of getting you out of there, but let's come back to that. For now, let's get you home."

Home of course was a joke. I had no home. I had nowhere to go. No one that would take me in or want to see me. As it turns out, that hardly mattered. As we pulled out of the hospital's parking garage and onto the crooked pavement of Ogden Avenue Maureen explained my situation to me.

"You're not going back Gavin. It's important that you understand that."

I nodded the affirmative, but of course I didn't really. I had no idea what she was talking about.

"I'm serious," she said. "Never going back. Not ever for any reason. Look at me when I talk to you Gavin."

I looked at her.

"You can't ever go back to prison."

"Maureen-"

"SA Adalet will do fine thank you."

That annoyed me.

"Fine, SA Adalet, is this some kind of medical release? Is it because I was stabbed?"

She laughed, hard this time. Real laughter, she found me funny.

"Jesus fucking Christ Gavin. You're dumber than I thought."

Now I was pissed. I hated being called dumb.

"You don't get it at all, do you? That was me. I made that happen so I could get you out. It was an act. A con. Good god, I really would have thought you'd figured that part out on your own. You're dead Gavin. You don't exist anymore."

I must have looked especially lost. Deer in the headlights kind of stare. I know I felt as though I'd been pulled out of my body and forced to watch the whole thing from above.

"I'm what?"

"You were shived Gavin. In plain sight of everyone. You fell on the ground, bled all over the floor. They rushed you down to the medical office, but sadly, they were unsuccessful in saving your life. You passed away, a tragedy of our violent prison system. Your family, such as it is, has been notified and a box of ashes is being delivered to their home."

"I died?"

"That's right. So, you see why it's so important that you don't end up in a situation where you would potentially be dealing with the judicial system again. It would be difficult to explain how you're out and about in the world when your fingerprints are associated with a dead man."

"But why," I said again. "I don't understand, why are you doing this for me? Did you find the video? Did you talk to Weather? Why not just let me go? Why is this happening?"

Adalet looked impatient. She checked her watch and glanced out the window of the car. We were leaving Congress Parkway, taking the on ramp to the Eisenhower expressway heading east.

"Look Gavin, we don't have a lot of time. In about fifteen minutes I'm dropping you off and then you'll never see me again. You'll get your answers, but that will have to be later. There's a reason you're out, but it's not because I like you. I need you and it's just that simple. You're out here to do something for me and when that thing is done, well, I don't know what will happen next, but in the meantime, there are rules."

I choked on a piece of laughter.

"Rules? What kind of rules?"

Maureen took a deep breath and stared me in the eyes.

"One, you don't leave the city. Consider it house arrest. You have the city limits of Chicago to move around in, but you never leave those confines. Ever. Two, you can't contact anyone you knew before. No friends, no family, no old teachers or guys you played tiddlywink with. No one knows you're alive, and that leads to rule three. You can't have a job. Dead people don't work. There's a death certificate on file with the state and your social security number is defunct. You can't fill out paperwork, take out a loan, get a credit card, sign a contract or do anything that requires an identity because you don't have one. Lastly, you stay out of trouble. If you're found wandering around doing petty crimes or so much as, I don't know, jaywalking; people are going to want answers. Your file says you're dead. Don't make me make it true."

The car pulled off the expressway. We'd left 290 and taken the Dan Ryan south for most of the drive. Now we were at 103rd Street, the deep south side of the city with cracked pavement and abandoned houses. We sat in silence for the rest of the trip. A couple miles down the road we took a left on Torrence Ave and came to a stop.

Outside the car was a small red wall with a green door. It was wedged between two shops but had no signage of its own. There was a red awning and a small window that was papered over from the inside, but nothing to suggest that it was inhabited in any way.

"That's it," she said. "Detective Hinde up there will be in touch. She'll let you know what's next. Don't try and reach me though. As far as you and I are concerned we're strangers."

"Where do you want me to go?" I asked.

She gestured with her head at the green door outside.

"You'll be safe in there. They'll look out for you for the time being. Now go, get the fuck out of my sight, and Gavin, don't fuck this up."

Detective Hinde opened my door and I stepped out. It was starting to rain, and the pavement had a glassy shine. I walked around the squad car and stepped up on the sidewalk, turning back just in time to see them pull away and disappear into traffic down the street.

I took a deep breath and thought about running. I really

could have. I could've hit the road and never been seen again. I could've been free, but something in me, something broken, wouldn't allow it. I stood in the rain, my sweatshirt and jeans getting soaked and looked at the green door on the red wall. A voice in my head said that something bad was coming, but I didn't see any other options.

I knocked on the door.

* * *

The door was heavy, solid wood, but old. The edges were starting to rot, dropping sawdust on the threshold and creating a gap at the bottom between the door and the ground. It was hand painted forest green with a brush. You could see the lines from the bristles in the paint and there were scattered chip marks where the color had come off and the battered wood shone through. It was the only green door on the block as far as I could tell, but it was locked, and no one was responding to my persistent knocking. I looked around. There were cars driving down the road which was Torrance Avenue if the street sign at the corner was to be believed. Pedestrians moved up and down the sidewalk, passing me without a second glance, or even a first one for that matter. Everyone was minding their own business, making a special effort not to notice the crazy man pounding on the door of the boarded-up shop.

My hand pulled back to bang again on the ragged obstacle when I heard a muffled grunt come from behind the door. There was a screech, like nails on a chalkboard and I heard a heavy click like a sturdy lock being unlatched. The door swung open.

In the door frame was a monster of a man. He was dressed casually in jeans, sneakers, a t-shirt and a half zipped up hoodie. He was intimidating, almost frightening. He had dark black skin with deep eyes and a wide round face. Standing at easily six foot four he had to weigh over three hundred pounds. His hair was trimmed close to his scalp and his nose looked like it had been broken at some point in the past. The deep eyes looked me up and down with an expression of surprise and something else. Was it worry?

"What the heck?"

His voice shocked me. It was deep, as it should be, but it was soft and had a child's slow measured tone. It wasn't aggressive, but rather concerned. An emotion that was mirrored in the expression on his face.

I glanced around to my sides quickly and back at the man.

"Hi, sorry, I'm..." I was stuttering. "I'm, well, I guess I don't really-"

"You're yonga than I thought."

"What?" I said.

"I thought you'd be olda," he said as if it was a criticism. "You'd betta get inside I guess."

I didn't know what to say, I was so confused, but I obliged quickly and without further comment. The door swung closed behind me and for a moment the room was pitch black. I wasn't crazy about the dark, it reminded me of the hole back in Statesville. Solitary confinement. A four by six-foot room with no lights, no running water, no cot. Just a stuffed mattress on the floor and a seatless toilet in the corner. This felt like that, but only for a moment before my eyes adjusted and the light spilling in from under the door and a flickering from somewhere in front of me cast sepia toned shallow contrast across the features of the space.

It was a narrow brick corridor. Not cinder block like the building around it, but real red brick, seriously old and worn smooth as if it were covered in fabric. It was so narrow I could reach out and place a flat palm on both sides at the same time.

There was maybe six feet of walkable length before it dropped off steeply down a short set of cobblestone stairs that led to a huge ornate wooden door with an unsettling wrought iron knocker and heavy black iron handle set between two wax candles in medieval looking wall sconces.

The giant was still in front of me, guiding me through the space. He pressed the thumb lever on the handle and swung the door open. I half expected the hinges to creak as the door opened, like it was some Vincent Price movie. I figured this must be The Pit so inside I expected to find The Pendulum. The door, however, swung open silently and smoothly and led into a rather nice, if slightly dated and run down, nightclub.

We stepped through to a raised platform, maybe fifteen feet on each side. A wooden rail with brass accents ran around it and there were chestnut benches with red leather cushions placed along the wall on two sides. At the far end was an ornate wooden host stand manned by a surprisingly young-looking twig of a man in a striped violet dress shirt.

Beyond the platform was an enormous space. Red brick walls with framed art. Red and gold patterned carpet like you would find in a hotel lobby covered spots and a long wood bar with a tattered leather bar rail and unmatched bar stools. It was dark and moody, like something from a Conan Doyle story that time forgot.

The mountain of a man that was leading me approached the twiggy guy. After greeting him, he stepped to the side to reveal me standing behind him.

"Can you tell him dat Mr. Gayle is here?"

"He's in the back, why don't you just take him back there?" the host said with a feathery effeminate voice.

"I gotta get back up to my door."

"Christ, no one's gonna knock on that door Nate. No one ever knocks on that door."

"He did." the man apparently called Nate said.

The scrawny host let out a long, exasperated sigh.

"Okay, fine, I'll take him back."

"Thanks."

Nate patted me on the shoulder, and it felt like someone hit me with a bag of flour. I let out a little groan.

"Drake'll take you back to see Mr. Simons."

With that, Nate turned around and went back through the wide doorway and back up the stairs. I turned back to face the fop called Drake.

"Mr. Simons?"

"He runs The Club." Drake said. "He's sort-of the manager. He has some clean clothes for you, and I imagine you'll want something to eat."

"Sort of the manager?"

"Eh, the owner of The Club is..."

Drake took an uncomfortable pause.

"Away. So, Mr. Simons is looking after the place until he gets back."

"And is Mr. Simons as vague and nonspecific as you are?"

"He'll tell you what he wants to, and not tell you what he doesn't. He's doing you a big favor here. I wouldn't look a gift horse in the mouth if I were you."

"I don't think it's me he's doing the favor for," I said, more to myself than to him.

"Yeah, maybe not. Still, I just wouldn't."

"Okay," I said. "Got it."

We walked through the dining room to an old-fashioned kitchen door on swinging hinges with a big circular window that was foggy with years of grime. On the other side of the door was a small kitchen with modern stainless-steel counters, tables, and appliances. In the back of that was another green door with a heavy looking round steel doorknob and a don't fuck with me looking deadbolt above it. Drake knocked on the door.

"It's open." Came the voice, from inside.

Drake turned the knob and opened the door as far as he could while still holding onto the knob.

"Mr. Simons, Mr. Gayle is here."

"Ah, okay, good. That's very good. Glad to hear it. Please, send him in."

Drake moved aside but kept his hand on the door. I looked at him with uncertainty, then looked back behind us. Deciding there wasn't an alternative I turned back around and walked past Drake into the room. The door closed behind me quickly.

I was in what looked like an apartment. It was small, but it was definitely a living space. I was standing on a five by five-foot square of emerald green floor tiles with flecks of white and another, darker shade of green in them. Directly to my right was a very small kitchen with a tiny electric stove, fridge, microwave, and a stainless-steel sink. In front was a forest green carpet, long stranded, but not quite shag. It looked old and worn and almost threadbare in spots. There was an ancient brown sofa in the middle of the room facing a brown tanker chest serving as a coffee table of sorts and an old wood tube television that was more a piece of furniture than an appliance.

Stepping into the room further I saw a short hallway to my right with three doors, one on either side and one at the end. A toilet flushed and a sink ran for a minute, then the door on the right side of the hall opened up and a man stepped out.

He was old. Not in his last days, but well into his seventies. He wore dress slacks, a blue oxford button-down shirt, and nice shoes. His hair was thin and salt and pepper but combed nicely and well cut. He took two steps forward and stuck out his hand.

"Hi, hello, hi there. I'm Greg. Greg Simons. You must be Gavin. Great to meet you. Glad you could make it."

He paused and laughed a little at his own joke.

"Glad you could make it. Right? Ha!"

"Nice to meet you as well Mr. Simons," I said without being convinced it was true.

"Please, call me Greg."

"Your friends called you Mr. Simons."

"Who, them?"

He nodded at the door. I nodded back.

"Ah yes, well, they aren't my friends. They work for me, so, yes, they call me Mr. Simons, but you, I'm hoping we can be friends. No reason not to; be friends that is. So you should call me Greg. Really, I would much prefer you call me Greg."

"Okay, Greg it is."

"Thanks."

"So, Greg."

"Yes?"

"Maybe you can explain to me what exactly is going on here."

Greg looked confused. He wrinkled his forehead and leaned in a little bit.

"Going on where?"

Now I was annoyed. I didn't want to have to play twenty questions, I just wanted some straightforward answers.

"Going on here. Here, right now, what is going on? Why am I here?"

He sighed, smiled, and nodded.

"Ah yes. I see. Well son, I think your first order of business should be to get cleaned up. I don't mean to point out the obvious, but you are kind of a mess right now."

I sighed now. Irritated that I was being put off again. Though, he wasn't wrong. Even with the new clothes, my hair still had blood in it and I was dirty and smelled like prison still.

"Right. Okay, but..."

"There is a shower and sundries in the bathroom there and I have some clean clothes hanging on the back of the door. I'll whip us up something to eat while you get cleaned up. Then we can eat and talk. There's an envelope with a little cash on the dresser. Won't be enough to live on, but that's what we're here for. There's a bed, a dresser, and some personal space."

I stared at him for a time with suspicious eyes, then with the calm that comes with acceptance, I dropped my shoulders, took a breath, and walked into the bathroom and closed the door.

Chapter Seven

June 12, 2012 5:21 P.M.

We ate tapenade and toast points with shaved garlic. It was good, very good in fact. I hadn't realized how much I missed good food. Prison had been murder on my pallet. My tastes had always been refined. That came from growing up with parents who had good taste. I was eating and enjoying foods that most people never tried when I was four years old, and by the time I was fifteen I could tell you what wine varietal would pair well with various dishes. I acknowledge I was a bit of a snob and a foodie, but I don't apologize for it.

The food we were eating, the tapenade, the toast points, rare lamb chops, hearty spinach salad and robust pinot noir were not the best I'd ever had, but they were close. I ate every bite with closed eyes, savoring the moment. I really hadn't realized just how bad the prison food had been until that very moment.

"So Gavin." Mr. Simons began after almost an hour of silence between us. "You have the room as long as you like. The kitchen is yours, during operating hours you can eat in the dining room. I'm supposed to remind you to stay in the city, stay out of trouble, and keep your nose clean."

"Mr. Simons,"

"Greg."

I sighed.

"Greg, I appreciate all of this, I really do, but if you don't mind too awfully much, what am I doing here?"

He leaned back in his chair and crossed his arms. He was a distinguished looking older man with good manners and a gentle disposition.

"I guess I don't really understand the question," he said with what sounded like sincerity.

"Well," I said, wishing this didn't have to be such a struggle. "I woke up this morning in Statesville. I was at the tail end of the first nickel of my forty-three-year sentence. Then out of, pardon my language, but out of fucking nowhere, in the middle of lunch I am pulled into some elaborate prison break scenario that was, apparently, orchestrated by the same woman who put me in there in the first place.

"Then I'm dropped off in front of your building with no explanation or direction, only to find out that everyone is expecting me. No offense Mr. Simons,"

"Please, Greg." he interrupted assertively.

"No offense Greg, because I really am very grateful for all of this, but I'd really like to know what the fuck is going on."

Mr. Simons looked pityingly at me. He took a sip of his wine and set the glass back down.

"Gavin, I wish I had the answers for you. I would love to tell you why you're here, why you were let out, and what the meaning of life is, but I don't have those answers.

"My boss, and good friend, called me. He said that we were going to have a visitor. He gave me your name and told me that every accommodation was to be made for you. He didn't say when you were coming, or how long you'd be staying, or how you'd get here, or even where you were coming from. He just said that we should do everything we could to make you comfortable."

"Who's your boss?" I asked.

"He's away."

I rubbed my eyes with my fingertips, then let out a long breath.

"Away is a where Mr.-"

He shot me a glance.

"Greg. It's a where, not a who."

He nodded. "I think that, given the circumstances of your visit with us Gavin, my friend would like to remain somewhat anonymous for the time being."

"Did he say that?"

"No, he didn't say it, but I am going to assume it. I know him pretty well, that's why I'm running things while he's away. I know what he would want without having to have him say it."

"Well, isn't that Butch and Sundance of you?"

"Yes, you might say that it is."

We ate the rest of our meal in silence, then he gave me a ring with two keys. One for the room he had put me in and one for the front door of the building. When Mr. Simons left to get things ready for opening The Club for the night I went back to my room and shut the door. I laid down on the small twin bed in the corner of the room and went to sleep.

* * *

10:36 P.M.

Maureen waited until the last A.SA poked their head in her office and said goodnight, the last lights had been shut off for the

78

night, and the last of the cleaning crew had rolled their carts onto the elevator. Then, at ten forty-five p.m. she walked out of her office and down the hall to the records room.

The room was a large rectangle painted zombie gray with row after row of butter white lateral filing cabinets. The end of each row was labeled with magnetic letters indicating the alphabetical range of the files in that row. She walked to the aisle labeled "Cu-Doc" and found the drawer containing the file on Kevin Dobson. She opened the drawer and pulled the file, then walked to the end of the row, leaving the cabinet open.

In the corner of the room was a massive industrial copy machine that everyone referred to as Once-ler. Maureen approached it and flipped the heavy toggle switch to turn it on. As the Once-ler warmed up she methodically went through the file and removed every staple, paperclip, and binder clip, then tapped the edges of the pile of papers to align them into one neat stack.

She set the documents in the feed tray, tapped the option for two sided copies, and hit start. The machine hummed, clicked, and began sucking in pages and spitting out the originals into a discard tray. Copies of every page landed in an angled bin on the end of the machine.

When the Once-ler was done, Maureen slid on a pair of latex medical gloves, picked up the copies and dropped them into a manila mailing envelope. She replaced the originals back in the file and carried it back to the file cabinet, replacing it exactly where it had come from and closed the drawer.

She grabbed the mailing envelope on the way back to her office. Inside, she dropped it on her desk and moved around to the back side and unlocked the top right-hand drawer. From inside she pulled out a clear plastic clamshell case and a small yellow bottle with a blue cap and red nozzle. The bottle was dropped into the envelope. After that she took a pair of scissors from a cup on the top of her desk and cut open the plastic container and pulled out a small gold Zippo lighter. She flipped it open and spun the wheel. It sparked but didn't light. It was, too, placed inside the envelope.

She closed the envelope without licking the glue and fastened the brass brad, then pulled a roll of tape from the top right drawer of her desk. The tape was opaque white with tiny red lettering printed across it that said eyes only over and over again. She peeled off a strip of the tape about seven inches long and pressed it across the envelope flap, sealing it shut. She flipped the envelope over and pressed a laser printed address label to the middle of the paper. Half a dozen no lick stamps of various denominations were affixed to the upper right-hand corner and then she dropped the envelope in her huge purse.

Maureen turned off her office lights, locked the top right-hand drawer of her desk, gathered the empty plastic container the lighter had been in, and walked out her office door.

Twenty minutes later she had dropped the envelope in a blue USPS mailbox ten blocks from her office in the opposite direction of her house. Then she walked back to her office, got in her car, and drove home.

* * *

11:50 P.M.

When I woke up it was dark. I didn't remember turning off the lights before falling asleep, but they were off now. My immediate assumption was that Mr. Simons must have turned them off while I was sleeping. I made a mental note not to expect privacy in this living arrangement.

I sat up and turned on the lamp that sat on the nightstand next to the bed. I rubbed my eyes for a bit, then my neck. After a minute I stood up and started looking around the room. I wasn't used to anything that big and it made me uneasy.

The clothes that had been provided by Mr. Simons were good enough. Department store brand jeans, black long-sleeved t-shirt, white discount store gym socks, and some brand-new Nikes. There was also a decent brandless canvas jacket that would be more than adequate for Chicago weather through the end of October. None of it was what I would have called my style but compared to the orange cotton jumpsuit I had been wearing for the past four years, anything else was a welcomed change.

I made my way back to the kitchen, which was now bustling with activity. There were two chefs cooking at the stoves and two workers of Mexican origin based on their accents, arranging plates for presentation. There were also two young ladies in black skirts and men's white button up dress shirts that appeared to be The Club's wait staff.

I looked around for a moment and spied a bowl of red apples on one of the stainless-steel countertops. I picked one up and polished it on my shirt. The food in prison had been mass produced for hundreds of inmates at the absolute lowest possible price point. The closest thing we ever got to fresh meat was an overcooked chicken breast maybe once a month if the prison's supplier had extra from a canceled order or some other mistake. Other than that, it was dried meat, soggy frozen vegetables, powdered mashed potatoes, and sometimes on very special occasions, white rice.

The only saving grace had been the apples. After I had dropped the weight on the skinhead mother fucker in the yard and the word got around that I had a short temper and nothing to lose things had changed for me. I had always avoided confrontation before that, now confrontation was avoiding me. The inmate buzz was that I had started taking security into my own hands. It turned out there had been lots of guards who felt, well, grateful. Some maybe even indebted. Giving me a long leash ended up making their jobs easier and arguably safer.

One of these guards had an apple tree at home. He began bringing in fresh apples for me in season. Every night when I got back to my cell there was a fresh, ripe apple sitting on my bunk waiting for me.

I began looking forward to lockdown each night. I would sit on my cot, meticulously polish the apple to a shine, then pull the stem out with my teeth and bite deeply into the crisp fruit. It was the best moment of my entire day.

Before prison apples weren't really my thing. I didn't dislike them, but I was pretty ambivalent. Apple pie was always nice, but raw apples, I could take 'em or leave 'em. But when the only fresh food I got were those apples; well, I found I savored them, and quickly developed a passion for the fruit. Now I felt that, put in Eve's place, I would have traded paradise for a bite as well.

I finished polishing the apple and popped the stem off with my teeth like I was pulling the pin on a round, red, grenade. I spit the stem into a nearby trash can and took a monstrous bite, closing my eyes and relishing the tart juice as it filled my mouth. It tasted just as good as freedom.

"You must be Gavin," said a melodic female voice. I spun around to see a gorgeous young woman with auburn hair, deep hazel eyes, and a perfect hourglass figure dressed in the server's uniform I had noticed earlier.

I took another bite of the apple and chewed it while sizing her up. I swallowed half of it with a gulping sound and said, "Mm hmm. I am indeed."

She smiled at me.

I smiled back and said, "And who might you be?"

She laughed a fresh, light, carefree laugh and said, "I'm Katie. I work here. I'm a server."

I hadn't seen anyone so at ease in a long time. I found it instantly disarming and felt myself relax.

"It's very nice to meet you Katie."

"Likewise, I'm sure," she said. "I hear you're going to be staying with us for a while."

"Not too long I hope." I bit the apple again. "Your boss has been very generous, but I don't want to overstay my welcome."

"Not likely," She said. "This is what he does."

That made me frown.

"What's that?" I asked.

"Take in strays," she said slyly.

"Oh. Is that what I am? A stray?"

"Well," she smiled again, and I felt more tension drop from my shoulders. "You're here."

I felt myself break into the first sincere smile I'd had in more than five years.

"Touché."

"Are you going to come out to the dining room and have some dinner?"

I hadn't thought that far ahead yet, but it occurred to me at that moment, by that question, that I could go anywhere. I could just run. Get on a bus and get out of town, or could I. It seemed unlikely that SA Adalet would go through all the trouble of sneaking me out just to let me go on the lamb my first night.

"Oh, not tonight I don't think," I said, testing the waters. "I just got into town, as it were, and I think I'm going to go out and enjoy the whole, fresh air of it all."

Katie laughed deeply and it made me smile.

"What did I say?" I asked, laughing a little myself.

"As it were? Of it all? Who talks like that?"

I cocked my head. She was making fun of me. She was,

maybe, flirting with me. I couldn't tell. It had been a long time since anyone had flirted with me.

"Well, I guess I do."

"Okay then Mr. Gayle, you can enjoy the fresh air of it all, all you want, but first you are going to come sit down and have dinner. Best food in the city here, and it's all our little secret. Come sit, have a drink, have a meal, and then go out and see the sites... as it were."

I sighed and let my shoulders fall.

"Whatever you say Ms. Katie, I am in your hands."

She smiled and tilted her head as if to say, 'follow me'.

The dining room felt very different during business hours. The room was dim, almost dark, and looked vastly bigger than it had with the fluorescent work lights on. The walls seemed to disappear into the shadows giving the impression that the room went on forever. The glassware all appeared old and worn, and from what I could see, none of the dishware matched. The bar itself looked like it was about a hundred years old. Most of the varnish had worn away leaving dry splitting wood in some places. Overall it felt like a classy place that had grown worn for lack of upkeep.

It wasn't what I would have called busy. About a dozen people in all, spread throughout the dining room, at the bar, tables, and sofas. The soft whispered conversations of the scattered guests were drowned out by a slightly out of tune piano playing a bluesy Tom Waits number but voiced by a deep throated red haired girl. Her voice was soft and alternated between smooth and scratchy. She sang passionately with her eyes closed, as if to herself.

Katie stopped at the bar and leaned over to ask the bartender something. She glanced at me, then nodded in the direction of the host stand.

"Wait here a second," She said and hurried away.

The bartender walked up to where I was standing. She was drying a glass with a white rag and eyeing me up and down.

"So, you're Gavin then."

I raised my eyebrows and gave a weak nod.

"It appears so."

"Can I get you anything?"

I eyed the glass she was holding and glanced at the liquor bottles lining the shelves behind her.

"What do you suggest?"

The barkeep looked at me thoughtfully, then reached under the bar and pulled out a tall skinny glass cylinder with a red label and black lettering that simply said Redemption. She pulled the cork from the bottle and poured the brown liquid into the glass she had been polishing and set it on the bar.

I reached in my pocket and pulled out the envelope of cash that had been left in my room, but the woman waved me off.

"No charge."

"Well, thank you," I said.

I picked up the glass and took a sip. It was warm and spicy with just a hint of sweetness underneath. I swallowed it and soft fire spread through my throat, chest and belly.

"That's good," I said.

The bartender smiled and handed me the bottle.

"Why don't you just keep this for tonight," She said.

"Oh, I couldn't."

"Sure, you can. You probably need it. Don't worry, we've got more."

"Alright," I said hesitantly. "Thanks." I took the bottle and another sip from the glass just as Katie walked back up to me.

"Mr. Simons said to give you the booth."

"Okay. The booth?"

Katie smiled.

"Yeah, we only have the one actual booth. It's in the VIP section."

She walked me over to what was undoubtedly the darkest corner of the room. There was a raised platform, just one step up, covered in wide mahogany floorboards and surrounded by a wooden rail. It was maybe twelve feet square and held one large corner booth with red faux leather cushions that faced out into the room and one highboy style table. There were no lights of any kind and the acoustics were such that the sounds from the rest of the room, the piano and its player, and the other customers, were all dampened to a barely audible background hush.

"VIP section?" I asked. "It seems more like the leper section. Is Mr. Simons trying to hide me?"

She laughed again. Either she liked me, or she found the world ceaselessly entertaining.

"Well, our VIPs generally prefer privacy. This is actually the best seat in the house."

I shrugged again and sat down in the booth. I set the bottle of Redemption on the table and sipped from my glass.

Katie said, "I'm going to go to the Kitchen and put your order in and I'll be right back. Is there anything else you need right now?"

"Uh, I haven't seen a menu yet."

Katie gave me a practiced and understanding look.

"We don't have menus, Gavin. It's not a restaurant, it's a private club. Lisa and Louise, our chefs, they decide on a menu each day and that's what it is. Our clients pay a substantial membership fee, and with it comes all the food, drinks, and privacy they want. There's no cover at the door, no check to pay at the end, no bar tab, and no questions. Only members are allowed in. No walk-ins, and no guests. New membership is by management invite only."

I got an oily sick feeling in my gut.

"So, it's a mob club?"

Katie laughed hard.

"No. No Gavin, it's not a mob club. No criminal element here at all in fact. Our membership screening is very thorough. Before our owner took over, there was a gang presence here, but it was just a speakeasy kind of place. A secret remnant of the prohibition years. But when the current owner took over, he kicked out all the gang bangers, drug dealers, and anyone that was questionable at all. He cleaned it up and stuck Nate on security. Now it's members only, and congrats, that means you."

Something about the scenario didn't sit right with me, but I didn't see any point in arguing with her.

"So," Katie said again. "I'm gonna go back to the kitchen and put your order in. It's Buffalo Carpaccio and grilled asparagus tonight. Is there anything else you need?"

"I don't suppose the bar has cigarettes?"

"Sure, what brand do you smoke?"

I paused.

"I haven't really thought about that in a while, but I guess I used to smoke Camels."

"Wide's or Lights?"

"Wide's would be great. Is there a back door or something to step outside?"

Katie smiled again sweetly.

"Gavin, it's a private club. You can smoke inside. I'll bring you an ashtray."

I shook my head in confused wonder.

"Sorry, thanks."

"No worries."

She walked off and left me sitting in the booth looking out over the room. I thought about the day and what was going to come next. I felt like I was treading water in the middle of the ocean as sharks circled closer and closer. So, this was going to be home. This weird little box that seemed to have as many secrets as me.

I sipped my drink and stared at the bottle. Redemption. The bartender was right; that was what I needed tonight.

Chapter Eight

June 13, 2012 10:44 A.M.

I was a little hazy when I opened my eyes. I'd been dreaming about Weather which was jarring. I hadn't really dreamed about her in years, though she was never far from my mind while awake. When I opened my eyes, I half expected a view of the dull grey grid of springs on the cot above mine in my cell. Instead the darkness of my new room under the cinderblock box surrounded me.

I laid there motionless for a long while, letting my eyes adjust. With no windows, the room never betrayed the time of day, and with no clock I had no idea how late the drinks from the previous night had made me sleep.

Katie had been right, the food had been excellent, and it had been nice to relax with all the drinks and smokes and food I wanted. It had been a pleasant night all things considered, and I had to admit I could have ended up in a worse situation.

I sat up and fumbled for the light next to my bed. When I could see again, I noticed a clear plastic dry cleaning bag hanging on the inside of the door to the room. Inside, it appeared, were the same jeans and shirt I had been wearing when I arrived. Privacy was definitely an issue here and it was already beginning to seem like a slightly better decorated prison. I decided the only way to know for sure was to try to leave.

I showered in my bathroom and inspected myself in the mirror. I needed to shave, but the razor that had been provided was a yellow and white plastic disposable with a single blade. I had been using that exact model in the joint for years, but I'd be damned if my first shave as a free man, if that was indeed what I was, would be with one of those.

I washed my face, hard, with a cloth and the bar soap on the sink and brushed my teeth with the orange plastic toothbrush whose bristles were too soft. The toothpaste left a stale chalky mint taste in my mouth. I rinsed with water from the sink until the taste was gone, then redressed in the clothes from the dry-cleaning bag.

I grabbed the envelope of cash from under the mattress where I had stashed it the night before; a holdover habit from prison where anything you didn't want to lose, had to stay pressed firmly against your body at all times.

I stepped out of my room and walked down the hallway and through the kitchen. Lisa and Louise were just getting in and unloading the day's fresh ingredients for the night's menu. From the look of it tonight would be oysters and endive salad. I had to admit, if this was to be just another prison, it was a lot better than where I had been.

The clock in the kitchen said eleven-thirty. I'd slept late. I grabbed an apple from the bowl in the kitchen on the way through, then thought better of it and grabbed two, sticking one in my pocket and biting deeply into the other while throwing a passive wave to the two chefs preparing their kitchen, then headed out into The Club.

There was no one in the dining room as I walked through,

and the host stand was abandoned as well. I opened the heavy door to the dimly lit stairs and walked through letting the door shut behind me and stood still until my eyes adjusted to the darkness, then slowly I climbed the stairs.

At the top of the stairs Nate sat in his tiny folding chair protecting the front door. I took two steps forward and he stood, stepping in front of me and in front of the door. I stood still and silent for a moment, then the big man spoke.

"Mr. Gayle."

I gazed up at his square face.

"Nate," I said.

"Can I get you a cab?" he asked in a helpful voice.

I stood dazed for a second, surprised at the offer. I think I had expected him to try and stop me from leaving. "No thank you Nate," I said. "I think I'll walk."

Nate nodded once and pushed the door open to the late morning sun and stood aside.

I looked at him with an unwarranted suspicion, then carefully stepped past him.

"Have a good afternoon Mr. Gayle," he said and shut the door behind him.

I looked back at the old green door and let out a long breath, then turned and headed north into the city.

I walked for two hours. It felt good, walking, being out in the sun without a fence surrounding me on all sides. Not a visible one anyway. I maneuvered my way unconsciously through commercial and residential neighborhoods, across busy and deserted streets and under leaky bridges. Eventually I found myself in The Loop, the area of downtown surrounded by the elevated train known simply as The L. This was what people thought of when they pictured Chicago in their heads.

It was also the part of the city that I was familiar with. The University of Chicago was south of here, I had passed it up a while ago without ever really getting close to it, but this was where I'd spent most of my time for the semester I was there. Shops, restaurants, parks and activities were concentrated in The Loop area and I immediately (and finally) felt at home. The comfort of the environment though, made me astutely aware of my discomfort with my clothes.

I dug into my back pocket and pulled out the envelope of cash Mr. Simons had left for me in my room. I counted it out again. An even two hundred dollars, not much you could get with that sum in this neck of the woods, but I decided to make it go as far as I could.

A few blocks west of Millennium Park I found a T.J. Max. I rustled through the mismatched racks of men's clothes until I'd come up with a decent pair of black wrinkle free dress slacks and a white button down. In shoes I found a pair of black slip-on loafers that would do until I could acquire some boots. Near the register I grabbed a ten pack each, of socks and underwear from a wire bin. The total for the whole endeavor was just over a hundred dollars.

I changed in the bathroom and left the old clothes in the stall next to the toilet, then headed out to see about finding something to eat. I couldn't afford a sit down joint, not unless I was willing to spend my last dime, so I hit a fast food burger place and got a slab of calories between a white foam bun. It wasn't as good as the food at The Club had been, but it was still better than the prison chow I was used to.

Then I roamed the city for a bit. I wasn't going anywhere or looking for anything in particular, just moving in space. I passed through a Walgreens and picked up a good razor, one with five blades and a head that pivoted as well as some expensive shaving cream that called itself shaving butter.

It was calming to just go. Just wander and think. I didn't have answers to any of my questions. My life was a tilt-o-whirl of people and events I didn't recognize or understand. My best bet, I decided, was just to go with the flow and see where the ride let off. It didn't take long to find out.

It was getting dark and I figured it was time to start heading back. It had taken two hours to find my way to The Loop from The Club and I didn't think it wise to try and make the return trip on foot. Not in that part of the city anyway. I stood on the edge of the street and hailed a cab, a process that took a lot longer than I would have thought.

I didn't really remember where The Club had been, but I knew it was south and maybe a little east and I knew it was on Torrence. I had the driver take Lake Shore Drive south until he couldn't anymore. Then we zig-zagged through the neighborhoods until we hit Torrence. A few blocks further, when the numbers on the meter were getting close to what I had left to spend, I had him stop. I paid him with the rest of the money in the envelope and hoofed it on foot the last block or so until I spotted the weary red building with the green door and went in.

Nate greeted me with a friendly tone and once again there was no one at the host stand. I stepped through the dining room and kitchen, grabbing an apple on the way and headed to Mr. Simons' office. I knocked gently and was invited in.

"Mr. Gayle, I thought maybe we'd lost you already," he said when he saw me.

"No sir," I said. "Just out doing the tourist thing."

"Ah, and doing some shopping I see," he gestured at my new clothes and the bag in my hand.

"Just trying to get comfortable," I said.

"Sure, sure," he said in an understanding tone. Well good to see you found your way back. Dinner is starting to come out now, oh, and these came for you today."

Mr. Simons reached under his desk and produced a manila mailing envelope and a large cardboard box. I stared at them with suspicion for a moment then stepped forward, reached out and took them.

"Thanks."

"No problem. Will we see you for dinner tonight then?"

I looked at the packages with uneasy distraction, then up at Mr. Simons.

"What? Oh, yeah, sure, tonight."

"Good then, see you tonight Gavin."

I turned and stepped out, closing the door behind me. I gazed back down at the envelope. It was addressed to me with no return address, sealed with white tape that had red lettering printed across it. The lettering read 'eyes only' over and over and over. One side was smooth and firm, the other felt lumpy, like there was something hard inside it. The box had no address on it, just a large sticker with Illinois Department of Corrections printed on top and my name and inmate number scribbled in black marker.

I thought about opening them right there but decided against it. No one knew I was there except State's Attorney Adalet. She had said answers would come, maybe these were part of that. I decided I wanted to open them in private.

Back in my room I set the envelope and the box on my bed. I gazed at them both trying to figure out what to open first. After a minute I decided to tackle the box. I pulled at the brown packing tape that sealed it shut and tore it off the seams. It came off in one strip pulling a good portion of the cardboard off the box with it. The contents nearly stopped my heart.

Inside there was a dark gray felt fedora that had seen better days, five white button-down dress shirts with French cuffs, two pairs of black slacks, and one pair of black wingtip loafers. There was a long black wool overcoat, a black leather Montblanc vertical wallet and two men's jewelry boxes. The first was polished walnut with my sir name carved in calligraphy on the lid. It held half a dozen sets of cufflinks, three tie pins, two quarters, and two men's wrist watches which I recognized immediately.

One was a black face with exposed gears under the crystal and a black leather band that my Aunt Paige had given my father for Christmas one year. The other had been a birthday gift to my dad from the whole family that my stepmother had bought their first year together.

The other jewelry box had a set of reading glasses and a solid black straight razor. I took it out of the box and opened it. The blade was thin, extremely sharp and flat black except at the very edge where a dull gray glean showed through. I closed it and set it back in the box. These were my father's things. I recognized the watches and the hat and jacket. The shirts and slacks were nondescript but every bit my father's fashion. At the bottom of the box was a note, handwritten in perfect cursive penmanship.

Gavin,

Your father would have wanted you to have these.

He loved you very much, and he never stopped believing in you.

You were a good boy Gavin, and I believe you can be a good man.

Love,

Uncle Kevin

I never saw my dad after my trial. He had died the day of my sentencing and I had always felt responsible in one way or another. I didn't go to his funeral, if he even had one, and I had assumed that everything he owned had been discarded, thrown away the same way I had been. Holding those items, I felt an overwhelming, crushing sense of sadness and guilt. I collapsed onto the bed next to the box and cried. I cried huge gagging sobs until the effort of it drove me, finally, to sleep.

* * *

The envelope was still waiting for me when I came to. I assumed it would be more heart-wrenching nostalgia; I was wrong. Inside I found a stack of papers, maybe thirty pages or so, several photographs of a young girl, beaten, bruised, and bloody. A photograph of a young man, a police mug shot in which he looked genuinely frightened. Below the papers and the photographs was a yellow bottle with a blue lid and a gold Zippo lighter. I turned the lighter over and over again in my hand, feeling the smooth edges and the seam at the lid. I flipped it open and spun the wheel. It sparked, but the pristine white wick stayed that way.

I set the lighter and the bottle on the nightstand and began leafing through the papers. It was some kind of criminal file. I pushed the materials around and pulled out the photos.

They were eight by ten color photographs of a girl. She was young, in her early teens and in bad shape. She had a huge purple swollen eye and brown dried blood around her nose and mouth. There was a cut on her forehead and the unbruised eye was bloodshot.

There were three photos of her. One of them was head on, the other two were from either profile. All showed the same damage. All were closeups of just her head.

The fourth picture was of a boy. He was young as well, probably about the same age as the girl. He was good looking and clean cut with sculpted hair and clean straight teeth, but the photo was a mugshot. He was standing in front of a wall with horizontal lines indicating height in feet and inches and he was holding a small black felt board with white plastic letters and numbers.

Kevin Dobson
   CPD - 562173489

I reached over, flipped on the lamp and sat down. There were at least a dozen newspaper articles clipped out in the pile. Chicago Tribune, Chicago Sun Times, The Daily Herald. I picked up the first one in the stack and began to read.

Justice Eludes Top Legal Eagle

Today a Cook county judge dismissed charges against a local teen for the brutal assault and beating of... Redacted content. The Judge stated that evidence submitted by the State's Attorney's office had been obtained illegally and that all state-ments by the accused and his associates submitted after the acquisition of said illegal evidence was inadmissible.

With no further untainted corroborating evidence to submit at the time of the hearing, the judge declared the accused free to go and...

The rest of the papers documented the assault of the girl in the picture by the boy in the mug shot. The evidence was pretty rock solid, especially the description of a video of the attack from the attacker's cell phone. Unfortunately, the boy had been released because the video evidence had been obtained illegally.

I was confused. Obviously, this came from SA Adalet. For one, she was the only one who knew I was here, and for another it was full of confidential police and county documents that only she and a handful of other people would have had access to, but why give it to me? Why was it important that I know about this girl? Clearly there was a parallel between her situation and that of Weather's, except-

Then it hit me. It's exactly what Jake, the other inmate, the one that had stabbed me had said. "I have a friend... She's got a daughter... She ran into some trouble, like what your friend got into... When you get out, I want you to help her."

Then I noticed the most important detail; the girl's name, it wasn't in the documents. The boy's name was. It was everywhere, but the girl's name was completely missing. But I didn't need her name, looking at the pictures again I could see the resemblance. I knew who this girl was, and I knew why I was out, but I still wasn't sure what I was supposed to do.

There was a knock on my door, and it opened before I could respond. Mr. Simons stuck his head in and looked around for a moment before finding me on the bed.

"Oh hey," he said with a slight tone of apology. "Uh, Dinner's starting to come out if you're interested."

I smiled and gave a nod.

"Thanks Greg, I'll be out in a minute," I said.

He waved and backed out of the room, closing the door behind him.

I shuffled all the papers together and slid them back in the envelope. I felt a deep sense of anger towards the situation and pity for Maureen and her daughter. As much as I hated her for sending me to prison, I couldn't help but feel a gut-wrenching sadness for what she must be going through. No one deserved to have to endure that kind of pain. It filled my belly and my chest and crawled up my neck. It sank its rotten teeth into my brain and that's when the anger took over.

I was out because of this. SA Adalet had set it all up for me because of her daughter. But why me? Because of Weather. Because it was just like what happened to Weather. Except, Maureen didn't believe my story about Weather. She didn't believe that I had saved her, she thought I killed that boy out of revenge.

Now I realized that clearly wasn't the case. She did believe that I was innocent, but still wasn't admitting it. If she knew the truth, she shouldn't have had to break me out of prison in some stupid elaborate heist, she could have just had the sentence overturned, but that wouldn't have helped her. She needed me under her thumb. She needed to control me because now she wanted revenge.

I should have felt some vindication and resentment, but I didn't. I was angry, but I also felt pity. Not for Maureen now, but for her daughter. All I could think about was how we let these things happen over and over again and the men, the boys who were responsible never seemed to have to face any consequences.

As I was putting the papers away, I noticed something I hadn't before. Taped to the top of the mugshot was a tiny piece of black plastic. It was rectangular with a small notch in one corner. It couldn't have been any bigger than the fingernail on my pinky. I frowned to myself and peeled the tape off the corner of the photo. I inspected the piece of plastic under the light. On the back it had four or five small metal strips at one end, but no markings at all. I had no idea what it was or what I was supposed to do with it, but I set it down on the desk with the photo and sealed the envelope back up.

I made my way down the hall and through the kitchen that was now bustling with activity. There were three cooks behind the line stirring and spicing pans full of simmering food on the stoves. A young Hispanic man was at a deep sink scrubbing pans and sending long white plates through a huge commercial dishwasher.

There were a couple of young ladies in white button downs with loose black neck ties and short black skirts. They were attractive and giggled as they loaded plates of food onto round server trays. Mr. Simons was in front of the line giving orders to the staff and garnishing plates with sides and silverware. He didn't even look at me as I walked through.

In the dining room things were more subdued. The dusty blonde piano was now occupied by the same red head, this time with a long braid down her back. She was playing some jazz piece and singing along, more to herself than for the benefit of the room. There were half a dozen occupied tables, all pairs of men eating and speaking in conspicuously low voices.

I walked back to the booth Katie had put me in the night before, sat myself down and took to watching the people in the room. It was an interesting show that would have made Scorsese proud. After a minute Katie stepped up into the section and approached me with a smile and a glass of bourbon.

"Good evening Mr. Gayle," she said sweetly. "It's so nice to see you again."

I nodded and thanked her for the drink. She gave me the night's dinner description; Duck a l'Orange and told me she'd be back with the first course shortly, then turned to walk away.

"Oh, Katie," I spurted out just having had an idea.

She stopped and turned back to face me.

"Yes Mr. Gayle?"

"I'm sorry," I said. "This isn't really part of your job, I'm sure, but you wouldn't happen to know what this is?"

I dug into my pocket and pulled out the small black chip of

plastic. I set it on the table and slid it towards her. She stepped up and leaned over examining it without touching it.

"Yeah," she said. "It's an SD card."

She sounded like a person answering an imbecile.

"I'm sorry, a what?"

Her shoulders fell as if in disappointment.

"An SD card. A memory card. Like for a phone, or a camera. It's actually a micro SD. Nothing really uses the big ones anymore."

I frowned.

"What's on it?" she said starting to sound interested.

I shrugged.

"I have no idea Katie. I have no idea."

Chapter Nine

June 13, 2012 10:50 P.M.

I ate my meal, which was excellent. The duck especially. It had a crisp skin and tangy apricot flavor. I drank a glass of bourbon and then Katie brought me a bottle of dark heavy zinfandel that tasted of black cherries and smoke. It was delicious and I finished the whole thing.

As I smoked a cigarette after dinner, I picked up the small black chip from the table and turned it over and over in my fingers. I couldn't believe that this tiny fleck of plastic was a computer disk. I knew I'd been away for five years, but had technology really advanced that quickly while I was gone? I stuck it in the breast pocket of my shirt and finished my drink and cigarette. I figured I would have to go out the next day and find a way to see what was on it.

A little after midnight I was feeling the weight of the day and I headed back to my room. I was just collapsing into the threadbare recliner when the knock came. I looked up expecting to see Mr. Simons stick his head inside, but nothing happened. A moment later there was another knock.

I stood and walked to the door, then cracked it a smidge before swinging it open. Katie leaned in the frame lit gently by the soft glow of the desk lamp. She was smiling nervously leaning on one leg with her hands clasped behind her back. When I smiled at her she bit her lower lip and glanced at the ground.

"Are you supposed to be back here?" I said.

"I dunno," she said. "Probably not."

There was a silence and then suddenly she blushed.

"Oh my God," she spurted apologetically while straightening herself into a more formal upright pose. "I'm not here to- I mean, I didn't come back here to-"

I laughed.

"It's okay," I said. "I didn't assume anything."

"I just- I thought you might want to use this."

She brought her hands from behind her back and produced a small shiny black piece of glass.

"It's my phone. I thought you might want to see what was on that card."

My eyes lit up.

"Wow, yes. Thanks," I said and started digging in my shirt pocket for the chip.

"Um, can I," she dropped her voice to a whisper. "Can I come inside? We're not supposed to have phones here. I don't want to get caught with it."

I flushed realizing it had been rude not to invite her in in the first place.

"Oh, of course," I said.

I stepped aside and she walked in shutting the door behind her. We walked to the desk and I sat down. The card was difficult to fish out of my pocket because it was so small. It kept getting caught in the corners of the fabric, but eventually I got a grip on it and set it on the desk.

She slid her fingernail along the edge of her phone and pulled out a small wire tray. Expertly she dropped the tiny card into the tray and pushed it back into her device. A few moments of fiddling around and she showed me the screen. It was a file directory just like I remembered from the PCs we used in school. The header read: External Memory followed by a single file name.

Kevin.vid

"It's a video," she said.

"Can we watch it?" I asked.

She laughed at that, clearly, I was way out of touch.

"Of course," she said and tapped the file name on the screen.

Her phone went black, then an image popped up. There were two people in the frame. A boy and a girl. The boy was pushing her gently on a swing set behind a small brick house. The video appeared to be shot from behind some bushes. It was dark and shaky and there was the sound of breathing and hushed laughter.

The girl was sipping from a clear plastic water bottle and the boy's hands were starting to move lower and lower on her back as he pushed her. Then the girl dropped the bottle and put her feet down on the ground. She said something, but it was inaudible on the recording.

The boy moved around in front of her and put his hands on her shoulders. She swayed back and forth and sideways in the swing trying to steady herself. He moved his hands to her waist and leaned his head in towards her's. She winced and turned away.

He followed her and kept moving in and she pushed him away gently. He came back in again and she wiggled off the swing and fell onto the dirt. He got on his knees and held her wrists over her head. He tried to kiss her again and she head butted him in the nose.

The boy backed off and held his face and there was the sound of laughter on the recording. Then the boy in the video leaned forward and slapped the girl hard in the face. He grabbed her shirt and tore it open exposing her bra. He reached down and grabbed her between the legs and said something that I couldn't make out.

At this point the camera moved out of the bushes and towards the two kids on the ground. There was shouting and arguing, and the boy looked back directly at the camera. He waved at it indicating that he wanted it off, then turned back to the girl. I saw his hands tear at the button and fly of her jeans and then the screen went blank.

I stared at the black screen of the phone and felt... nothing. I'd had a few drinks, a bottle of wine, half a pack of cigarettes and my fill of fear, anger, and rage for the day. The video was horrendous. It was appalling and disgusting, but somehow, not surprising. I had read the police reports and news articles. I knew what had happened to the girl, the video was just too much. It was gilding the lily and it just made me tired.

I'd seen it all before. With Weather. The injustice of the privileged and the disregard for women. The way we let boys behave and swept away girls like garbage. I knew that there was no justice for girls like her. She would be scarred forever. There would be something broken in her for the rest of her life and the boy would get to go on and do it again. More girls broken, more women learning never to trust a man. I felt helpless in the most profound way.

"Oh God," the voice next to me said.

I looked up. I had forgotten that Katie was there.

"I'm sorry you had to see that I said," putting a hand on her shoulder.

She jerked away from me, then looked me in the eye with regret.

"Sorry, just a reflex," she said.

"It's okay," I said. "I understand."

She gave a short sarcastic grunt.

"I doubt it."

I felt a kind of shame.

"You're right. Of course, I don't."

"So, what are you going to do?"

I looked at her puzzled.

"Do?"

"Yeah, what are you going to do about this?"

I gave a vacant shrug.

"Nothing. What am I supposed to do?"

She laughed angrily.

"Well, is he in prison?"

"No," I said. "They couldn't convict."

"Right," she said sardonically. "Of course, they couldn't. Or they didn't want to. Same shit different day."

"Well, I'm pretty sure they tried. The girl is the daughter of the State's Attorney."

Katie looked at me horrified.

"Where did you get that?" she asked.

I looked at her phone and pulled the envelope from my back pocket and set it on the table.

"It came for me this morning. I don't know exactly where from, but I have my suspicions."

She opened the envelope and flipped through the contents.

"You have to do something," she said. "Someone gave this to you so you could do something. You have to do something."

"Okay Katie, what? What do you want me to do?"

She looked at me with frozen eyes.

"Gavin, right? Gavin, I don't know if you've figured it out

yet, but this place, this club; it's not for the good guys. Good people don't come here."

"But I thought you said-"

She was angry and annoyed and was starting to shout.

"What? I said what? That it wasn't a mob club? That there were no criminals here? There aren't. The world isn't binary Gavin. It's not good guys and bad guys. The people who come here aren't criminals, but they aren't good. Maybe they think they are, but we don't live in a world of white hats and black hats, we live in a world of shades of gray and sometimes you have to do something bad for good reasons. In this world the best you can hope for is dark white."

"What are you trying to say?" I whispered.

Her expression went flat.

"Jesus Gavin. Kill him. You have to kill him."

* * *

June 14, 2012 1:12 A.M.

According to his booking report in the file Kevin's address was on the North side of the city. Katie dropped me a few blocks away and I hiked the rest. It was a long walk, but it was a nice night, and nobody worries about walking around the north side after dark. Besides, I needed time to think.

What Katie was asking me to do, what the package was asking, was outside of my moral comfort zone. It's true, I had killed before, but somehow this was different. When I killed the kid attacking Weather it was in a haze of fear and rage. I wasn't thinking and barely had any idea what I was doing.

The guy in prison, he had already killed someone else and would likely do it again if it benefited him. His death was a kind of revenge, but also a kind of preemptive self-defense. Not only for myself, but for everyone inside and I still got an extended sentence and a month in the hole for it.

This kid. This Kevin, he hadn't killed anyone. Not yet at least. Sure, he had the personality type, the kind of person that could try to rape a teenage girl and then leave her in the dirt, killing wouldn't be a huge escalation for him. Still, it felt wrong. A premeditated, cold blooded murder because the justice system had failed. It was a lot to consider.

When I got to his building, I grabbed a spot across the street with a clear view of the front door. I leaned against the building's facade and pulled out a smoke. It was the last one in the pack Katie had given me. I spun it between my thumb and index finger deciding if I should burn it then or save it for later. I flipped the gold lighter from the envelope open and spun the wheel. Sparks flew, but no flame.

"Damn," I muttered to myself.

I stuffed my hands in my pockets and drew out the yellow bottle. I pulled the lighter out of its thin gold housing, flipped it over, lifted the dense wool bottom and squeezed the contents of the bottle into the loose cotton inside. I closed it all back up, put the bottle back in my pocket and spun the wheel again.

This time a long orange and yellow flame danced around the cotton wick. I put it to my face and dragged on the cigarette. I closed the lighter with a satisfying click and stood there, looking at the building and smoking.

The envelope was back in my pocket. I pulled it out and read through the pages again. I was starting to feel something. My heart was pumping, and adrenaline was starting to work its way through my system. My muscles were tense and the hairs on the back of my neck were standing up. I looked at the file again and back at the building, then I gave a quick glance down the street and another in the other direction.

There, a block away and on the other side of the street was a payphone. I stuffed my hand in my pants pocket and fished out a handful of loose change Katie had given me.

"Call me when you need a ride back," she had said. "You may have to search a bit for a payphone, but they're still around."

I crossed the street and stepped up on the curb just as the door to the building opened and Kevin stepped out. I nearly ran into him. I lowered my head, muttered an apology and turned in the opposite direction of the kid. After a couple steps I spun on the balls of my feet and started casually following him.

Kevin was a lowlife. A rich kid, popular, lots of money, but no empathy for anyone. That much was clear from the documents in the envelope. He was one of those kids who only kept friends that could do something for him. Anyone else was cast off as a worthless reject. He bullied and dismissed anyone with less money, status, or power than he had. Girls were objects to be used and then when they could no longer elevate his status, dismissed as sluts and whores.

He walked with the strut of someone who was never questioned. He had the air of someone who always got his way. I hated this kid already, but that wasn't good enough. Not good enough by far for what they were asking me to do.

The kid took a sudden right down an ally and I paused. I stared ahead at the empty sidewalk and thought. It was late and the foot traffic in this neighborhood was light. I didn't know what was down the alley, but if it wasn't at least more crowded than the street it would be pretty obvious that I was following the kid. I decided the best decision was to walk past the alley at a casual speed. If it was clear I would double back and investigate it. If I saw the kid, I'd just keep walking, cross the street and grab a dark corner to watch the opening from.

I started moving again. As I passed the alley, I gave a quick glance that revealed an empty inlet dead ending into a low loading dock. I stopped and waited a moment then backed up and slowly started down the alley.

It was narrow, only about twelve feet wide at the opening then it seemed to widen out a bit before the dock doors. My feet were crunching on the loose gravel and broken glass that was strewn across the rough asphalt ground. I tried to stay quiet, but the sound seemed to echo off the narrow brick boundaries of the space. As I passed the end of the path the alley opened up at the left. I turned to check my blind spot and caught a fist, hard, in the side of my face.

Real life fights don't look like they do in the movies. No one gets thrown across rooms or makes melodramatic grunts. Punches don't sound like a bat hitting a cantaloupe. In real life they're almost silent except for the faint snap as the small bones in your hand break against the other guy's skull. I heard that sound as I collapsed on the ground.

I felt the tiny rocks and debris tear the fabric of my pants and push up into the tissue around my knees. There was searing pain in my cheek and eye and I could tell there was blood soaking into my slacks.

I laid a hand on the ground and staggered backwards a couple steps as I tried to stand up. I was in a daze and shook my head trying to come back. I looked up just in time to see Kevin pouncing forward. I took another blow to the face, this one just above my left eye. The skin opened up and blood ran down my face and into my mouth.

Another swing came in fast, but I managed to duck under it and I shot a straight punch hard into the kid's lower ribs. I heard a slight crack that could have been his bones or mine and the kid staggered back gasping for breath. He tried to straighten up but couldn't lift his torso. I pulled myself up straight and cracked my neck; first to one side then the other. I wiped the blood from my eyes and looked at it on my fingers. I wiped it on my pants.

"Kevin, right?" I said in a breathy wheeze.

The kid stared at me with hate masking the pain that must have been shooting through his chest. He coughed and stood as straight as he could.

"Who the fuck are you?" he asked.

"Me?" I chuckled and shook my head slightly. "Kid, I'm no one."

I stopped and thought about the unintended irony of that statement.

"Yeah," I whispered to myself. "I'm no one and chances are if you hadn't come at me like that, I would have stayed no one."

The kid stared at me. He leaned back against the brick wall behind him and stuck his hands in the pockets of his jacket.

"Why don't you tell me about the girl." I said dabbing the cut above my eye with my sleeve.

The boy squinted at me and leaned forward a little.

"What?"

I sighed.

"Adalet," I said, starting to feel better and simultaneously starting to get annoyed. "Tell me about her. What's the deal there?"

The kid leaned back again and closed his eyes. He let out a breathy sigh and lifted his head again.

"Shit. That's what this is about? The lawyer's slut daughter? Really? Fuck man, that's old news. What'd she send you out here?"

I just stared at him and bled on my shirt.

"Look, she was all there. She was totally into me; she just wouldn't pull the trigger. I mean seriously, a total cock tease. What was I supposed to do? Girl like that? Indecisive! What? I'm just supposed to let her keep leading me on? Get me all the way to the edge and then just change her mind? Fuck that man."

I felt that pounding feeling in my chest again. This douche bag was not helping his own cause.

"So." I said.

"So what? So, I helped her decide. Girls needs to learn you can't just keep leading a guy on like that. I didn't want to be the one to teach her, but someone had to."

I nodded. It was a sad gesture filled with regret.

"Look, I get it. Mom's upset, but I guarantee you, at some point she got the same lesson."

He coughed and started straightening up. His rib was broken, but it was a small fracture and hadn't done any internal damage. He was getting his wind back and his confidence.

"It's a part of growing up. Girls all have to learn at some point. They have to deliver on what they advertise."

I tilted my head and took a step forward. The kid pulled his feet in closer to the wall he was propped up against and stood himself up a little straighter. I took one more step and the kid sprung. He shot up straight with a wince and pulled a heavy looking snub-nosed pistol from his jacket pocket and aimed it at my chest.

I didn't know much about guns. Not back then. I had fired a shotgun a couple times at my grandparent's Wisconsin cabin. It was a terrifying experience and I'd declined to make it a ritual. I'd also seen a couple basic revolvers come and go through my Mom's house as a kid, but I had never held, let alone fired an actual handgun, and I certainly couldn't tell one kind from another. That being said, this gun had what seemed to be an unusually short looking barrel and an unusually large looking hole at the end of it. All of this made me unusually scared. Scared shitless in fact.

I took a half step backwards and turned sideways with one arm extended towards Kevin, palm flat out.

"Okay kiddo. We don't have to go this route. Like I said, I'm nobody."

Pleading for your life is something you get used to in prison. It not working is another thing you get used to.

"If you hadn't jumped me tonight you probably would never have even known I exist. I was just checking you out. As a favor. Just seeing who you were. This doesn't have to end with someone shot."

Kevin smiled a little.

"I've got a cracked rib that I'm going to have to account for somehow. This ain't nothin' now, and you ain't nobody."

He turned the gun sideways in an attempt to be threatening and winched as the action torqued the muscles in his chest.

"And why is it," he coughed, "the person at the wrong end of the gun is always saying nobody has to get shot? The only person looking to get shot tonight is you."

I inched forward a bit holding the same position. He was weak and hurt and I suspected playing at being stronger than he was. I also figured there was a sixty-forty chance the gun wasn't even loaded. Of course, it could just have easily been forty-sixty. Kevin put his thumb on the hammer of the pistol and pulled it back. The click as it locked in place seemed very loud in the muggy early morning air. I stopped moving.

"We're really in a spot now," he said. "See, you may be telling the truth, but you know what they say about ifs and buts."

I nodded cautiously.

"Candy and nuts," I said.

"That's right, and I don't see any reason to believe that if I let you go, you won't just turn up again, ya know?"

I nodded once.

"I am a bit like a bad penny."

"So here we are."

"Yup," I said.

"Well then."

I watched his eyes. He was definitely hurt worse than he was letting on. His pupils were opening and closing trying to hold focus. I made a quick judgment and dropped like a stone. My side hit the concrete with a thud, and I swept my right leg in an arc in front of me. It caught his ankle causing it to snap in two. He fell hard on his cracked rib and the gun went off like a firecracker.

I felt my left shoulder tear open and blood sprayed across my face and down my chest. My arm burned and everything went black for a few seconds. Pain spread up my neck and through my brain like wildfire. It felt like someone was sticking ice picks in my eyes.

Slowly it shallowed out and my vision came back. I could move my hands, then my legs and finally my head and body. The city swam back into focus and I saw Kevin.

He was gasping on the ground, alternately trying to breathe and cry at the same time. His eyes were clamped shut and tears were streaming out of them. I stood up, wincing and holding back tears myself. I stepped over the kid and reached down to the ground-up pavement and grabbed the gun from his hand. The kid didn't fight, he just let it go.

I stood over him looking down at his broken body.

"I told you it didn't have to go this way."

Kevin pried his eyes open and looked up at me. He gasped a couple short breaths and held the last one in.

"And I told you that it is what it is."

He took a deep breath and rolled under my legs onto his back and reached his hand into his other coat pocket. I just pointed the gun and clicked the trigger.

The round in the chamber exploded and fire flashed out the

barrel. The kid's head flattened out like a pizza and sprayed the gravel and asphalt beneath it.

The kid was dead.

I dropped the gun on top of him and staggered out of the alley. I was limping and blood ran down my face and shoulder, soaking my clothes and leaving a nice scarlet thread on the ground behind me. I made it the two blocks back the way I had come and pulled that handful of quarters out of my pocket. I fed the payphone and pulled the envelope out of my pocket. On the front was the number Katie had written down to reach her at. I stared at it for a long time, then pulled out the police report and dialed the number at the top of the page. The phone rang four times then beeped.

"I uh, I think I need help." I slurred.

I dropped the handset without putting it back on the hook and started to walk. I was getting dizzy and as the night got darker everything began to swim. I ducked behind a building and found an empty dumpster. I sprayed down the file folder with the lighter fluid, lit it up, and dropped the blazing folder into the dumpster. I watched it burn until it was just ash then took a stick from nearby and scattered the ashes inside the bin and closed the lid. I sat on the ground leaning against the dumpster and closed my eyes.

Sleep came fast and when it did, I dreamed of Weather.

* * *

4:45 A.M.

"We're going to need to stop meeting like this Mr. Smith."

It may well have been the same room, I'm not for certain either way, but the woman standing over me when I woke was most surely the same nurse. She had her hand wrapped around my wrist and she was staring at the clock on the wall, watching the red second hand sweep past eight o'clock. When it reached nine, she let go and smiled at me with the look of a parent bandaging a child after the umpteenth skateboarding accident.

"You seem to be prone to bad luck Mr. Smith. Perhaps you should consider a slightly less dangerous hobby. Skydiving comes to mind."

"What am I-"

"You had a run in with old number two," she said, interrupting me.

I frowned.

"We dug a piece of lead out of your shoulder."

I stared at her, then it came to me. A piece of lead. A bullet. I'd been shot.

I moved in the bed and a searing pain shot through my left shoulder, down my arm and up my neck though my skull. It was terrible. Like being stabbed with a white-hot knitting needle, or so I'd imagine. It took a moment, but the memory came back, re-emerging in chunks as if over a slow internet connection.

"How'd I get here?" I said in a groggy voice.

"Your detective friend brought you in about an hour ago. She's really looking out for you, you're a lucky man."

I gave a sardonic chuckle under my breath.

"Yeah, that's me. I should buy a lotto ticket."

Less than twenty-four hours before I had been in prison, but I had been safe. Well, safe-ish. I had a cell to myself and even though I was looking down the barrel of another thirty-eight years, I was taken care of. Despite the legal ramifications of my actions inside, the guards appreciated my removal of what they considered a person of extreme professional annoyance. From the moment I swung that free weight into the side of Benson's face I was given carte blanche by the guards who felt I had done them a massive favor.

Now, for the second time in less than a week I was being stitched up after someone had tried to kill me. Lucky was not the way I was feeling. Truth be told, the only thing I was feeling was tired.

"Well, you're looking okay. The pencil seems to have missed any bone or major arteries. Honestly, with a pencil that size I would have expected it to blow right through you. You've got some tough muscle tissue. It'll heal up eventually, but you'll probably always have some soreness there. Weather will make it worse."

I looked up, startled.

"I'm sorry, what?" I said feeling a chill run down my neck.

"When it rains son. The humidity, pressure, they may aggravate the injury. It'll hurt more in bad weather."

I let out a long, relieved sigh and slumped back into the bed.

"Right," I said. "Got it."

"Advil will help."

"Okay. Thanks."

She smiled and scribbled something on the pad and dropped it in the slot at the end of the bed.

"I'll go let your police officer friend know you're awake."

"Oh- you don't have to..."

But she walked out the door. It swung closed and clicked into place.

Things had not gone as I had planned that evening. I had no intention of hurting, or even meeting, the boy that night. I just wanted to observe him. Get a feeling for what I was dealing with, what my job was supposed to be. Now that it had happened though, that my hand had been forced and I had committed yet another sin against society and mankind; now that I had to live with what had actually happened, I didn't feel bad at all. Not a bit. He had been a blight on humanity, and we were all better off without him.

The door opened.

Detective Hinde, the same cop that had brought me in before, stepped into the room and she did not look happy. She shut the door delicately and strode over to the side of my bed on silent feet, then quietly extended a single finger and drove it into the bandaged wound in my left shoulder.

I tried to howl in pain, but she quickly pressed both hands across my mouth, stopping me from screaming, or even breathing for that matter. She gazed at me, directly into my eyes with a terrifying expression, and I believed in that moment that she was truly trying to kill me.

I choked and tears ran down my cheeks. Slowly she took her hands away, opening up my airways and letting my eyes pull back into focus. She was mad, murderously so and I felt a sense of confused rage rush over me like a cold bucket of water.

"How the hell did you manage to fuck up on day one?" she shouted at me in a broken whisper.

My mouth hung open, but I couldn't make any words come out.

"Do you know what you did asshole? Do you know how hard this is going to be to clean up?"

"I- I don't understand," I said, sounding like I was going to cry at any moment. "I thought this is what you wanted."

She looked at me like I was an idiot.

"What?" she said, sounding genuinely surprised. "How in fuck would you think we wanted this?"

"You- I- I mean- You left that envelope. All the pictures and articles and- I- well, what did you want me to do?"

Her shoulders dropped and she rolled her eyes. She let out a long sigh and glanced back at the door, then looked back at me.

"We wanted you to not get shot, you dumb motherfucker."

I grimaced and tried to sit up. Pain fired through my chest and abdomen and I collapsed back against the pillows.

"Do you have any idea what a pain in the ass it is to bury these hospital records. This is going to be my week now. Like I don't have better things to be doing than cleaning up after you."

She paused. She was thinking, tilting her head as she looked at me as if deciding something.

"Ass hole," she said with a slightly warmer tone.

She walked over to a small backpack that was sitting on an uncomfortable looking stuffed chair in the corner of the room. She lifted it and carried it over to the bed, dropped it on my legs and unzipped the top. After rooting around in it for a moment she pulled out an ugly piece of black metal. A gun. The gun. The gun I had been shot with and subsequently had murdered Kevin Dobson with.

She tossed it in my lap.

"It's yours now fucker," she said. "Certainly can't go into the system. Besides, from the look of how things went tonight, you're going to need it."

I choked, holding my hands up above my head, squirming like I was trying to get away from a snake.

"Fuck, no. No thank you," I shouted. "Get that thing away from me."

The detective burst out laughing.

"Seriously," she said. "It's a little late now to be getting squeamish don't you think?"

I froze, still posed like a pitcher about to be clobbered by a line drive up the middle.

"I don't like guns," I said.

Megan let her laughter slow to a chuckle, then regained her calm.

"No? Hm. No, I don't either kid, but I'm here to tell ya, you better get used to 'em. You better get used to 'em pretty damn quick."

* * *

6:07 A.M.

The ride back to The Club was silent. Megan was still mad, and I was hurting and confused. I didn't like what had happened, didn't like my part in it. I still didn't mind that the kid was dead, but it upset me that I had been the one who pulled the trigger. I had let my feelings take over again and when that happened, I was always left with a bag of regret hanging on me, tugging at my shoulders and making me feel a hundred pounds heavier.

Detective Hinde pulled her car up in front of The Club and put it in park, but left the engine running. She looked at me with frustration and disappointment. There was a long moment of silence before I finally spoke.

"So, what now?"

"Now you get out of my car and you go to sleep," she said.

"What about tomorrow?" I asked. "And the day after that? What happens now?"

She shrugged.

"I don't know. This isn't my party, I'm just your chaperone. It's not my call."

I felt tears forming behind my eyes and I fought them back.

"But I'm done right? I did what you-"

She shook her head.

"Fine, what she wanted. I did it. I'm done now?"

Megan looked down at her lap and gripped the steering wheel tightly, then turned to face me and looked me dead in the eyes.

"Gavin, I'm not part of the plan. I don't know why she got you out or what she expects you to do. Yes, you took care of something she wanted... taken care of, but if I had to guess; I don't think you're done. I don't think she would have gone through all of that just to off the kid that hurt her daughter. That could have been taken care of in a million different ways, all of them much easier than getting you out to do it."

My best efforts failed, and I felt the water push past my lids and leak out onto my face. I wiped my eyes with my sleeve and choked back a sob. I stared at the detective with desperation. I longed for her to tell me she would help, that she would find a way to get me out of whatever Adalet had planned, but that's not what happened.

"You need to get out now. You need to go inside and go to sleep. When you wake up you can tell yourself this was all a bad dream."

"And when will I know what's next?"

Megan shook her head.

"I don't know Gavin. Maybe never, but I wouldn't count on it. Now open the door and get out of my car."

I hesitated.

"Now."

I pulled the handle and swung the door open. It was so hot outside I felt like I was stepping into a sauna. I stepped out of the car and closed the door. I didn't look back at Hinde. I couldn't. I took a step towards the curb and froze at the sound of her horn.

I looked back and she rolled down her window.

"Gavin," she said sternly.

I just stared.

"You're forgetting something."

She lifted her hand off the passenger seat and held out the snub-nosed .45.

I shook my head.

"No," I said adamantly.

"It's not an option."

I didn't move.

"Gavin, take the gun. Now."

My heart was pounding, and my shoulder was burning and aching. I felt sick and exhausted and terrified at the same time. I didn't want the gun. I didn't want any gun. If I had my way, I'd never see another gun in my life, but the look on her face told me that there was no negotiation here.

I stepped back to the car and put my hand in the open window. She placed it in my palm and began rolling the window back up. I jerked my arm out and watched as she put the car in drive and disappeared around the corner.

I looked at the weapon in my hand and felt myself begin to shake. I felt the cold metal slipping between my sweaty fingers and jumped back as it eluded my grasp and fell clattering to the pavement. I looked at it for a long time, lying there on the street between my feet. I almost walked away, leaving it there for someone else to deal with, but my better judgment took hold and I bent down and picked it up.

I wasn't familiar with guns, so it took me a moment, but I figured out how to eject the clip and un-chamber the last round. I stuck all the pieces in my pockets and glanced up the road to the church at the corner before turning and walking back in the unmarked door of The Club and back to my bedroom.

I slept quickly, but when I woke there was no pretending. I killed that boy and though he was a piece of human garbage, it was not my right to end his life. I laid in bed and stared at the ceiling, feeling the worst kind of hopelessness, that of knowing what's right, and knowing that you will do wrong anyway.

Chapter Ten

June 15, 2012 8:30 A.M.

The nurse Loretta had been right. It took almost three weeks before I could even begin to move my shoulder.

The day after I got out of the hospital I woke up and found a package on my desk. It was wrapped in brown paper with a tiny white paper envelope laying on it like you might find on a bouquet of flowers, it read:

"Thank You"

I opened the package and inside found a brown leather shoulder holster like you see weathered old detectives wear in gritty hard-boiled mystery movies. I looked at it closely and felt the hard leather in my hands. I ran my fingers over the thick stitching at the edges and felt that all too familiar oily sickness churn in my stomach. I stuffed the thing under the mattress of the bed and went to the kitchen to steal an apple.

I asked Mr. Simons for a safe, and without a question one arrived the next day. I placed it at the foot of the bed and set the combination as Weather's birthday, then stashed the gun, ammo, and the new holster inside and slammed the door.

During my weeks of recovery, I spent a lot of time at The Club. It was easy there. People were nice and they treated me like I was important, like I was special. I became friendly with the kitchen staff, the wait staff, and bartenders. I got comfortable in the dark corner where Mr. Simons preferred that I sit. It was nice. It was quiet. It was peaceful.

Every week or so an envelope appeared on my desk with two hundred in cash inside. Two hundred dollars a week was hardly enough to live on, but with free housing and free meals it did prove enough to get around on. It bought me cigarettes and train tickets which, since I didn't really have a job, and didn't really have any friends, was really all I needed day to day.

As soon as I could move it again, I started exercising the shoulder to prevent it from locking up and developing arthritis. Once it was working better, I resumed my regular workout routine I had developed in prison. One hundred pushups twice a day, fifty chin ups twice a day, and a five minute plank first thing in the morning and again right before bed. After a couple weeks I was back in shape.

I wasn't sure when I would hear from Hinde again, but I had grown used to the idea that I probably would eventually. The holster for the gun had made that clear. The encounter with Kevin Dobson had gone badly and that was mostly my fault. I hadn't been prepared. I hadn't been on guard. I'd been thinking like a free person, not like an inmate, always on the lookout for a potential threat. That wouldn't happen again. Next time I would be bigger, stronger, more alert, and more prepared.

It was six weeks after the incident with Dobson that the next manila envelope arrived. Thinner for the lack of the lighter and fluid, it contained a simple file folder with about twenty pages of material in it. The man featured inside was a two-time loser working on his third strike. The evidence in the file suggested that he had stalked a young girl named Penny, a barista at his local Starbucks.

She was nineteen and a student at DePaul. Her parents were in their late fifties and she was the first in the family to go to college. Her mother was a server at a diner in Nashville and her father was a plumber who had taken a second job as a used car salesman to help pay for her tuition.

The man had followed her for weeks, then began calling her until she had to change her number. Then one night as she was walking home across Grant Park, dressed in black and wearing a ski mask, he attacked her at knife point. He stabbed her twice in her abdomen, barely missing any vital organs and left her for dead in the bushes next to the band shell.

The prosecution had him dead to rights and he would have gone away for life on his third strike, but the defense produced a prostitute who took the stand, visibly beaten, and testified that he had been with her the whole night of the attack. They produced a receipt for services which made the entire court-room break out in laughter. The testimony was enough to hang the jury and now the State's Attorney's office was going to have to retry the case. But with an alibi already in place and with weeks, if not months, for the defense to clean up and rehabili-tate the girl and make her an even stronger witness on the stand, SA Adalet feared that he would walk.

I read the file over and over again the whole night sitting on the hard, twin mattress in my room, going over and over every detail. I ordered dinner to the room and thought about what would happen if I refused to follow through on this. Was this even an order, or was it more of a request? Maybe that was even strong. Maybe it was just the SA saying 'hey, if you feel like doing something about this, no one is going to stop you'. I rolled it over and over in my mind and eventually fell asleep with the file on my chest.

In the morning I went to the kitchen and made breakfast, then took a shower and changed into fresh clothes. I grabbed the cash from my desk and headed up to the street to hail a cab to Harold Washington Library.

I spent the afternoon researching the man in the file, starting with the computers, but it was hard to find anything substantive. Anything that would be useful was hidden behind a paywall and required a credit card to access. Eventually I landed on the old microfiche newspaper files. With a lot of patience, I was able to sift through old stories in the city crime section of the Sun Times and put together the background on the perp.

Both of his previous strikes had been violent, and both had been against women. One was a domestic abuse situation where the girl had ended up with a broken collar bone, the other was an attempted date rape. The second girl had been able to fight him off with the help of a keychain bottle of pepper spray, but not before ending up with a black eye and a bruised rib. In both cases his attorneys had been able to plea bargain the charges down to simple assault and he had served less than half of his sentences with parole.

This third case would have put him away for good, but with a hung jury and the new alibi it was looking like he was going to walk until he raped or murdered some other girl. I wondered how often this happened. How many girls; wives, daughters, girlfriends, nieces, and friends were hurt, or broken, or killed because the system was set up to protect the animals among us. How many times had a family lost someone because some sub-human monster that should have been in a cage was, instead, drinking a latte in an overstuffed armchair picking out his next victim?

I flipped the switch on the microfilm projector, put the film back in its canister, and put away the trays. Outside I walked the steps up to the 'L' platform and swiped my CTA card through the turnstile. It took two trains to get me within walking distance of The Club.

Nate was at the door and greeted me as I followed the steps down into the dining room. Drake nodded as I passed the host stand and cut through to the kitchen. Lisa was chopping mushrooms when I came in and grabbed an apple from the bowl. In my room I spun the dial on the safe holding the apple in my mouth. Month, date, year; Weather's birthday. The dial clicked, the lever turned, and the door opened.

The holster fit over my shoulders surprisingly well. It was comfortable and light, with my jacket on I could barely tell I was wearing it. I fiddled with the gun for a second to find the magazine release then filled the clip with ten rounds from the red box before sliding the gun into the sleeve of the holster and snapping it shut. I picked up the file from the desk, rolled it up, and slid it in my coat pocket, then put on my hat, pulled the chain on the desk lamp, and walked back out of The Club.

I waited quietly, patiently this time, outside the man's shitty apartment building smoking half a dozen cigarettes and stuffing the crushed-out butts in an empty Altoids tin. When the guy came out of the building, I unsnapped the strap on the holster and pulled out the gun, pulled back the slide to load the chamber and replaced the gun in the holster.

I waited until he was a block away before starting to follow him. I waited and walked and waited and walked. Patience, precision, persistence. Finally, when we were alone on a desolate boarded up street, I picked up my pace. When I was close enough that I could almost reach out and touch him I called the man's name.

"Bobby!"

Then I didn't wait. I didn't wait for the man to answer, or for him to throw a punch. I didn't wait to tell him why I was there or to ask him to explain his actions. I reached into my jacket, pulled the gun, took half a step backwards and pulled the trigger.

The sound of the gunshot echoed off the abandoned brick buildings for what seemed like seconds. The man's chest erupted like Mount Vesuvius at Pompeii and he fell backward like a board. His head smashed into the pavement and cracked open like an overripe watermelon. Blood pooled everywhere, and quickly.

I stood there for what felt like forever, looking down at the corpse, watching the blood pool grow and move towards me. I took a step backwards as it approached the soles of my shoes. I breathed deeply the heady July night air and felt the wind on my cheeks. Without thinking about it I flipped the safety on and holstered the gun back under my left armpit.

What was surprising was the silence. No screams or sirens or tires screeching. Nothing. No response at all. The only sounds I heard were the wind skimming the rooftops of the warehouses and my heart beating a slow steady rhythm in my calm, easy chest.

I turned around and walked slowly back to The Club. Surprisingly I wasn't thinking about the man, or the victims, or the police or Weather. I walked back to The Club in silence thinking about what to make for breakfast in the morning.

* * *

July 5, 2012 7:17 A.M.

Eggs Benedict, sourdough toast, and strong coffee is what I decided. I ate it sitting down in my booth while reading the Chicago Sun Times. There was no mention of the shooting the night before.

By ten days later I'd settled into a routine. I'd make my own breakfast, skip lunch and walk around the neighborhood. I'd hit the library and do some reading and then make my way back to The Club for dinner. I checked in with Mr. Simons every couple of days just to be polite and I'd be in bed by eleven.

I hadn't heard anything from Detective Hinde since the night in the hospital, but I was sure I wasn't done with her. Megan had given a not so subtle implication that there was no definable end date to this arrangement.

That Friday when I got back to The Club for dinner, I went to my room to get changed and saw what I'd been waiting for. On the desk were two envelopes. One was my customary white legal envelope stuffed with the standard two hundred in cash. The other was the manila envelope I'd been dreading the arrival of. I opened the white one and stuffed the bundle of twenties into my father's Mont Blanc wallet, then picked up the larger package. It was lighter than the last two with a heavy bulge at the bottom. I tore the top off and dumped the contents out on the desk.

Two items fell out. The first was a set of car keys on a ring with an alarm fob hanging off it. The second was a small white card with neat handwriting on it. It read:

Thank you.
Love,
Penny

I stared at the keys on the desk. What was I supposed to do with these? What were they even too? I picked them up and played with them in my hands. The key fob was new, pristine, no smudges or nicks in the plastic; but the keys themselves looked old. Yellow brass showed through the silver coating and the hard edges were worn and rounded.

I stuck them in my pocket and headed out through The Club.

"Not staying for dinner?" Katie asked as I headed towards the door.

"No no. I'll be right back. Just, uh, checking on something," I said. Katie gave a shrug and continued setting places at the tables for the night's dinner crowd.

I headed up the stairs past Nate and walked out onto the street and looked around. There were maybe a dozen cars in view. I pressed the button with a picture of a closed padlock. Nothing.

Nate stepped out of the door and stood on the sidewalk next to me.

"Wha'cha doin' Mr. Gayle?" He asked with a sincere curiosity.

"Uh," I glanced at him then back into the street. "I'm not really sure."

"I didn't know you had a car."

"What? Oh, no, I, uh, I don't."

Nate looked baffled.

"Why do you have car keys then?" he asked.

"I'm, hmm."

I stopped and dropped my shoulders. I turned and looked at the big man for a moment then walked back to the door. "I honestly don't know Nate."

He frowned

"I just got these, but I don't know what they are for."

I pressed the button on the fob again and heard a loud horn go off and it made me jump. I looked up at Nate and he looked back at me. I pressed the button again. Another honk and a flash of yellow light on my right. We both turned our heads in the direction of the sound, and I pressed the button again.

Sitting, parked at the corner and across the street, was a

beautiful, gleaming, smooth as butter black Chrysler 300. Its horn honked and its lights flashed and my jaw dropped.

"Is that your car?" Nate asked.

I just stared at the beautiful machine.

"Mr. Gayle, is that really yours?"

"Um, yeah," I said hoarsely. "Yeah, I guess it is."

Part Two

Weather

Chapter Eleven

<hr>

October 5, 2019 8:12 P.M.

She was a wreck. Split lip, black eye, and she was pretty sure her nose was broken. When she woke up in the apartment, she wasn't sure where she was, her head was pounding and she was terrified. That was hours ago, now she remembered... some of it. The confusion had worn off, but the fear had only amplified.

The heavy steel door swung open with a crash and she sat bolt upright at the sound. Without thinking she tried to stand and was abruptly yanked back down into the hard metal folding chair under her by the handcuffs around her wrists. They were tight, digging into her skin and fastened to the dull gray metal table in front of her by a loop welded to the center of its surface.

She winced in pain and curled herself back over the table. It was cold and hard, and it made her skin crawl to touch it. The whole room made her anxious in fact. Small, poorly lit, painted an unsettling off gray with a huge corner to corner mirror taking up one whole wall, it was exactly what she would have thought an interrogation room would look like, but she was surprised at how it made her feel.

Two men stepped through the door. The first stormed in red faced and full of steam. His shirt was unbuttoned to the third position and he had tiny beads of sweat clinging to his blotchy face like rain on a window. She assumed that this was meant to intimidate her, make her feel unsettled. In reality it did the opposite. It made her angry. She felt her insides harden at the idea that they would try and scare her when she was already terrified out of her mind.

The second strolled in casually, flipping absentmindedly through a small black notebook and chewing on the end of a worn-out pencil stub. He was soft skinned, tan and still had a tie knotted up under his collar. Both wore plain blue suits with leather backed brass badges hanging from their breast pockets. The CPD was there at last.

The sweaty man circled the table a few times inspecting her suspiciously while Mr. Cool found a comfortable place to lean against the wall. When he was settled in the first yanked out the chair across from her and dropped into the seat like a bag of bricks.

"Weather Kimberly Rose," he growled, making her name sound like and accusation.

She looked at him trying to mask her anger with an expression of confusion. He stared back at her with steely eyed conviction and let the silent answer to his question hang in the air. After a while he said it again.

"You are Weather Kimberly Rose. Correct?"

She looked back at him feeling his condescension as a physical jab. She parted her lips as if to speak, then thought better of it and sealed them again. They gazed at each other and Mr. Cool removed the chewed-up pencil from between his teeth and jotted something down in his notebook.

The moist man sitting across from her let out a long sigh and leaned back in his chair. He crossed his arms and seemed to look her over like she was a bizarre piece of modern art. Weather was nervous, but her frustration with the show they were putting on took president and gave her determination to stay focused and present. She bit the inside of her lower lip and let the pain clear her mental fog.

"Maybe," she said, finally trying to hide the quiver in her voice with abhorrence. "We should start with who you are and what, exactly, I'm doing here."

The man's expression didn't falter. He looked her in the eyes and nodded once, waited for a moment as if reconsidering, then nodded again.

"Okay," he said. "I'm Detective Jacobs. This," he gestured sideways with a lilt of his head, "is Detective Stiller."

He stopped talking.

Weather nodded and waited.

The silence stretched out.

One of the fluorescent lights in the room began to flicker obnoxiously then stopped again.

The Detective didn't move. Weather didn't either.

The light flickered again.

"And why am I here?" Weather reiterated with mock calm.

The Detective narrowed his eyes.

Weather knew what was coming but waiting to hear them say it was making her crazy. She felt the tension in her chest growing like a balloon being inflated past its capacity. There was a ringing in her ears now and the room started to wobble in her periphery. A small tingle appeared in the middle of her back and slowly grew to a huge numb spot spreading between her shoulder blades. Her fingers got cold and brittle. In the widening silence she felt her breath getting shallower and her heart started to beat harder and harder in her chest. To be safe, she ran through the checklist of stroke symptoms in her head and then-

"You're here, Ms. Rose, because you're under suspicion for murder."

Pop!

There was a quick sound of water rushing past her ears and then everything stopped. The ringing in her ears was gone. Her vision was clear, and her body was fine. No numbness, no pain, her breathing was normal, and her heart rate was stable, but she was cold and a long chill made itself home in her spine.

She stared coldly back at the detective, looked over at Mr. Cool taking notes and gazed at herself in the eight-foot-wide mirror taking in the battered reflection.

She wore orange pants and an oversized orange shirt provided to her by the city of Chicago. Her face was yellow and brown and black and blue. There was rust colored dried blood smeared across her face and her nose was pointing in an unnatural direction. Her hair was a rat's nest, all clumped together in sticky patches. She looked like she'd gone a full ten rounds with an MMA champ and lost.

She let out a laugh, but it wasn't genuine.

"Grayson, right?"

The Detective didn't respond.

She shook her head.

"Have you looked at me Detective? I'm five foot nothing. I weigh a hundred and five pounds soaking wet, and I look like I just played three periods against the entire Blackhawks bench without pads. You really think I killed someone from the FBI?"

The detective uncrossed his arms and straightened up in his chair. He looked at her long and hard, then leaned in across the table.

"Yes Ma'am, I do."

He looked to the other man.

"Stiller," he said.

The man with the notebook closed it and stuck it in his pocket. He stuck the remains of the number two behind his ear and stood up straight.

"Weather Kimberly Rose," he said. "You are under arrest for the murder of United States Special Prosecutor Brandon Grayson. You have the right to remain silent..."

* * *

October 5, 2019 7:11 P.M.

Hinde stood on the sidewalk in front of the building for a few moments before reaching out to knock on the door. It was dark now and the rain had stopped, but the cold autumn wind whipped around her and fought its way down her collar sending sharp chills down her spine and appendages. She rapped hard on the chipped wooden door and stood back waiting for Nate, The Club's only security, to appear.

It took several moments, and Megan was ready to knock again when the door finally swung open and Nate stepped out into the evening air. He was a big man, six four and probably three hundred pounds. He wore a charcoal suit that fit him remarkably well considering his heft and it blended perfectly with his obsidian black skin. He looked at Detective Hinde for a moment with apprehension before recognizing her and smiling warmly.

"Detective Megan," he said sweetly with a childlike voice that betrayed his enormous stature. "It's so good to see you. Do you have something to drop off?"

Hinde smiled. She couldn't help it. Nate was a sweet guy with a crap job, a lot like herself. His soft voice and friendly demeanor put her at ease and made it less stressful to say what she had to say.

"Not today Nate. I'm here to see Gavin," she said in an easy-going tone.

Nate's smile vanished and, in its place, sat an expression of worry.

"Mr. Gayle?" he said.

"Yeah," Hinde responded casually, or at least an approximation of it. "Yeah, I've got some news for him."

Nate shook his head.

"But not here Detective Megan. You guys don't meet here. You don't meet here, not at The Club. You don't meet Mr. Gayle here."

Detective Hinde put out a gentle hand and laid it on Nate's monstrous arm.

"I know. I know Nate, but this is important. I don't have time to set up something somewhere else. Do you think you can let me in to see him?"

Nate ran his wide palms and long fingers across his face and over his bald scalp. He was anxious about the request and clearly didn't know what he should do.

"It's okay," Hinde said. "It's okay Nate. She sent me. She has something he needs to know. It's pretty important. I promise, I won't be long."

Nate seemed to be weighing his options. He wasn't the kind of guy who was used to making decisions. He had one job, let in the people who should be there and keep out those who shouldn't. Trying to make judgment calls in specific circumstances was well outside his pay grade and his comfort zone.

"I promise," Hinde said, even softer. "It's okay, I'll be in and out."

Nate nodded.

"In and out," he said.

"That's right Nate. I'll be in and out. No one will even know I was here."

"Okay Detective Megan. Okay, in and out. Okay."

The huge man moved aside and held the door open for the detective. She stepped in and he followed, letting the door swing closed in the process. The space fell to blackness and Hinde reflexively put her arms out for balance.

The entryway was small, no wider than the door frame with red brick walls and a rough cement floor. She couldn't see anything, but her hands easily touched the surfaces on either side of her and she was able to maintain her footing.

"Watch your step," Nate said, and she felt his heavy hand rest gently on her shoulder.

He gave her a slight nudge and she moved down the corridor slowly, inching her way towards the stairs she knew led down to the main level of The Club. She felt the hand leave her shoulder and heard the soft voice advise her to look out for the steps ahead. When her toes found the ledge of the platform, she saw a dim light glowing below her. Still holding the walls on either side of her she made her way down the half dozen or so stone steps to a landing in front of an ornate oak door.

The small cobblestone floor was about four feet square and there were wax candles burning in elaborate sconces on either side of the door. She wrapped her hand around the cold iron handle and depressed the lever with her thumb. The sound of a latch lifting echoed through the cramped space and the door swung free into the room ahead of her.

* * *

October 5, 2019 6:38 P.M.

It was dark in The Club. I liked it that way and so did everyone else. It wasn't the kind of place you'd go to be seen, more like a place you'd go to hide. When I walked in, I was cold, wet, bloody and in need of a drink. Lauren, the dark-haired misanthropic bartender, held up a bottle of my usual Seascape Pinot Noir when she saw me. I grimaced and shook my head indicating it was a night for something a little bit stronger. An understanding nod came back to me.

I snaked through the maze of low two tops and through the kitchen to my room in the back. I washed up, bandaged my ribs and put on fresh clothes, then headed back out to my booth in a shadowy corner of the dining room. There was a large glass of bourbon waiting on the table when I got there. I took a gulp and let the satisfying burn wash over me. By the second glass I was starting to feel normal again.

On my third the heavy old door at the front swung open with a rusty squeal that it had been developing over the past several months. I didn't know the people who came to The Club, but I knew the kind of people they were; rich, powerful, important and arrogant. They were the people who ran the city for the people who ran the city. They were the deal makers and agreement enforcers. I knew who they were, but not who they were, and I didn't want to know either.

I sat in my private booth, quiet and alone, drinking and smoking and waiting. I was always waiting for the inevitable just one more time. For the request that wasn't really a request. The favor that was really a debt. I'd sit and I'd wait for the package that always eventually came. This time though, it wasn't a package. It was a person and that meant it was so much worse.

Detective Hinde and I were not friends and we weren't

what you would call friendly. We were colleagues at a job that neither of us applied for. I didn't dislike her particularly, but I know the feeling wasn't mutual. She hated me, and with good reason I suppose. Hell, it's the same reason I hated myself and we both knew it wasn't my fault. Not really, but who else were we going to blame?

When she walked into the room it went silent for a moment. Lauren stopped polishing glasses and set one down on the bar with a thud. Amelia, the pale buxom redhead that played, sort of, the worn out upright piano next to the kitchen doors stopped. The whispered conversations at the tables all paused for just a moment as everyone acknowledged the presence of a cop in the room.

For her part, Megan did her best to put them at ease. She wore civilian clothes; a skirt half a size too small and heels no cop would ever wear to work. She also made a show of not noticing there was anyone else in the room. She had daggers in her eyes, and they were pointing straight at me. No deviation. Not even for a second. After a moment the low murmuring music of the room resumed, and I was left staring at the detective as she stepped up to my table.

We were both quiet for a bit, gazing at each other like two wild animals sizing each other up over a stray scrap of meat. She had sweat on her forehead and just the slightest anxious tremor in her hands. Obviously, she didn't want to be there. She was sent and that meant something bad had happened.

"Detective," I said, opening my cigarette case and pulling out a smoke.

"Gavin," her voice was cold, hard and unpleasant.

I clicked open my lighter and spun the wheel as I pulled it to my face. One long drag off my coffin nail got the thing lit. My free hand found my glass without the aid of my eyes and I let a swallow of booze fill the uncomfortable silence for a moment, then finally I let out a long sigh and dropped my defensive posture.

"Are you going to have a seat?"

She eyed the chair across from me and considered the offer. It would have been better for her to stay standing, to keep her elevation and hold on to some sense of authority, but she knew she wasn't supposed to be there and no matter how she approached the confrontation, that was my space, and I was in charge. Eventually she acquiesced and pulled the chair out, dropping into it with defeat.

"So, is this business or pleasure," I grinned when I said it. Megan was a good-looking woman. Small around the waist with hips just wide enough to fill out a dress. She had a professional sensibility that could've been sexy if she ever wanted it to be and eyes that you really could get lost in under different circumstances.

"You don't really deal in pleasure, do you Gavin?"

It was a halfhearted stab at me, and she knew it was aimed in the wrong direction. I gave her a wounded expression and put my hand to my chest.

"What I do always makes somebody happy."

She grunted.

"Happiness and satisfaction are not necessarily the same thing."

I gave a slight nod. That was true enough.

"So what's this about?"

She bored into me with her hard, penetrating gaze. I felt it crawling over my skin and it made me shiver. When I was suitably uncomfortable, she leaned back in her chair and surveyed the room for the first time since she'd walked in. An angry frown not even trying to hide disgust pulled down at the corners of her mouth.

"Wow," she said. "This place really is a dive."

I sucked hard on the last dregs of my butt and crushed it out in an overfull ashtray. I followed her stare around the room. She was right of course, well, almost. It was less of a dive than a dump, all tattered at the edges and well past unrefined. The truth, it was old, very old and no one had ever bothered to keep it from falling into squalor. There wasn't any point really. It wasn't a place for tourists. Hell, it wasn't even a place for locals. The Club was a place people went to be invisible. At that, it succeeded.

Dark and warm with little in the way of air circulation or ventilation gave it a mustiness mixed with the strong smell of old pipe tobacco. The walls, all stained with cigarette and cigar smoke matched the floors that were usually sticky. Two top tables were battered and worn matching the bar with its weathered blonde boards. None of the glasses matched and the cheap booze sat in reused unlabeled bottles. Even Amelia, the piano player, looked worn out by a life that didn't go her way.

"Yeah," I said. "It's a dump, but it's my dump and you're not supposed to be here. So, what is it Megan? What's she want?"

Megan crossed her arms. She knew that was coming. It was standard posturing for two vultures circling a kill. She may have known she was in the wrong place, but I knew I couldn't bully or intimidate her. In truth, we were a couple of pawns and we both worked for the same Queen.

"It's-" she started but cut herself off.

"It's what?" I frowned.

"Well Gavin," she paused again. "It's Weather."

She spat out the words like they were poison.

I didn't say anything at first. It'd been a long time since I'd heard that name spoken out loud and it shocked me hearing it come out of her mouth, but I'd been dealing with these people for a long time and I knew what a surprised look could do to a power balance. My expression didn't change. I sat holding her eyes with mine, letting the sentence hang in the foggy air between us.

"It's about Weather how?" slow, deliberate speech.

"She's been arrested."

I reached for my bourbon and sipped. I was getting to the end of the glass and I inspected the few remaining ice cubes floating in the yellowing liquid.

"For what?" I said finally.

She looked me dead in the eyes, clearly feeling the control of the situation swinging her way.

"Murder."

I took a deep breath, the kind of breath you take when you're not ready to speak in a moderate tone. I sat back in my seat then twisted and pulled myself back up to the table. The flat silver case found its way into my hands and I pulled out another long brown cigarette and screwed the gold foil tip between my lips. Again, the snap of my narrow Zippo, the scrape of the wheel on the flint and the crackle as it ignited and did its job. I puffed twice then clicked the lighter shut and pulled hard on the butt.

"Let her go," I said finally, blowing smoke as I spoke.

"Gavin-"

"Tell the Lieutenant to let-"

"Gavin, he can't."

I stopped speaking. I was rigid and I felt my pale Irish face redden as my blood pressure started up the ringing in my ears that always came before I lost control.

"He can't," she said again. "Gavin, she killed a Fed. Grayson! Gavin, fucking Brandon Grayson."

I shook my head.

"Who the- I don't have any idea who that is, and I don't care either."

"Seriously?" She looked at me with awe. "He's the spe- He's

the FBI lawyer investigating Chicago corruption. We've got her now, but the FBI is on the way down there. They're going to take her; we can't do anything here."

Another shake of my head.

"No. No she didn't do that. Come on Megan," I was shouting now, standing up and leaning across the table palms flat on the surface. "You fucking know she didn't do that."

Detective Hinde put on a wincing smile and nodded understandingly.

"Maybe. Probably. You're probably right, but it doesn't matter. They found her at the scene, Gavin. They found her there naked. There's no way we can let her go. There's nothing we can do."

There was a soft moment of tense quiet. My breath was heavy and hot across the expanse between us. Slowly I sat back down and smoked my butt.

"And Gavin, you can't-"

"What?"

She stopped.

"What Megan? I can't what?"

She flinched ever so slightly at my anger. That slight twinge, that single moment empowered me. I felt a rush of adrenaline, a surge of entitlement.

"I can do all the other shit you guys ask me to do!"

The detective shifted and straightened up into an authoritative posture. She recognized the ground I'd gained and was trying to get her footing back.

"Gavin, I never-"

"Bullshit!" I screamed.

The restaurant went quiet. The music stopped again, and the various guests of the establishment started to silently get up from their seats and retreat out the front door one by one.

"Don't tell me it's not you," I shouted. "Do you think I

differentiate? Do you think I care who's fucking office those little packages come from? Ask yourself, Detective, if you think I see any difference between you and her."

I said the word with a terrifying contempt.

"You go down there. You go down there and you let her go. You fucking do it. Fucking do it right now!"

Megan looked at the floor. Her cheeks flush and her jaw set. She stood up silently and, after a pitying sigh, walked towards the door. At the step to the main dining room she stopped. She paused just long enough to gather herself then turned.

"I'm really sorry Gavin. We can't help her, and if you get into it with the feds, well, we won't be able to help you either."

I felt something snap inside me. The same kind of snap as I felt years ago at the party. The tissue thin barrier I'd built up and protected over the past thirteen years, the wall between my deepest feelings and my conscience actions; I felt it tear and shred and everything I'd spent a decade suppressing came pouring out like water from a fire hose.

I roared and lifted the edge of the table in front of me then smashed it back down to the ground. The legs of the table split and debris crashed to the floor. A cloud of ash filled the space between the two of us. Hinde didn't flinch this time. She showed no surprise, no fear. She simply turned away and walked across the room and out the door making it squeal and slam shut behind her.

Chapter Twelve

October 5, 2019 8:13 P.M.

For thirteen years I had worked on two things: staying calm and forgetting Weather Rose. The latter was a fool's errand. I knew that. I could never forget a person who changed my life so completely, but the goal was never success oriented, not consciously anyway. It was about the effort. Trying to put her out of my mind was the important part. Loosening her grip on my heart, my mind, and my actions.

The former, though, staying calm, that was a real objective. That was important. I recognized that my anger played too big a role in my life. It had probably always been there, but the point at which I know it came to control me was my parent's divorce.

My parents split up when I was seven years old and to call it traumatic would be like calling the ice caps melting away to nothing a bummer. It broke me. We were a close family and I never knew that they were having problems. To me it seemed as though my entire life up to that point had been a grand illusion. A mirage in a magician's glass and they shattered it in a single instant.

It broke me for trust and for faith and for love. It let the anger out, and when it got out it consumed me, and I became its vessel. From that point on my anger was my compass and rage my true north. Ironically it was Weather that helped me keep all that in check. She was my anchor and my guide through the troubled waters of my inner self.

Of course, the double irony was that it was my anger, my rage, my unchecked fury that took her away from me and set me adrift. Lost at sea, drowning in my own failures. It became up to me to find a way to right the ship and calm the riptide of my emotions. It took me the five years I was in prison to find that calm, and the next five to finally feel I had mastered it and tamed the monster inside myself.

Now it was loose again.

I gathered my strewn things from around the splintered pieces of the table and retrieved my coat and hat from my room. On a final impulse I opened my safe and took out my gun, a battered old .45 I hated to look at. I stormed through the kitchen and dining room and up the dark stone steps to the street level door of The Club. Nate was there, a huge imposing brick wall of a man.

"You look angry Gavin. You probably shouldn't-"

"Out of my way Nate," I said.

"Uh, Detective Megan said I shouldn't-"

"Nate," I said calmly, but with a voice sharp as glass. "Move."

He looked at me sadly and stepped aside. I squeezed past him in the narrow corridor and threw the door open. It was late and the traffic on Torrence Ave was light. I crossed the street against the light and found my car.

It was a dark and angry ride from The Club to the nineteenth precinct where I assumed they were holding Weather. It wasn't a random assumption. The nineteenth was Megan's precinct, that's where her desk was, and she had said we have her, not they have her. I could have been wrong, but in my experience when she said we, she wasn't talking about the police.

It was almost nine p.m. when I made the hard right off of Marquette onto Lake Shore Drive. I'd been doing seventy on the side streets and out of concern for sheer physics let the 300 drop to fifty-five before making the turn. Once on the straightaway of LSD however, I pressed my foot to the floor and was doing ninety miles an hour before I made it off the Jackson Park peninsula. My rage was running the show now and I knew that that was never good.

Part of me was still crying out to let it go, to calm down and regain control of myself, but my emotional core was impenetrable to logic now. It didn't want to level out. It didn't want to think critically. What it wanted was to kill every single person that had made my life into the nightmare that I lived in every day.

That was a lie too though. If I listened to my better angels, the ones that hid in the dark narrow recesses of my soul, I knew that revenge wasn't my goal. I wasn't really mad at the people who held my greasy marionette strings, not any more than I was yesterday at least, or even an hour ago. I didn't want to hurt anyone, I never wanted to hurt anyone. Not really. All I really wanted, all I had ever wanted, was to protect Weather.

That's what it all boiled down to. The only thing that had ever really mattered was her. She was my impetus, my reason for being. I was weak without her and she was strong even despite me. If I had it all to do over again, every moment of the last decade and a half; if I could take it all back and change that one night, I knew I wouldn't. I knew that, no matter what, any time Weather was concerned, I would do whatever had to be done, and that would always lead back to where I was at that moment. Cresting a hundred miles an hour around Deadman's Curve on Lake Shore Drive heading for what would almost certainly be my own undoing.

* * *

8:38 P.M.

State's Attorney Maureen Adalet sat at the small metal table in the center of the off-putting gray room in the rear of the District 019 Headquarters. Weather sat across from her. She knew this girl, but she hadn't seen her in almost thirteen years. Maureen was quiet, and mindful, watching Weather's face, her eyes, the small lines just forming at the corners of her mouth. She was patient, precise and methodical.

For her part Weather was unflinching. She sat peacefully in her orange scrubs, staring cockeyed at the mirror that covered the whole wall to her right. She seemed a million miles away, and Maureen, to her surprise, felt bad for her.

"How have you been Weather?" she said.

Weather turned her head and looked coldly at Maureen. She tried to lean back in her chair, but the chain between her wrists caught on the loop and tugged her shoulders uncomfortably, so she leaned forward instead and rested on her elbows. She gave a long questioning look at the State's Attorney, then a brief judgmental glance at the detectives, let out an exasperated sigh and began picking at her fingernails silently.

Maureen grimaced. She was trying to be nice, but she didn't have time to play games. The FBI would be here any minute and Maureen needed answers before they took control of the situation.

"Okay then, down to business. Miss Rose, how did you know Mr. Grayson?"

Weather dug a small piece of dirt out from under one of her French manicured nails and wiped it on the table in front of her.

"Miss Rose, were you having a sexual relationship with Mr. Grayson?"

A slight head cock and she began working on the next nail.

"Weather, have you spoken to Gavin recently?"

Weather stopped her nail cleaning and looked up at her. She gave a startled frown, sipped the air, paused and gave a long exhale before returning to grooming her nails. The detective with the notebook scribbled something in shorthand then put the pencil back in his mouth.

"Miss Rose," the other detective said. "Did you kill Special Council Brandon Grayson?"

Weather wiped another piece of debris on the table.

Maureen sighed. She was getting agitated and every second that passed brought her control of the situation closer to its end. She rubbed her temples with her fingertips for a moment then folded her hands on the table.

"Maybe it would be easier if we start with what we already know. Ya know, get the ball rolling."

Weather stopped picking and looked up again. She shrugged and tried again to lean back in her chair but ultimately found herself mimicking Maureen's position.

"It's been almost thirteen years since I last saw you, during the trial right, or just before. You never showed up in court."

Maureen opened a file folder and flipped through some mostly blank pages.

"You've been pretty quiet since then. You don't have an arrest record. No parking tickets. No speeding tickets. Your driver's license says you don't live in the city, and you don't appear to be married."

Weather gave a 'maybe, maybe not' shrug and tilted her head in a way that said 'anything else'. Maureen stared at her silently and she shrugged again and went back to picking her nails. She was starting to get a small pile of nail gunk building up on the table in front of her despite having had her nails cleaned out into a small plastic evidence bag during her fingerprinting.

"The rest of what we know at the moment doesn't look good for you. You were found in the victim's apartment, half naked, covered in his blood. A gun that we're pretty sure is going to end up being the murder weapon was laying right next to you with bloody fingerprints all over it. I have a detective heading over to the prints lab right now to confirm that those prints are yours, but that's pretty much a formality, right? They are your prints, aren't they Miss Rose?"

Weather did her best not to show any emotion, any reaction at all, but she could feel the flush in her cheeks. She knew that her face blushed red and then white very quickly. She didn't remember how she got on that floor, or for that matter, anything at all after she had walked in the door of Grayson's apartment, but she was pretty certain that the detective was right. When the police got the results on the fingerprinting it would indeed be her prints on the gun.

They would find her skin under the victim's fingernails, and his' under her's, and there would be gunpowder residue on her hands that much was a certainty. She was certain because she deserved this. This was karma for what she did to Gavin, and for some reason this lawyer seemed to know that too.

* * *

8:55 P.M.

Special Agent Kyle Flannery's SUV was FBI issued, however, it didn't have lights and siren. He was a white-collar investigator and never had the occasion, in this assignment anyway, to chase bad guys through the streets of Chicago like in the Blues Brothers. Tonight, however, he was flying through traffic with one hand leaning on the horn and the other tugging repeatedly on the lever next to the steering wheel that flashed his brights.

The message from Grayson had been strange. He sounded weird. Not exactly scared, but definitely off.

"Kyle, you're not going to believe this. Ya know your guy, well I've got his girlfriend here and she's fucking crazy. Get over here. My place. Fast, like fucking now."

There was a loud crack that followed and a fuzz in the speaker, then a rattle and the line went dead. That was it, and it would have been enough, but it wasn't what had Flannery playing Grand Prix through LSD traffic on his way to the north side of the city. It wasn't Grayson's message at all. It was the eight missed calls from his SAI.C. and the one text.

Grayson is dead. Homicide. 745 Buckingham.

Brandon Grayson was the Special Prosecutor in charge of the investigation that had brought Agent Flannery to Chicago five years ago. He was a straightforward Type-A personality in an expensive suit and pricey shoes. Flannery had liked him immediately.

Grayson took a moralistic view of the law that Flannery shared. Not one of religious convictions, but simply that the law was the law. Were there laws that were wrong? Sure, but there was a process, a legal process, to fix them. A person obeyed the law because it was the right thing to do, for society, and flaunting the law was wrong. Period. This made what Flannery and Grayson did especially right. There could be no greater calling in life than to enforce the laws of a great democratic society. Flannery felt that way, and Grayson felt that way too, and Flannery respected him for it.

The feeling was mutual. Grayson had picked the agents that were brought into his investigation by hand. Flannery had previously been assigned to a team that was working with the D.E.A. shutting down marijuana farms in the west. This was a controversial and unpopular program in the press and increasingly in society as a whole. Already there were several states legalizing the use of marijuana for either medicinal or recreational purposes, and many of the agents on the assignment approached it with little more than halfhearted attention, but Flannery took it very seriously. He never shared a personal viewpoint on the subject of legalization, he just did his job with zeal and determination, taking down farm after farm, warehouse after warehouse, and dealer after dealer. Not because he had strong feelings about the dangers of pot, but because it was the law and it was his assignment.

Grayson was impressed with Flannery's moral dedication to his work and requested to have him transferred to Chicago to work on his corruption task force. Flannery hadn't been thrilled with the idea of moving to Chicago. City government corruption didn't sound that interesting, especially compared to the work he had been doing, but a personal request was a good mark on his record, and the idea of working for someone who thought enough of him to specifically ask for him was appealing.

The case had been only slightly more interesting than Flannery had predicted. Days raiding drug warehouses had given over to days of sitting at a computer looking over city contracts and financial documents. Flannery barely left the office now except to go and visit someone else's office. Usually an alderman or some small business owner who had received a no bid contract with the city. The tasks were mundane and the information only just interesting enough to keep him from falling asleep at his desk.

He did enjoy working with Grayson though. Grayson had a fascinating career and knew interesting people. Their work conversations often detoured into old stories of previous cases and scandalous tales of amazingly inept people. Flannery spent most of what you would call his 'free time' with Grayson in his office engaging in these meandering discussions. They had become close, well as close as two people without a social life can become. Flannery thought of Grayson as more than his boss. He thought of him as a wise and experienced mentor who taught him things he would need to know to someday become that man with the stories. Stories like Flannery's ghost, the ghost of the south side, the ghost called Gavin Gayle.

Flannery first heard, or rather read the name Gavin Gayle in an old hospital report. He had been working with Michael Carrigan, the Postal Inspector-in-Charge for the U.S. Postal Inspector Service in Chicago. Together they were investigating government employees who were using the U.S. Mail to commit fraud. Bribery and corruption at the city level were a gray area for the feds, but as soon as something went through the mail, bingo! Suddenly it became a federal crime. The night before Carrigan was scheduled to testify in court to evidence that a North Side alderman and several city inspectors were colluding to shake down local businesses in a widespread bribery scheme, he was shot dead in an alley off of Fulton Market in the Meat-packing District.

That was problematic enough, but the real kicker was that the person who shot him was dead too. A teamster that was also on the payroll for a West Side alderman, one of the ones named in the indictment. His body was found just thirty feet away from Carrigan with three holes in his chest and still holding the gun that killed the Postal Inspector. Carrigan on the other hand was unarmed and had no powder residue on his hands or clothes.

There were no witnesses, and the ballistics report couldn't match the bullet that killed Carrigan to any previous shootings. The other body though, that was different. CSU was able to pull a single .45 caliber bullet from the body. The other two had been through and throughs and both had mushroomed into useless pancakes against the brick wall behind him. The bullet in the body though had little in the way of mushrooming, it was in fairly good condition and was matched easily in the ballistics lab. The file on the match was less straightforward.

The bullet matched a single previous shooting which had occurred about two years earlier. The Forensic report referenced the case number from that incident as Chicago Metropolitan Police Department Case 07-1-087483-4. Flannery had visited the local precinct that had filed the report, but the case file was missing, replaced with a marker indicating that the file had been relocated to the state's attorney's office. When he requested access to the file at the SA's office he was told that it was unavailable except by subpoena.

The subpoena process had taken a week, and he waited another week for a copy of the file to be sent to his office. When it did arrive, almost the entire content of the file had been redacted. A word here and a word there still shown in rough manual typeface, but line after line of the Xeroxed document was crossed out with wide black marker leaving no indication of the original content of the document.Flannery flipped through the thick folder, growing increasingly frustrated as page after page revealed no new information. Finally, three pages from the end of the report there was a brief reference to an ambulance and a trip to Stroger Hospital with a time two forty-nine a.m. and date stamp June 14, 2012. It wasn't much, but armed with a warrant he visited Stroger Hospital's records department and in the friendliest way possible, demanded the admittance record for a GSW June 14, 2012 arriving in the ER between two a.m. and three a.m. Luckily there was a single incident that whole night of a gunshot wound intake and the record was not only available on site, but also completely un-redacted. The patient's name, originally typed in as John Smith, was crossed out and handwritten in as Gavin Gayle. He was a twenty-eight-year-old white male.

There was no phone number listed, Flannery wondered how that had happened, but there was an address, and the charges had been billed back to an insurance account that ended up linked to a City of Chicago Medical Savings Account. Flannery photo-copied the file and gave the originals back to the woman at the records desk.

The address listed wound up being an SRO public housing unit on the near west side, and the apartment number was unoccupied, and had been at the time of the hospital report according to city housing records. The MSA ended up being a pool account. It was a sort of petty cash or slush fund for covering the medical expenses of uninsured people that the city wanted to control or keep quiet for one reason or another.

It was a totally illegal operation that led directly to seven indictments of city officials and a dozen or so more indirectly, which, while providing no real progress on the identification or location of the mystery patient from that night, did earn him a little bit of latitude in his investigation from his superiors.

That latitude didn't change the fact that the only thing Agent Flannery had to go on was the name on the admittance form. Clearly whoever filled out the forms didn't want the identity of the patient known, what with the name John Smith originally entered and the bogus address. Also, whoever was protecting this patient was high enough in the Chicago political machine to have access to the totally illegal health insurance account entered on the patient's charts. Apparently, however, someone had, at some point, slipped up and given a different name for the patient, and someone else had been good enough to hand write that name in the file. Gavin Gayle. It could have been another fake name, but why replace one fake name with another. Flannery believed it was real and it was all he had.

Running the name through the FBI database provided a slightly smaller pool of leads than simply Googling "Gavin Gayle". Narrowing the search to Chicago and the immediate surrounding suburbs, however, reduced the list of people with that name or alias to more manageable six identities, and when he removed the individuals who were either dead, or in prison he got the number down to two. Two suspects was a nice easy number, maybe a little too easy, but he moved ahead anyway without holding his breath.

The first of the two turned out to be an eleven-year-old, living in Wheaton, IL about thirty miles outside the city. That seemed unlikely given that he would have been nine at the time of the shooting. The other was a seventy-eight-year-old Irish immigrant with lung cancer currently living in a nursing home in Oak Park. Flannery had no doubt that a seventy-four year old could have pulled the trigger on a man in a dark alley if he felt he needed to, and it wasn't out of the realm of possibility that the age on the admittance form had been fudged, but this particular Gavin Gayle had been out of the country, in Ireland visiting family at the time of the shooting. He had passport stamps, airline records, and dozens of alibis in his homeland to vouch for the fact that he wasn't in that alley on that night.

So, he was back at zero. Flannery decided to dip back into the pool of unlikely suspects. Though dead or incarcerated individuals rarely managed to overcome those obstacles and commit murder, the task of doing a background check and crossing them off the list seemed easy enough, and at the very least, a good mental exercise to kill some time until the next lead came along. Of the six names on the list, five of them landed firmly in the "dead" category. One of them landed tentatively in both.

It was at that point that Flannery brought the information to Grayson. Grayson had looked at what he had, had asked valuable and insightful questions, and had heard him out thoroughly, and after all that, Grayson had dismissed it.

While the trail of documents was suspicious, it ended in a name that was literally a dead end, and Flannery's theory that it was a conspiracy was wild speculation at best. Ultimately his main point was that it was bad press to waste tax funded resources chasing the bogeyman.

Grayson had dropped it at that point. No FBI resources were to be used following up on Gavin Gayle, but Flannery still felt there was something there. He decided to push forward, asking questions and following leads in his evening hours. This meant that time with Grayson and his war stories grew less and less frequent until it disappeared altogether. Their relationship became cooler and more professional.

Then two days prior to Grayson's death Flannery had learned of The Club. He didn't yet know where it was, but he had heard that Gavin Gayle owned it, or ran it, or at the very least acted like he did. He apparently spent every night there, and if you could get past the front door, you could see the man himself.

Flannery called Grayson to fill him in on this new information, but he hadn't been able to connect with him, so he resorted to leaving several messages with Henry, Grayson's assistant. With no response, Flannery decided to pursue the lead alone and bring Grayson the proof afterwards.

Except now Grayson was dead. Not just dead, murdered, and the address in the text message was his home. It was the same place he had just told Flannery to meet him, where Gavin's girlfriend was apparently going psycho. Flannery had a hard time seeing this as a coincidence. As he screeched to a stop in front of Grayson's building he was filled with anger. He was angry at this direct attack on his team, angry at the immorality of the crime itself, angry at the effect on his investigation, but mostly he was angry at losing a friend.

The elevator doors opened with a chime and Flannery stepped off. The entry room was full of hustle and bustle. There were Chicago P.D. detectives, SWAT team members, FBI, and State and Federal Attorneys all speaking to one another, taking notes and comparing information. The door to the apartment was open and Flannery could already see the commotion inside. Half a dozen steps later he was standing next to Special Agent In Charge Michaels at the edge of a pool of coagulating blood.

"I called you eight times."

"I know, I'm sorry. I was in a meeting."

SAI.C. Michaels looked at him with a frown.

"A meeting with whom?"

"Probably best if we talk about it later." Flannery said. "So, what the hell happened here?"

"Looks like a lover's quarrel. Chicago PD Got a call about a disturbance. Loud shouting, things breaking, then gunshots. Two beat cops show up and climb the stairs to the apartment, but as they got to the entry way out there," he gestured to the door Flannery just came through, "there's more gunfire and two shots come through the door. One hits the elevator doors the other catches one of the officers in the vest. They freak out, call for backup and SWAT and then wait. Apparently after that it stays quiet for a while. Just as SWAT shows up, they start hearing movement inside again."

Flannery looked frustrated.

"Cops never identified themselves?"

"Nope."

"And they didn't try to enter until SWAT got there?"

"Uh uh."

"Got it, so then?"

Michaels sighed.

"So, then SWAT breaks down the door, everyone rushes in. Grayson is on the floor in a pool of blood. One in the chest, and one in the head. The girl is lying on the ground in front of him in nothing but her skivvies, covered in blood spatter, gun about a foot and a half away from her."

"And her clothes?" Flannery asked.

"In a pile next to the bed. They're on the way to the lab to check for DNA."

"Any I.D.?"

"Yeah, driver's license. Name was Weather Rose. Address outside the cit-"

Flannery flinched.

"Name was what?"

"Uh, Weather Rose."

Michaels looked down at his notebook to double check.

"Yeah, Weather Rose, age twenty-nine. Lives..."

"Yeah, yeah okay."

Flannery's heart was pounding now. Grayson had said it. He had said it on the message.

"...your guy, well I've got his girlfriend here and she's fucking crazy."

This was all too big a coincidence.

"Where did they take her?"

SAI.C. Michaels looked at Flannery like he was having a stroke.

"Uh, Addison I think. Chicago PD took her before we got here. I was going to go down and pick her up as soon as I was done here."

"I got it." Flannery said already halfway out the door. "Finish up here and meet me back at the office. I'll take care of moving the girl."

"Yeah, okay, sure."

Michaels watched bewildered as Flannery flew out the door and jumped in the elevator.

"Whatever that was," He shrugged and squatted down to inspect the floor.

Chapter Thirteen

October 5, 2019 8:56 P.M.

I felt sick as I rolled the Chrysler up to the curb. I hadn't felt like that in a long time. I'd gotten over the nausea of the job years ago. I'm not proud of it, but it's true, and my boss made sure I didn't run into any legal entanglements on a day to day basis.

She also made sure that I was comfortable if not happy. She provided my room and board at The Club and passed on, well, I'd guess you'd call them gratuities from grateful families. Gratuities like my cigarettes and my car. I couldn't have a real job, not one that paid, and I couldn't have I.D. so a driver's license or automobile title was out of the question. Those gratuities were what made my life what you might call normal. The conditions of all this had become so routine that I hardly noticed them anymore.

The feeling in my stomach then; that rotten putrescence, was something I'd managed to forget somehow. I didn't like it, I hated feeling it work its way up my throat and spreading that brassy acid across my teeth, but more than anything, I realized, I didn't like that it had gone away in the first place.

It was bad to be there. I shouldn't have been. Couldn't have been actually. It was against the rules. It violated every condition of my work release agreement. I thought about that as I stared at the squat brick and glass building and it brought back that feeling of oily fever that had plagued me at the beginning. The thing to do was step on the gas and get back to my neighborhood, instead I killed the engine and stepped out of the car.

I slipped out of my overcoat and threw it and my hat in the back seat. I slipped my gun out of my shoulder holster and locked it in the glove box and removed the holster and dropped it on top of the coat. I shouldn't be walking into a police station in the first place, I certainly wasn't going to do it packing heat. I grabbed a pre-knotted necktie from the passenger seat and slipped it around my neck.

I saw in a movie somewhere that a clipboard and a confident wave will get you into any room in the world. I sure hope that's not really true, but it stuck with me, and in my experience it's more or less accurate. I threw in a lanyard with some large credentials hanging from it, busy with design and print so it's difficult to read or make out from a distance. People, even people who should know better, rarely question someone wearing ID around their neck. It turned out the boys in blue at 850 W. Addison were no exception.

I pushed open the front door of Townhall, the Headquarters of the Chicago PD Lakeview district, and with a big friendly grin, waved my metal clipboard and strode right past the Desk Sergeant and through the double swing doors on the left side of the room.

Inside I collapsed against the cream-colored cinder block wall and nearly threw up. I took a white linen handkerchief from my pocket and wiped my forehead and the corners of my mouth while surveying the surroundings.

I was in a corridor about forty feet long. The floor was standard beige speckled industrial tile and there were bare fluorescent tube light fixtures on a drop ceiling. I counted three doors on each side of the corridor, the same cream white as the walls, with stainless steel door knobs. Each had a twelve-inch square glass window at eye level with a crisscross of wire inside. At the end of the hall was another set of double doors, but not swing doors. These looked solid, steel doors with solid handles and no windows.

I regained my composure, tucked the now damp handkerchief back in my jacket and began making my way down the hall. At each door I stopped and peeked through the small window. They were all the same. Ten by ten rooms with a gray metal table, three chairs, a microphone hanging over the table, and a small camera in the upper right-hand corner of the room. They were all empty. Interrogation rooms, I guessed I was headed in the right direction.

At the end of the hall I grabbed the knob of the right-hand door and tried unsuccessfully to turn it; locked. I tried the left-hand door as well with the same result. I had to push down panic again as I stared at the sturdy barricade. I gave a quick glance behind me, then back to the doors. I reached again, more out of frustration than expectation. As I gripped the handle on the right it spun inside my hand and pulled away as the door swung open.

That surge again. I instinctively dropped my eyes to the floor and stepped aside. A pair of women's legs in stockings and black heels passed by and I quickly caught the door. I pivoted and started to step through when the sharp click of the footsteps behind me went silent. I tried to fight the urge to turn, but instinct prevailed and my eyes met the stare of Detective Megan

Hinde. I feel my heart stop. I looked at the door in my hand and quickly tried to slam it shut between us, but the heavy slab slammed against her hand.

I stepped backwards and spun, walking down the hall at a speed that bordered on running. After about ten steps the detective shouted in a raspy whisper.

"Gavin!"

I froze, my mind flashing through options, possibilities, scenarios where I could get out of this without the whole goddamn world crashing down around me. I took another step.

"Gavin!"

Frozen again.

"Oh my God, what the fuck are you doing here? Are you fucking crazy?"

Slowly I turned to face her.

"Look, I specifically told you to stay the fuck away. I mean, holy shit, how did you even get past the front desk? You can't be here. They have Weather in interro- Fuck, Maureen is here, and the feds are on their way! Seriously Gavin, you fucked up, you need to leave."

A blank stare was all I could muster, trying to decide between the dual urges of fight or flight. Hinde was clearly panicking, breathing hard and glancing around like a paranoid.

"Gavin, she killed Grayson. When they found her she was damn near naked, covered in his blood, and the gun was right next to her. I'm supposed to be on my way to the prints lab now to see if they got a match, but you know they will."

I shook my head.

"No."

Hinde rolled her eyes.

"Fuck," she spat. "I don't know if she killed him or not, but it looks that way and with it looking like it does, well, I don't have to tell you. This is Chicago Gavin, and with it looking like it does, they just aren't going to look much fucking further."

"I have to see her."

"Abso-fucking-lutely not. She isn't alone. No, no you have to leave. Seriously, fucking go!"

"I will, right after I see her." I said doing my best to sound confident and defiant.

"Fuck man! Fuck, aren't you listening to me? You can't walk around a police station. You can't do that ever, but seriously, no way you can be here while fucking Weather Rose is being questioned for the murder of member of the FBI!"

I decided the conversation was going nowhere and turned to start walking down the hall.

"Okay, okay, okay! Fuck, just fucking stop for a second."

I stopped but didn't turn around.

"Okay." she sighed. "Okay, come on, come with me. You can see her, but you can't talk to her. She's in the big interrogation room being questioned. If there's no one in the witness room, I'll let you see her through the glass."

"Thank you," I whispered.

"Yeah, thank me. Fuck, if anyone sees us together, I don't fucking know you. You get sixty seconds and then I want you out of here. You got yourself in, so you can find your way out. I'll drop you off, then I'm heading to the prints lab to get the report on the gun. When I get back you better be gone."

"I'll be gone."

"Yeah, you fucking better be."

She stuck a key in the door and swung it open. The room was narrow and dark and smelled faintly of old coffee and sweat. I stepped in and stared through the glass.

"Before I'm back," she said again.

I nodded and the door clicked closed behind me. I was alone, but not really. On the other side of the glass was Weather.

I hadn't seen her in thirteen years and the sight of her gave me chills. I leaned against the mirror taking it in. It was the same girl, broken and bloodied, chained up in orange prison scrubs, but still the same girl. My girl. A tear ran down my cheek and fell with a tiny splat on my shirt collar.

* * *

9:15 P.M.

Weather was getting restless; antsy. She was trying to play strong, but she knew there was no way out of that room. Not without talking to somebody. The door to the interrogation room swung open and a woman walked in followed by a tall gentleman in a dark suit. The woman was wearing a smart professional skirt, white blouse and carrying a brown file folder that she handed to one of the detectives. Another cop she assumed.

He opened it and skimmed through the contents, flipping pages quickly and nodding. The man in the suit stepped forward and held out a hand to Maureen.

"Madame State's Attorney," he said formally. "Special Agent Kyle Flannery. I'm with the Justice Department."

And there they were. The FBI had arrived. It was faster than she had expected and good news too. Chicago was dirty, corrupt, anything that the powers that be wanted would happen sooner or later, more likely sooner. This lawyer, SA Adalet, she could manipulate people and situations and make things go the way she wanted them to. She was the big fish in that little pond. The FBI, however, was out of her control. Having them swimming around in her waters was like having a Great White make its way into Lake Michigan. They had their own agenda and the Cook County State's Attorney wasn't even a blip on their radar.

Maureen bit her lower lip a little sideways and nodded at the agent.

"FBI?" she asked.

"Yes ma'am," he confirmed.

She took a deep breath, stood up and shook his hand.

"Nice to meet you Agent."

The agent gave a nod to each of the detectives in the room, including the woman that had walked in with him. Then turned his attention to Weather.

"Ms. Rose, how are you? Have you been treated well by the CPD?"

His tone was formal, not friendly, but it wasn't aggressive either. He wasn't speaking to her like a criminal, but rather like an object. He was neutral and unaffected. Weather just gazed back at him with an untrusting stare.

"Well, we'll certainly have to get you cleaned up. I'll make sure you get a shower and we'll see if we can find you some more comfortable clothes."

Weather tugged at the chain between her hands.

"Oh, of course. We can take those off I think."

Flannery turned to the sweaty detective and gave a head gesture towards Weather.

"Detective, would you mind?"

The detective straightened up.

"As a matter of fact, Agent, we have strict rules about suspects in custody. They must remai-"

"It's fine Detective," a slight change in tone. Subtle, but noticeable.

"Ms. Rose is no longer in your custody. As of now the FBI is taking jurisdiction on this event and Ms. Rose will be in my custody from this moment forward. Now, if you will kindly remove her handcuffs, and perhaps get her a cup of coffee I'd appreciate it immensely."

The police looked astonished. They glanced at each other open mouthed. At first, no one moved, then slowly as if he was unsure of himself, the sweaty cop in the wrinkled shirt moved to the table and released the clasps on the bracelets around Weather's wrists.

"Thank you, detective. Thank you all for your service tonight. You are now dismissed."

The female cop and the two men all looked at Maureen. She nodded and, begrudgingly, they made their way to the door and out of the room. Maureen sat back down, crossed her legs and stared at the Agent.

"I'm sorry Ms. Adalet, I'm afraid I'm going to have to ask you to step out as well. This is a Federal issue and I'm going to need the room."

Maureen's face flashed red. She stood up with an agitated huff, gave a menacing glance at Weather and, still holding the file the woman had delivered, stormed out of the room. The agent watched the door swing shut then let out a relieved sigh. He turned back to Weather and smiled.

It was odd to see him smile. It seemed out of character. Weather had only known him for those few short minutes, but already she felt as if she had a sense of who he was, and that sense said he wasn't a smiler. Cops will smile or act friendly with a suspect in order to develop a rapport with them. She'd seen it on TV. They do it to make the suspect feel comfortable and at ease. It encourages an atmosphere of sharing, but this wasn't that kind of smile. This was more of a; you just found your car keys in the sofa cushions kind of smile. It was a gotcha smile.

"Well, that's got to be a little better, no?"

Weather rubbed at her wrists where the cuffs had been digging in. She gave a little shrug.

"We'll see," she said.

The agent nodded. The smile on his face straightened out and he went back to his all business attitude.

"Well, let's start with this Ms. Rose. You've been charged with the murder of my boss, United States Special Prosecutor Brandon Grayson. He was my direct supervisor here. I've been working with him in Chicago for almost three years on city corruption. He handpicked me out of a pool of hundreds of agents, so I appreciated him. He'd become a friend too. We were close is what I'm trying to say, so you can understand that I'm pretty upset right now."

His tone was unshakeable. No pitch changes in the voice, no stammers or increases in speed. He was calmly talking to her like he was giving the weather in San Diego. Seventy-five and sunny today. Seventy-five and sunny tomorrow. Seventy-five and sunny for fucking ever.

"Things don't look too good for you," he went on. "It would be easy to just let this all fall on you. The FBI could simply extinguish its anger and send you to the chair."

Weather didn't flinch either, though it took effort. She stared back at him matching his intensity.

"So, you were found at the scene, next to the body. You were, well, basically naked. You had the victim's blood on you, and you were in proximity of a firearm that is believed to be the murder weapon."

No reaction.

"That folder that the detective had when she walked in, that was the ballistics report on the gun. I haven't seen it yet but based on the reactions from the officers in the room I'm pretty sure it said that it was the murder weapon and I'm pretty sure it said your prints were on it."

Weather flinched a little at this, just the slightest twitch then covered it quickly. She ran her fingers through her hair and pulled it back as if she were going to put it in a ponytail; without a rubber band though, she just let it fall again.

"It may have also had findings of powder residue taken from your hands at the time of arrest. I'm guessing now, but it seems reasonable. All of that seems enough to put you on death row. It would be a slam dunk case, but here's the thing Weather, for some reason I'm not convinced."

This did get a reaction from her. She looked up. She looked the agent in the face and for just a moment there was a flash of something that looked like hope across her pale eyes.

"Not one hundred percent. We'll call it ninety-nine, but that's not even the worst of the evidence against you. There's something that even the cops don't have."

The agent reached into the breast pocket of his jacket. He pulled out a flat rectangle all silver on one side and black glass on the other. He pressed a button on the edge and the screen of his phone lit up. A few more touches and swipes and he set the phone down, screen up, on the table. He touched a button and it began to speak.

"Kyle, you're not going to believe this. Ya know your guy, well I've got his girlfriend here and she's fucking crazy. Get over here. My place. Fast, like fucking now."

There was a sound loud enough to fuzz out the speaker and then a clattering sound. Then just silence for a few seconds and a soft thumping. Then the recording stopped.

Weather was white. She wasn't breathing. There was water gathering in the corners of her eyes and her hands were trembling.

The agent stepped closer to her and said softly, but in the same business-like tone, "Weather, do you know who he's talking about? Do you know who my guy is?"

Weather coughed. She was moving her mouth, but no words

were coming out. She just choked and coughed. Then she started to cry.

"It's okay Weather. Take your time. Do you know who he means?"

Weather nodded.

"Who?"

"Gavin," she whispered. "Gavin Gayle. But..."

Agent Flannery sat down across from her. He leaned in and firmly, but gently put his hand on hers."

"But what Weather?"

She coughed and cleared her throat holding back the tears, then sat up straight and pulled her hands away from his. She wiped her face with her hands and straightened out her crumpled orange shirt.

"But, Agent," she said as dignified as she could. "I'm not his girlfriend. No one is Agent Flannery. Gavin Gayle is dead."

Chapter Fourteen

October 5, 2019 9:45 P.M.

Agent Kyle Flannery stared at the girl with soft sympathetic eyes. He believed her, or at least he believed that she believed. She wasn't lying, and in truth, her truth, she wasn't wrong. Not on paper anyway. He had seen the death certificate himself. He'd seen the report from the prison stating that Gavin Gayle had, in fact, died in the ambulance en route to Stroger Hospital, from blood loss due to a stab wound in his abdomen. Gavin was truly, officially, dead.

The problem was Flannery didn't believe it. He had been in Chicago too long, investigated too many corrupt officials, and seen too many faked documents to take anything in this city at face value. To him, anything with an official stamp, or signature from a government employee was not to be trusted.

What he did trust were the clues. The hints and mistakes that appeared where they shouldn't. The dark matter that couldn't be seen directly but pulled at objects in space with its mysterious gravity. There was evidence that Gavin Gayle was alive. Fragments of paperwork and patterns of events that told

Flannery he was out there. Those clues, those accidental breadcrumbs were the things he trusted.

Flannery nodded at Weather.

"Okay," he said softly.

She heaved and let out a stuttering breath.

"Okay, but here's the thing. I think maybe he's not. I think maybe he's alive and if he is, if he's out there somewhere, then he's in trouble. He's in a lot of danger Weather, and I think; I'm pretty sure, Weather you're the only one that can help him.

Weather stared at herself in the two-way mirror. Her battered broken face made her look like a monster. It was demonic, misshapen and exactly what she expected. It was the face she pictured in her mind every time she thought of herself. She was a monster, and this was the face she deserved.

Flannery's words sloshed around in her head like a glass of water on a ship at sea. You're the only one that can help him. She let out a low chuckle to herself. Gavin didn't need her help now. Gavin was dead. Thirteen years ago, that's when Gavin had needed her help.

She thought about him as she did every single day since that night. Then she thought about herself, her life. She reflected on her cozy two-bedroom apartment in the suburbs, her cushy job teaching creative writing to well behaved students at an affluent high school. She pictured her new car with GPS and Bluetooth and considered the expensive bottles of sweet white wine that she polished off each night by herself.

Gavin had loved her. He had loved her more than she had loved him. He had doted on her and spoiled her and ultimately given up everything for her. He had thrown away his life to save her from an unspeakable event and when it came time to step up and tell the world the truth, she had shut down and clammed up. She had let him down, let him fall, let him die. Because of her he had been murdered in that stone fortress for nothing but loving her too much.

She hadn't lied. Not exactly. It was true that she didn't remember what had happened. She didn't remember being with that boy. Not in his bed, not in his room. She didn't remember Gavin bursting in or tearing the boy away from her. She didn't remember him throwing the boy into the brick wall or beating him until he was unidentifiable. She didn't remember any of the violence, but she did remember the drugs.

"Are you here alone?" the boy had asked.

"No," she said. "I'm with my boyfriend."

He had given her a doubting nod.

"Who's that?"

"Gavin," she said proudly. "Gavin Gayle."

A look of recognition passed across his face then replaced itself with a wry smile.

"Oh yeah, I know Gavin. You must be Weather."

She had felt herself exhale with a sense of relief at that. He knew Gavin. He'd heard of her. They were probably friends; she didn't have to worry about him coming on to her.

"Where is our buddy Gavin?"

She smiled.

"Off, locating drinks."

"That's gonna take a while," the boy teased. "Knowing Gavin's tastes. Not many places at a college party to find twelve-year-old scotch."

Weather had laughed at that. It was true, Gavin's tastes were unusually developed for a boy of his age.

"I'm sure he'll end up settling for anything brown."

The boy smiled a wide grin that sent a shiver down her neck.

"I know what he'd really like," the boy said. He reached into the pocket of his jeans and pulled out a small baggie of white tablets. Weather laughed.

"Oh, I don't think Gavin needs Viagra."

The boy gave a mocking chuckle.

"No, I don't suppose he does, but this is something else. This is for you."

She eyed him suspiciously, then cocked her head to the side and waved him off.

"I'm okay, thanks. I don't really do, uh, what is it anyway."

The boy smiled.

"Ex."

Weather frowned and he rolled his eyes at her.

"Ya know, Ex. Ecstasy. Molly. It makes you horny."

"Oh, ha, right," Weather giggled nervously. "Yeah, no worries, I've no problem with that."

"Yeah?" he said with that same oily grin that gave her the willies. "Well this makes it better. It makes it wild. Gavin used to do it with his last girlfriend. They loved it."

Weather's face flushed.

"I'm sorry, what? Who? What other girlfriend?"

The boy raised an eyebrow.

"Oh, sorry. I thought you knew. He didn't tell you about the other woman?"

Weather felt a strange sensation boil up in her belly. An emotion she was unfamiliar with. Jealousy. They had agreed to see other people while they were apart, but something in her had assumed he wouldn't. She had assumed he would be dutifully waiting for her, and he had never said anything to indicate that he hadn't.

"I see," she had said, and then, she had put her hand out.

That's all she remembered. No blurry images, no half details. The boy had drugged her and led her to the room and would have done awful things to her, but for Gavin finding them. The last time she talked to him was the morning after the police brought her in for questioning. He had been in lockup, not yet transferred to a proper prison. She looked at him for a long time through the bullet-proof glass before finally asking the only thing she could think of.

"Was there someone else, before? Before I graduated, did you have another girlfriend?"

He had looked so confused. She started sobbing, crying uncontrollably. He had called out to her silently behind the glass, but she ignored him. She had turned and walked out of the building and never saw him again. She didn't remember what had happened and that was all she would ever say, and Gavin would end up dying in prison.

"Well, Agent-" she turned and stared at Flannery. "I couldn't help him thirteen years ago; nothing has changed since then."

* * *

10:00 P.M.

I leaned against the glass, my forehead against my right arm, my left hand in the pocket of my slacks. I'd been out of prison for eight years. Eight years of laying low and keeping my nose clean, or at least as clean as I was expected to. I followed instructions, did what I was asked, and obeyed all the rules. So why was this agent asking about Gavin Gayle?

How could he know that name? I mean, my identity wasn't a secret exactly. I didn't use an alias. I couldn't, another part of the deal. Aliases are always broken eventually even if only accidentally, and when they are, the fact that you're using one in the first place is suspicious.

It didn't matter though, the Gavin Gayle that walked those

streets of Chicago was not the same Gavin Gayle that had gone to prison thirteen years before. That Gavin Gayle really was dead, gone, buried, and the only people who know about any connection we had to each other were State's Attorney Maureen Adalet, and Detective Megan Hinde.

No one else knew who I was. My identity was concealed, my actions covered up, and my instructions untraceable. So, if the FBI had my name then something big had gone wrong. The head of the Justice Department investigation into Cook County corruption had been murdered and my former girlfriend was found at the scene. It was like two corner pieces of a jigsaw puzzle without the intermediate ones that connect them.

Exhaustion crashed over me in a sudden overwhelming wave. I stepped back and leaned against the wall of the observation room. Weather, too, looked tired and defeated. It was clear that the Agent's battering had had an effect on her, but she wasn't yet sure what to believe.

I felt a surge of anger towards him. He was using her, using her guilt and pain to whittle away her sense, her logic. He was trying to push her to give him something under the guise that she could fix the past by saving me in the present, but she couldn't. She didn't have anything to give him, nothing to trade. Weather couldn't save me, no one could.

I looked at my watch and choked. Forty-five minutes. I had promised Megan sixty seconds, I was well over my time. I took one last look at the former love of my life; shattered, pale and drained; staring into space while the Agent stood over her speaking gentle, muffled, manipulative words. I about faced and walked out the door.

Heading down the hallway I tried to think about what to do next, but the fatigue of the day hung on my mind preventing me from any sort of critical thought. My whole body felt heavy and slow. I craved a bottle of bourbon and the hard mattress of my twin bed at The Club. I reached into my pocket for my keys and froze.

The knob on the double door in front of me turned and the door, as if in slow motion, began to swing open. I took a step back and turned my head looking for an escape. My eyes locked, through the small glass window of the cream-colored door, with Weather's.

My heart nearly exploded. Weather's face went white and she jerked up to her feet. I broke our gaze just as the Agent turned following her stare. The doors in front of me were now fully open framing the persons of Detective Hinde and SA Maureen Adalet.

* * *

I suddenly knew what the phrase no win situation meant. I was stuck in a narrow corridor inside a police station between the woman I loved, who thought I was dead, an angry FBI agent with an axe to grind, and my evil puppet master who swore she'd kill me if something like this ever happened. A fleeting wish for a utility belt full of smoke bombs passed through my head. There was no escaping this situation, no disappearing. I wasn't going to be able to talk my way out of it, and since I'd left my gun in the car, I couldn't shoot my way out either, though that would have been a ridiculous notion in any case. My choices were narrowed down to which devil to join. As I've said before I generally ascribe to the axiom the devil you know, but something told me my devil was way worse than the other.

The door behind me swung open and I heard footsteps and the sound of the door clicking shut. Maureen and Meghan were standing in front of me staring at me with daggers. It suddenly occurred to me that they couldn't do anything. They couldn't admit to knowing who I was. I was kryptonite to them, a trojan horse in their walled city. Right now, in this one moment I was actually safe.

"Mr. Gayle?" the deep voice came from behind me, I didn't move.

I stared at Maureen and she stared at me. Our eyes were locked in a cold glare that was beginning to give me brain freeze. That's when I saw it. For the first time ever, I saw something new in Maureen's face, something I'd never seen before. I saw fear. She moved ever so slightly. I couldn't even pinpoint what it was. A hand, a twitch of the leg, she moved then stopped herself. She was completely rigid, and I smiled. Maybe I didn't need to pick a devil at all.

"Gavin," the voice behind me again.

I turned around to look at the agent. I studied him for a moment. He looked like a man staring into a magic eye poster. Like a man seeing a dead relative. He looked like he was seeing a ghost.

"Who me?" I said. I frowned. "Sorry man, wrong guy."

"You-"

I turned and walked forward.

"Gavin Gayle," the voice came again, this time with authority, demanding my attention. I didn't give it to him. I pushed through the middle of Maureen and Megan. They parted easily and without resistance. I twisted the knob and walked out the double doors of the corridor.

Then I ran. I ran through the small hallway and out the doors into the precinct lobby. I bolted through the lobby and out the front door as the desk sergeant yelled at me to slow down. I darted the dozen or so feet to my car, threw open the door and fell forward into the seat. I turned the keys to the ignition, leaned out the open door and threw up on the pavement. After that I wiped my mouth with my sleeve and slammed the door shut. I squealed away from the curb just as Agent Flannery,

Maureen and Detective Hinde ran out the front door of the station.

I was worried about Weather. She was still inside the station. She was still in arms reach of Maureen and her goons, but she was also in FBI custody. Being held by the feds for suspicion of murder, especially murder of one of their own, was not a good situation to be in, but I suspected it was better than being in Maureen's hands. If she was convicted, she'd get the death penalty for sure, but first they'd have to convict her and I believed Agent Flannery saw a more useful course of action for her custody. At least for the time being.

I knew nothing was over yet. I knew I'd have to face up to Agent Flannery sooner or later, but I needed time. I needed to make a plan; to get my ducks in a row. I'd face him soon enough; I'd have to because I knew too that my grace with SA Adalet was over. There was no going back to the status quo now. Things had changed, she was a frightened animal and frightened animals were dangerous. I was going to need Agent Flannery. I would need him to save Weather, and also, I'd need him to save me.

Chapter Fifteen

October 5, 2019 10:11 P.M.

Weather thought she was going to be sick. The room was spinning and upside down. Everything was topsy-turvy and she had no anchor point to hold on to. She remembered, now, some of the events. She had been contacted by this Brandon Grayson guy. He was a lawyer, she thought, but not a trial lawyer. He was with the FBI and he had called her, several times in fact, saying he wanted to talk about Gavin. Weather didn't know what it was about, but she didn't really want to know either. Gavin was a part of her life that she tried to put behind her. She'd never forget about the man himself, obviously, but all the other stuff, all the tragedy and pain, that was something she didn't want to revisit. Whatever this FBI lawyer wanted to talk about, it would almost certainly involve talking about that night, so she avoided it. She avoided him and his calls and his messages.

It wasn't until he showed up at her school, at her job, that she had to give him the time of day. He walked into her classroom right after the third period bell and cornered her at her desk.

"Miss Rose," he said firmly.

She recognized his voice from the phone calls and voicemails.

"It's nice to finally meet you. I've been trying to reach you for some time. Can we talk for a bit?"

Weather was shocked and appalled that he would show up at her job. It seemed very unprofessional to her. On the other hand, she hadn't given him much of an alternative. She supposed in hindsight that it was unlikely that the FBI would just drop something simply because you didn't answer the phone.

"Look," she said. "You can't be here. I have another class in three minutes and I'd rather not have a cop hanging around my classroom when the students start filing in. You can call-"

He shook his head.

"No. First of all, I'm not a cop. I'm a lawyer."

"You're with the FBI?"

"Well yes-"

"Yeah, you're a cop. Call me after-"

"Right, so you can blow me off again. No, I'm sorry. Look, you're not in trouble, I just have some questions for you."

"And I don't have time."

"When do you suppose you will," he asked with a bit of bite in his tone.

"I don't know," she sighed. "It doesn't matter anyway. You want to know about Gavin? I don't have anything to tell you. He died in prison, and I don't know anything beyond that."

He nodded, then gave an interesting tilt to his head.

"Well, that's what I want to talk about. I have an agent under me that thinks there may be more to the story. I was hoping-"

The door to the classroom swung open and two teenage girls in pink sweatpants and matching white glitter t-shirts walked in. They gave a curious glance at the two adults talking, took seats in the back of the room and started whispering to each other.

"Okay, you need to go now. My class starts in one minute."

The lawyer glared at her.

"Look, I'm a teacher. I really don't want to get involved in an investigation, and I really, really don't want my students finding out about my past."

"We can do it off the record," he suggested. "I'm just looking for some background. Can you meet me after school?"

Weather bit her lip. She could feel tears starting to well up in her eyes and she didn't need running mascara during class.

"Yeah, okay," she said reluctantly.

"Great," he said and dropped his card on her desk. "Call me when you get out and I'll let you know what time to come by the office.

By the time she finished marking papers and entering grades in the computer it was four thirty in the afternoon. She packed up her belongings and headed out of the school. She thought about blowing off the meeting with Grayson, but she figured he would just come back to the school again. She didn't need anyone asking why the FBI kept visiting her classroom.

She got to her car and dropped her purse and briefcase in the back seat then climbed in behind the wheel. She fished the business card out of her jacket pocket and dialed the number for Grayson's cell. It rang four times before being answered by a woman. She was breathy and agitated and seemed in a hurry. She said she was Grayson's assistant and that he was unavailable, but that Weather should come by his home office for a chat.

That's about the time things got foggy. She remembered the drive there, the elevator, the door, but that's it. Everything after that was just black. It was just like the night of the party. Things got hazy and then she woke up and everything was a disaster. Her life torn to pieces and she couldn't even remember how it had happened.

Now it was worse. It hadn't been long, just a second, but she knew what she had seen. Standing outside the door of the room she was locked in had been Gavin. He was older, bigger, and more tired looking, but it was him. Their eyes had met, and her heart had stopped. She had just finished telling the Agent that Gavin was dead, and then POW! There he was.

Gavin was alive. He was alive and he was out of prison. He was out of prison and he was here, in this building while she was being accused of murder. The world was upside down and she was more terrified than she had ever been in her life.

* * *

Agent Flannery watched as the black Chrysler 300 spat smoke from its rear tires and shot down Addison Street away from the station. His heart was pounding, and he felt a casserole of excitement, anxiety, and anger start to bake in his brain. He turned, jaw set, and stared down SA Adalet and Detective Hinde. "Either of you have anything to say about that?"

Hinde took a breath as if to speak, but the State's Attorney cut her off.

"Your guess is as good as mine," she said in a flat toneless expression.

Flannery dug a small notebook out of his suit coat and jotted down the plate of the car from memory. He noticed the State's Attorney's color pale as he did so. Then he slapped the book closed and stormed back into the station.

He found Weather right where he'd left her, though her demeanor was significantly shifted. She was pale and jittery.

188

She was nervous, frightened even. Before she'd seemed calm and regretful. On edge as much as anyone would be during a police interrogation, but not suspiciously anxious. Now she was a wreck. Puffy red eyes and tear marks down her cheeks. This was a girl in trauma. Flannery knew he was onto something.

* * *

Maureen looked at Detective Hinde with contempt. Her face was red and the lines at the sides of her eyes had sunk into canyons. She shook slightly and had a hard time making words come out.

"This," she said in staccato. "is-so-very-fucked."

"I really don't think she knows anything," Hinde said in a reassuring tone.

Maureen wrinkled her brow. "What?" she said.

"Weather," the detective clarified. "She really thinks he died in prison. She doesn't know anything about Gavin or us or the city or, well, anything."

"Are you fucking joking," the SA said with an expression of utter disbelief. "Who gives a shit. Fuck Weather Rose. I mean, she probably didn't know, but she sure as fuck does now. She knows he's alive, she can identify him, she can place him here tonight, and you don't think she'll say anything she has to to mitigate this murder charge? She killed a fucking fed. She'll fry for that. She'll agree to anything they ask her to."

Hinde shifted uncomfortably. She hadn't thought about it in those terms.

"And now, now, I have an FBI agent asking her questions, taking her into custody, and in possession of the plate number of Gavin's car. His fucking car whose last recorded title holder was the CPD impound."

Megan squirmed again and ran her hands behind her neck.

189

"So, what do-"

"Shut up."

She did as she was told.

"Okay, go inside. Start putting together an APB. Description only, no name. Perp is wanted in connection with the murder of the federal prosecutor. Armed and dangerous. Then call me before you publish it. I need to do something first."

"We're going to arrest him?"

Maureen laughed.

"Arrest him? I kind of doubt it."

* * *

Half a mile from the station I hit the brakes hard. The Chrysler jittered and bounced as it came to a stop in the middle of the street. I held the steering wheel with both hands and tried to control my breathing. I was in a jam. Everything was a mess and I suddenly felt for the first time since I'd been out of prison like things could actually get worse. I was screwed any way I looked at it. Maureen was certainly not going to let me just go back to the way things were. I had seen to that pretty succinctly. I wasn't going back to prison and I wasn't going to be going back to work either. She probably already had plans in motion to take care of me.

The FBI wasn't a much better option. They wouldn't kill me, but they weren't going to cut me much of a deal either. I could give them Maureen. I could give them Detective Hinde. I could give them The Club too, but I doubted they'd care much about that. That's all I had though, Maureen and Meghan. That's all I knew and even that would be tough to prove. They'd been good about insulating themselves. It was just my word that they'd done anything and the anythings they'd done really just pointed to my own criminal actions.

If I did give them the SA they could try and make a corruption case, but it would be weak and based mostly on the testimony of me, and my own crimes would make me less than credible. They'd never give me immunity, that would hurt their case even more. I'd be back in prison, federal prison this time and there'd be no early release.

The problem was Weather. I wasn't sure how she'd gotten herself caught up in this, but I knew she didn't do what she was accused of. She had no motive and even if she did, she just didn't have it in her.

Agent Flannery seemed to know it too, but he wasn't ready to let her off the hook just yet. He needed her for another reason. He wanted her to get to me. He'd made that clear in his interrogation. He knew about me somehow and somehow; he knew I was important. She was his bargaining chip and he was going to hold her until he had what he wanted, which of course was me.

I beat my hands on the steering wheel trying to wrap my head around it all. I didn't know where the fuck up had happened, but it had, and I was never going to find it on my own. There was also no way I was going to be able to get Weather out of this mess out here on the street. I really only had one option. One way to clear Weather and find out exactly what Agent Flannery knew and how he knew it.

I grabbed the gear shift knob and threw the 300 in reverse. I backed up fast, stepped on the clutch and spun the wheel, dropped the car into second and dropped the clutch. One minute later I passed the station again and swung around the corner parking in a disused garage in the alley just past North Reta Ave. I killed the engine, climbed out and grabbed my coat and hat, then walked to the end of the alley and watched the station.

Chapter Sixteen

October 5, 2019 10:39 P.M.

I watched the front door of the precinct station from the alley across the street for almost twenty minutes. It was getting cold out and I was running low on cigarettes by the time something happened. A black SUV pulled up in front of the station and two men in dark suits climbed out. The driver walked around the car and up to the front of the building while the passenger stepped back and opened up the back door of the vehicle.

A moment later the driver pulled open the glass door of the station and Agent Flannery walked out with Weather. She was in handcuffs again, her wrists pinned behind her back. She looked alert, scared and confused. She walked slowly with short stabbing steps like she was crossing a narrow bridge over a deep canyon.

Flannery had his hand on her shoulder and was talking into her ear. She didn't show any reaction to whatever he was saying, just kept walking carefully with her eyes fixed on the ground in front of her. When they got to the car the agent at the door took her hand and helped her into the backseat. They were gentle with her, treating her more like an aged grandmother than a murder suspect.

Once she was in, the agent closed the door and faced Flannery. They had short words then shook hands and the two new agents climbed back into the SUV and drove off. Flannery just stood there a moment watching them go, then he dug his hands in his beige trench coat and pulled out a set of keys. I took that as my cue. I stepped out of the shadows and crossed the street walking directly towards him.

"Agent," I called out in a loud whisper.

Flannery looked up, but apparently didn't see me yet. He looked around trying to determine where the voice had come from. A few steps later I was in the shallow pool of light poured out onto the pavement by the streetlight and I caught his eye. He looked at me thoughtfully but with no surprise.

"Mr. Gayle," he said. It made me stop. It frightened me to hear him say my name, which in turn surprised me. I'm not sure why. Obviously, I knew that I would have to confirm my identity in order to have the conversation that needed to take place, still, the sound of him saying it sent a chill down my spine and made my stomach flip.

"Seems like we may need to have a chat," I said.

He didn't say anything, just looked at me as if he was studying me. I felt like a frog pinned to black wax before being dissected. Finally, he gave a small shrug and said, "Ya wanna go inside."

I looked at the door to the station. Obviously, that wasn't what I wanted. Going inside was the exact opposite, it's what I wanted to avoid. I shook my head and gestured down the street.

"Not really, I thought maybe I could buy you a drink."

"It would be better for my report if the interview was in an official location," he said.

"Well I'm not quite ready for an on the record conversation. I'm here to talk, not be interviewed."

I could see him chewing on the inside of his lip. I was still half a dozen paces away from him and if I wanted to, I could run. He was weighing his options, trying to decide what he could get away with.

"Off the record, but I can record the chat for my own personal record."

I thought about this and nodded.

"Okay," I said.

I started moving again, away from the station and down the block. That part of Chicago was quiet in the autumn when the Cubs weren't in the playoffs, which was most of the time. It was getting cold, but not uncomfortable yet and you could still walk outside without bundling up. Flannery caught up with me and we walked together, letting the night air flow over us in silence. We weren't in a hurry and sometimes silence can communicate more than words.

I reached into my coat pocket and pulled out my cigarette case and lighter. I flipped open the case and drew a long brown cigarette out and screwed it between my lips, closed the case gently and felt the satisfying snap as it clicked shut. Then I flipped open my gold lighter and spun the wheel to light the flame. I stopped walking for a moment while I pulled the light to my face and took a few short drags. The lighter shut with a snap and I dropped both items back into my pocket.

Flannery stopped a few steps ahead of me and waited. With my smoke lit I rejoined him and the two of us kept walking.

"Why is it guys like you always have Zippo lighters?" he asked.

I dragged on the cigarette and exhaled.

"What kind of guy am I?"

Flannery chuckled to himself.

"The dark and mysterious kind. You guys always have Zippo lighters and cigarette cases. Isn't it more work to move the cigarettes into the case than to just carry the pack? And what's wrong with a Bic? It can't be cheaper to maintain a Zippo, so what gives?"

I gave him a sideways glance.

"Why do all you FBI types always wear raincoats? I don't see any clouds in the sky."

"Touché."

"They were gifts."

"What?"

"The lighter and the cigarette case. They were given as gifts. Someone gave them to me, so I use them out of respect."

"I see. Gifts from whom?"

"People."

"That's specific," he said, sounding agitated. "And what kind of cigarettes are those? I don't think I've ever seen a cigarette quite like that before."

I sighed.

"You seem to have an unhealthy obsession with my smoking habits, Agent."

"I was just making conversation."

I dragged again, then spun the cigarette between my fingers and flicked it out into the street. I exhaled the lungful of thick white smoke and stopped walking. Agent Flannery took another step and stopped himself. He turned back towards me and we stared at each other across a puddle of yellow light.

"They're Treasurer Blacks. They're imported from the UK."

"Ah, so I'm not going to find them at the Shell station across the street here?"

"No."

He nodded. "And where would I find them?"

I felt like the interrogation was starting a little early. I really wanted to be in control of the conversation and so far, it wasn't working out that way. I tried to steer things back to where I wanted them.

"I wouldn't know. They were a gift."

Flannery smiled.

"They were a gift as well?"

"Yes."

He stepped closer to me.

"And who were they a gift from?"

I took a step forward as well.

"A person."

"You get a lot of gifts."

"Well, people like me."

Flannery leaned forward just slightly and lowered his voice.

"And what about your freedom?"

I matched his tone.

"What about it?"

"Was that a gift as well?"

This made me laugh out loud.

"Agent Flannery, despite what the government likes to tell itself, freedom is not a gift."

"What would you call it then?"

"In my case?"

"In your case," he said.

I glanced back in the direction we had come, back at the police station, then back at Flannery. I pulled my coat tighter around my body and stuffed my hand into my pockets.

"Well Agent Flannery, freedom's just another word for nothing else to lose."

I was done talking about myself. I walked past Flannery and turned right down Broadway. Just a few paces south was a small bistro style restaurant called Ristorante Angelina. It was a storefront place with black and white striped awnings and no outdoor seating. Inside it was golden. Not metaphorically, literally. The walls were a golden yellow hue and painted to look distressed. The lighting was all incandescent, coming from small glass chandeliers hanging from decorative chain throughout the space, which added to the gold tones. It was filled with small two-top tables, some pushed together to make four-tops covered in white cloth tablecloths. It was long and narrow and very cozy and classy. There was a short brown wooden bar in the back with four stools. I was already sitting at one when Flannery walked in behind me.

He pulled a stool out beside me and sat down. The bartender, who was also the only waiter in the place, was at the only occupied table jotting down an order in a small notebook. He glanced over his shoulder at me for a second, then, after a subtle double take, apologetically touched one of the customer's shoulders and walked briskly back to the bar.

Flannery followed him with his eyes and was prepared to ask for some privacy when the young man approached us but was cut off by the server's apology.

"Mr. Gayle, I'm very sorry to keep you waiting."

The young man set a rocks glass with half a dozen small ice cubes in it on the bar and filled it to just above the ice with Redemption Rye from underneath the bar.

"Is there anything I can get your guest here?"

I tried to give a warm smile.

"No apology necessary Brent," I said. "Agent Flannery here would like one of the same please. We have some things to discuss, so feel free to leave the bottle and take care of your table. We will take care of ourselves."

"No problem," said the server, and set a glass in front of Flannery and walked away.

"You come here a lot?" Flannery asked.

"I told you, people like me," I said.

"Why?"

I swallowed some whiskey and looked Flannery in the eyes.

"Why do people like me?"

"That's right."

"Um, Agent Flannery, don't take this the wrong way, but not knowing the answer to that may be your main problem."

He smiled.

"I'm almost sure that's true."

I shifted in my seat to face him.

"So, Agent, here we are. I have things to say and you have things to ask. I'm not certain that those things are going to line up, but if we stay calm and focused, I think we can maybe make them meet in the middle."

"Tell me about your time in prison. How long were you in for?" he said, jumping right to the point.

"Agent, I think you may have me confused with someone else. Perhaps if I knew where you were going with this I could be of more help. What exactly are you investigating?"

Flannery leaned against the bar and took a sip of his drink. He made a sound indicating he was impressed with it and took another sip. He looked at the glass, held it up to the light and turned it in his hand. He brought it down, sipped again and set it back on the bar.

"That's very good," he said, "That is really very good. How much does..."

I grimaced and looked away.

"Right, a gift, got it. Let me ask you something else. Do you pay for anything? What about your car?"

I looked up from my drink.

"My car?"

"Yeah, that was your black 300 parked outside the station, right?"

"Yeah, I guess you could say that. Why?"

"Well," he said, sounding like he was winding up for a curve ball. "I was just wondering how a flashy black car could park illegally outside a police station with expired plates and not get a ticket."

I feigned surprise.

"Crap, are my plates expired?"

"Expired? Yes Mr. Gayle, your plates are expired, by a couple of years. Also, it's not registered in your name. According to the DMV it's registered to a Leroy Brown."

I chuckled to myself. I actually hadn't known that. I knew there was some kind of code attached to the registration that let the cops in the city know to leave my car alone, but registering it under the name of the infamous South Side baddie from the Jim Croce song was pretty clever.

"Really?" I said. "Leroy Brown? Ha, that's, that's very funny. Well, chalk another one up to the Illinois Secretary of State's office. They do seem to have trouble over there."

Flannery was starting to look annoyed with this game.

"The Secretary of State's office?"

"Obviously." I smiled.

"Obviously. And can I assume that the car was a gift as well?"

I nodded, unsurely at first then with some certainty.

"Yes, that would be an accurate assumption, Agent."

"And would I be way off base guessing that it was a gift from no one in particular?"

"No, no it most certainly was from someone in particular."

Flannery looked surprised.

"Really? Great! That's great. Who, in particular, was it a gift from?"

I shook my head.

"Oh, I really couldn't say." I said, having a little fun.

"You couldn't say?"

"No."

"Because you don't want to tell me, or because you don't know."

I leaned way back on my stool and stuck my hands in my pants pockets and gazed at Flannery for a bit.

"Well Agent..."

"Flannery."

"Right, Agent Flannery. I couldn't tell you why I wasn't ticketed. Maybe they just didn't notice. I was in a bit of a hurry and didn't notice that I was parked illegally."

"Okay, now we're getting somewhere. Let's talk about that. You were in a hurry. In a hurry for what? To get into the police station? Let's talk about that."

"You want to talk about the police?"

Flannery smiled.

"No Gavin, I want to talk about Weather."

"What is it you want to know Agent Flannery?"

The agent picked up a small cocktail straw from the bar and stirred his drink.

"I want to know what you were doing at the police station tonight. You said you were in a hurry, so clearly it was important."

"I was filing a missing pet report. My cat ran away"

I wasn't sure why I was being evasive. I knew I'd have to get to the point sooner or later, but something in me just wasn't ready to get down to it yet.

"In the interview rooms?"

"I got lost."

"Do you know why Weather is there?"

I frowned.

"Who?"

"She murdered my boss Gavin. Special Prosecutor Grayson, she shot him twice. Apparently, they were having an affair or something. They found her near naked in his apartment, covered in his blood with the murder weapon laying right next to her. So now she's ours. The FBI's. It's a federal case. She'll probably get the death penalty for it."

I shifted in my seat, slid my coat off my shoulders and let it half hang on the stool and re-adjusted again trying to get comfortable.

"Are you okay Gavin? You look upset."

"Well, I'm not entirely sure what you're talking about, but I can say with a good deal of certainty that if you are referring to that nice girl you had chained up like an animal back at the station, I don't think she did it. She didn't look like the type."

"Oh?"

"No, not a bit. I would say she's innocent."

"That's a remarkable talent you have," Agent Flannery said.

I took a sip of my drink.

"What's that?"

"You can tell if someone is guilty or innocent just by looking at them through a piece of glass. We should hire you for all our cases. We could save a lot of time and money."

"Hey, I'm just giving you my opinion," I said defensively.

"Okay, and I'm just listening. Look, my boss, my other boss, he's still down at the crime scene collecting all the evidence against your girlfriend. I've already got her in federal custody where she'll be indicted, tried, sentenced, and go to death row. They'll stick a needle in her arm and take her out of this world all before she turns thirty-one. Now, you're sitting here telling me that she didn't do it. In my professional reasoning, there are only a handful of ways you could know that for sure, and none of them is by glancing at her through a two-way mirror.

"So, I'm giving you a chance. I'm giving you a chance to help her out. Tell me how you know she didn't do it. Tell me how you know that the girl we found naked in my boss's apartment covered in blood, next to the murder weapon, tell me how you know she didn't do it. Convince me. Convince me now and I'll go back to my office and have her released."

I stared at him. I really wasn't ready to be having this conversation now, but now was when it was happening, and it didn't seem likely that there'd be a better time in the future. I knew it wouldn't end well. Not for me, that was for sure, and it probably would end up being pretty bad for several other people as well. Powerful people who weren't going to let it happen without a fight.

What I really wanted was time. Time to think, to go over the situation in my head, to line up the facts and figure out the best course of action. Unfortunately, time was what I didn't have. I had to decide. I had to say something to this FBI agent who had already found the breadcrumbs and was hot on the trail of the whole gingerbread house.

I decided that the best choice for the situation was to give Flannery something. Just a little something. Something that could keep him busy hunting more breadcrumbs long enough for me to put together a real plan.

"Her name is Weather Kimberly Rose," I said. "She used to be a friend, a long time ago, but I haven't seen her in about thirteen years."

"The years you were in prison." Flannery suggested.

"You keep saying that."

"Are you saying it's not true?"

I weighed this question in my head. It wasn't that I cared whether or not I lied to Flannery, but a half-truth would keep him busy longer than an out and out lie.

"Yes, I'm saying that's inaccurate. I knew her a long time ago, I don't know her now, but I can speak to her personality and I tell you that she doesn't have it in her to kill anyone, and she wasn't having an affair with your boss."

"That's a lot of knowledge about a person you haven't spoken to in over a decade."

"People don't change that much."

"You think not?" he said surprised.

"A person can change habits or behaviors, but who a person is inside; what they are ultimately capable of, that doesn't really change."

"That's a frightening point of view," Flannery said.

"The world is a frightening place, Agent Flannery."

"How did you get out of prison Mr. Gayle?"

A pause.

"You've got that wrong Agent."

"We both know that isn't true."

I picked up my drink and finished it, then set the heavy glass back on the bar and looked at the agent with tired eyes.

"Agent, I've had a long day, and I'm really tired. I need a cigarette and a good night's sleep. We both know you aren't going to let her go tonight, and I'm sure you have a lot of jack-booted questioning to do, so how about we call it a night? I'll be around, like I always am, and always have been. What's say we pick this up again tomorrow or the next day. Let me go home and get some sleep."

"Go home and get your story straight, you mean?"

"Whatever you have to tell yourself, Agent."

He looked at me with deep suspicion. He didn't trust me, and he didn't like the idea of letting me out of his sight again. Still, he had nothing to hold me on. Nothing that would stick. Reluctantly he nodded.

"Okay Mr. Gayle. Tomorrow evening," he took a business card out of his coat pocket and slid it across the bar to me. "Call me on my cell and I'll meet you so we can go over whatever Ms. Rose says tonight."

I mustered a weak smile and stood up. I put my coat back on

and reached into my breast pocket to produce my wallet, took out a crisp fifty and laid it on the bar. I stuck out my right hand for Flannery to shake.

"Good night Agent."

"Good night Mr. Gayle. See you tomorrow."

"Looking forward to it."

Flannery gave a doubtful grin and I turned and walked out of the restaurant.

* * *

11:02 P.M.

Flannery turned back to the bar and finished his drink. He sat alone for a while, until the bartender came back, picked up the fifty and cleared the bottle and glasses.

"What's his deal?" Flannery asked.

The bartender looked up at Flannery.

"Who? Mr. Gayle?"

Flannery tried to act casual, friendly.

"Yeah, is he like a regular?"

"I guess. Not like every day, but he comes in a bit."

"And he doesn't get charged?" Flannery asked.

The bartender's face shifted to one of unease.

"Well, I mean tonight, this is, that was his bottle, so yeah, but no, he doesn't usually get a bill. But he always leaves money."

"But that's a tip, right?"

"A tip?" The bartender repeated like he'd never heard the term before.

Flannery looked at his watch, his tone changed from casual to interrogatory.

"Yeah, you aren't putting that fifty in the register, are you? It was for you. So why doesn't he get charged?"

The guy looked nervous. Clearly, he didn't know if he was supposed to be talking about this but didn't know if he could just blow this guy off.

"I don't know man; I think he's friends with the owner or something."

"Friends?"

"Well, not like friends. Not like they hang out on the weekends or anything. I think Mr. Gayle did a favor or something for the owner. I think he helped or something and now he's comped."

"Who's the owner?" Flannery asked, taking his notebook out of his jacket pocket.

The kid looked unsure if he should be answering these kinds of questions, but he did.

"Well, there are a few. The main owner is Chef Devon, but he has some investors too. I don't know who's friends with Mr. Gayle, it could be any of them. They all have people they take care of here."

"What's Chef Devon's last name?"

"That's it. Devon, I don't know his first name. Everyone just calls him Chef."

Flannery nodded and wrote it down.

"Do you know who the investors are?"

The kid shook his head.

"Nah, not all of them. There's a bunch. One of them's a TV guy on channel two I think, and a bunch of city people."

This caught Flannery's attention. He looked up at the kid.

"City people, like city officials?"

"Yeah, ya know, like an alderman, and someone with parks or something, and like the State's Attorney, there's a bunch more. I think like maybe-"

"The what?" Flannery almost shouted.

"What?" the kid looked as scared as if Flannery had pulled his gun on him.

"Did you say the State's Attorney?"

"I don't know. That's just what I heard. I don't know any of them myself."

Flannery jumped out of his seat and stormed out of the restaurant dialing his phone as he went.

* * *

October 6, 2019 3:44 A.M.

I was cold and wet and still in a foul mood from my conversation with Agent Flannery when I stepped into the dining room of The Club. I'd spent the last few hours driving and thinking about my situation. There was too much going on to process in my state. What I needed now was sleep to clear my head and give me a fresh perspective. The sun would be up soon enough, and the place was empty. The candles on the tables had all burned themselves out hours ago.

The woman was standing behind the bar inspecting the bottles and running her fingers over the dusty shelves. She was exactly as I remembered her; tall, slender but not skinny, blonde hair in a bob that ended just above her shoulders. She was dressed formally and held herself with an air of confidence. I crossed the floor, the heels of my boots making an authoritative clicking sound on the scuffed-up hardwood floor. She turned towards me deliberately and leaned against the bar.

"Maureen," I said, sounding tired and annoyed.

"Gavin," she said, matching my tone. "It's been a while."

I pulled out a bar stool and took a seat, slumping myself on one elbow.

"A while," I agreed. "But far short of forever. I thought that was the arrangement. I thought we were strangers. You said we'd never see each other again."

She let out a long sigh and nodded.

"Yes, yes that was the plan, but you kind of blew that tonight. Didn't you?"

I rubbed my eyes in exhaustion then looked at her blankly.

"I didn't do anything. I didn't arrest Weather or invite in the FBI. I was just taking care of your shit and drinking here, minding my own business. I was staying out of trouble."

"You sure?" she asked. "You sure you weren't uptown putting a bullet in the guy that was sleeping with your ex?"

My neck prickled at the accusation.

"What?" I said indignantly. "You think that was me?"

She shrugged.

"I don't know what to think Gavin. It is interesting that every time Weather is with a guy that's not you, he ends up dead."

I felt cold fury starting to set in.

"First of all, I don't know that that's even true. I imagine she's had other men in her life over the last thirteen years. They can't all be dead."

She gave me a condescending glare.

"Bullshit Gavin. You know damn well she's had exactly zero involvement with other men. Don't act like you don't know exactly what's going on with her all the time. Don't treat me like I'm stupid."

It was true of course. I had kept tabs, quietly, on Weather since I had been sent away. I told myself it was out of love or out of concern for her safety, but I had quiet moments; moments when I'd had one martini too many, when I knew. I knew it was out of some strange possessiveness. A sense that my time in prison was payment for my ownership of Weather rather than for what I had done to that boy. It was those moments that I realized what I had let myself become. That I was, in fact, a truly bad person.

"Whatever, Maureen. I was here all night and you know that. You have all your little spies watching over me all the time. You know exactly where I am at any given moment and you know damn well, I wasn't uptown killing that Fed."

She looked down at the bar and gave a slight nod, then she looked at me again.

"Yeah, I know."

"And you know Weather didn't kill him either. I doubt very strongly she was even sleeping with him for that matter. I don't know why she was there," a subtle lie. I really didn't know, but I had my suspicions. Flannery had been looking into me and it only made sense that they would talk to Weather, but it didn't explain her presence at his boss's personal residence. "But it wasn't to go to bed with him and it wasn't to kill him," I said. "There's just no reason."

"You're probably right," she agreed. "But as I'm sure Detective Hinde told you, that hardly matters. What matters is that you stay the fuck away from it all. That's been the deal since the beginning. You stay out of the spotlight. You stay quiet and invisible or else I have to make you disappear for real, and you fucked that up."

I took a breath to interrupt, but she shut me down with a finger in my face.

"Hinde told you to stay out of it. She told you to stay away. Let the pieces fall and pretend you didn't know, but no, you show up at the fucking police station. You have a sit down with the FBI? The fucking FBI? Jesus Gavin! What the fuck were you thinking?"

I was mad now. The whole evening had been building and building the agitation, the resentment, the simmering rage and it was that moment that it all came bursting out at the seams. I sat up, rigid and alert and slammed my fists on the bar.

"I'll tell you what I was thinking, you murderous psychotic bitch. I was thinking that I spent five years in a shit hole prison and another eight doing your evil fucking clean up jobs because I wanted to protect Weather, and now, now it looks like that was all for shit. All for nothing. She's going to get a fucking needle in her arm for something she didn't do and I'm supposed to sit back and let that happen? I'm supposed to live with everything I've done, everything you've made me do and have it all be fucking meaningless? Fuck you!"

I was screaming at her. Shaking my fists and getting red in the face. My anger was blowing itself out and there was nothing I could do to stop it.

"I'm not doing it Maureen. I'm not letting her go down for this. You want to kill me? If that's what you think you have to do, you do it. You go ahead and try. But who are you going to get to do that? Huh? Who do you have that's going to kill me, because I fucking know you won't do it yourself."

She was red too at this point. Her hands were flat on the bar and she was shooting daggers with her eyes. Rage was oozing from her pores and she looked like she wanted to slap me.

"I didn't tell the FBI anything," I said, trying to slow my breathing and recapture my composure. "I told them they've got the wrong guy, but it doesn't matter. They already know Maureen. He knew my name. He knew my car and he knew my history. They've already got all the pieces and they aren't stupid either. They don't know it's you pulling the strings, but that's what they're looking for and you know they'll get there eventually. How long did you think this was going to be able to go on for? What was your exit strategy for this whole fucking mess?"

She stared back at me with blank fury.

"God Maureen, I sure hope you have one, because now, now is the time to use it."

She took a deep breath. She ran her fingers through her hair and put her hands in her pockets.

"You're right," she said. "You're right, it's time."

She pulled out her phone and laid it on the bar. She tapped the clock on the face of it and a timer app opened up. She tapped a few buttons and hit the big green start button. A timer for five hours started counting down.

"You have five hours to be gone," she said coldly.

"What?"

"In five hours, I'm sending your photo and license plates to all the precincts. You are an unknown potential terrorist and should be arrested on site. You are considered armed and dangerous and deadly force is authorized in your apprehension."

"You can't-"

Her eyebrows went up and her pupils blazed.

"I can't what? I want you to think about that statement. Think about what I did for you? You think about what I can and can't do. In five hours, you are Chicago's most wanted fugitive. You want my exit strategy. Here it is motherfucker. I'm not playing games. You disappear, you leave Weather to the Feds and you fucking vanish. Forever, or the next time a cop sees you you'll be slid into a freezer with a blank tag on your toe and no one will ever think of you again."

I looked into her eyes trying to determine if she was bluffing, but I knew. SA Adalet didn't bluff. She didn't make empty threats and she never ever lost. Not anymore. Not in the past eight years.

Chapter Seventeen

October 6, 2019 4:06 A.M.

A shiny black BMW drove into the parking lot at 2111 W. Roosevelt Rd. and slid into an open spot just a few yards from the front door of the gleaming silver glass building. The building was the Chicago field office for the Federal Bureau of Investigation, and the spot was marked Reserved.

The engine cut off and the door swung open. A pair of black four-inch heels hit the pavement and carried a tall woman with deep black-cherry-red hair and ridiculous posture through the early morning darkness and across the short distance to the entrance. Inside, she strode with absolute confidence across the marble floor of the lobby. The guard at the front desk glanced at her and nodded approvingly as she slid her ID card through the scanner and walked briskly through the turnstiles that led to the elevators.

She punched the up button and the car in front of her dinged and the doors slid open. She stepped inside and pressed the button for the tenth floor. An agent came around the corner reading something in a file and walked quickly to the open elevator car. As he approached, he took his nose out of his reading and glanced up. Seeing the woman standing in the car he stopped in his tracks and took a step backward, allowing the elevator doors to close with him still outside of them.

The car hummed as it moved up the ten levels of the building. Another ding and the doors slid open revealing a plush lobby with leather furniture. The low hanging moon was still visible through the tall windows. The woman stepped off the elevator and onto the soft deep carpeting of the executive office level of the FBI's Chicago Headquarters. She walked quickly and with purpose down the hall to the office suite of SAI.C. Colin Michaels and pushed open the door.

Michaels' assistant looked up from her desk with dreary and tired eyes and saw the woman standing in front of her. She took a quick breath and composed herself brushing her hair down with her hands and then picked up her phone.

"Hello Ma'am, just one moment."

She dialed two numbers and waited a moment. The woman could hear the phone ringing behind the thin wall in front of her.

"Yes, sir, Assistant Director DeBruin is here sir."

* * *

Maureen walked out the front door of The Club. At this time of morning the man they called Nate, the security, wasn't here. The place was quiet and empty and the air outside was cold. She took a long breath and watched the fog escape her lungs as she exhaled. Everything was a mess and it seemed like it was only going to get worse. She hoped that Gavin had taken her seriously and would be gone soon. Just gone. Erased like he'd never existed. That's what she hoped, but she didn't expect as much. She could feel him like a thorn in her side and the pain was getting worse.

She crossed the street to her car and climbed in. She wasn't really a smoker, not anymore, but she kept an old pack of Marlboro Lights in her center console for emergencies and this felt like it qualified. She dug out the battered pack and drew out a long white stick and slid it between her lips then lit a match and pulled it to her face. The smoke filled the car and she leaned back in the driver's seat and let it roll in and out of her lungs.

Just go, she thought. Just get out of town and get on with your life and leave me to mine. She knew this was her fault. She should have ended this a long time ago. Hell, she should probably never have started it, but at the time she didn't see anything else to do. It had all been for her daughter. It had all been for her, and maybe, just maybe it would have been okay if she had left it at that. If she hadn't gotten greedy and kept using the tool she had built.

Her phone rang and she glanced at the screen. It was Detective Hinde's burner line.

"Yeah," she said when she swiped the answer key.

"Everything's ready," the detective said in a steely robotic tone.

Maureen took a long breath. She swiped the screen on her phone bringing the timer back up. Four hours thirty-nine minutes. She stared at it for a long time watching the seconds counting down.

"Ma'am," the detective finally said.

Maureen hit the square button on the timer stopping it and swiped to clear the countdown.

"Send it now," she said. "Send it now and add in the address for The Club as a known location."

"Ma'am?" came again.

"Now Hinde. Send it out now!"

* * *

Flannery flipped through his notebook in the elevator. Until tonight he had never heard SA Adalet's name mentioned. Well, not never, obviously she had been in the news rather regularly being the State's Attorney and all, but never in connection to any of his investigations. A quick phone call had confirmed what the kid had said, Maureen and Jason Adalet were on the restaurant's investors list.

Now that he was heading up to confront her in her office, he wished that he had taken a little time to do some research first. Maybe learn her career history. He pulled out his phone and tapped the Google search bar at the top of the screen and typed Illinois State's Attorney Maureen Adalet and hit search. The six colored dots spun in their tiny circle then spat back a white card that said, 'no internet connection'. He glanced at the notification shade at the top of the screen.

No signal.

Figures.

Elevator.

He dropped the phone back in his pocket and stared straight ahead. He heard the bell chime and the steel doors slid open in front of him. It was dark in the offices and he immediately realized his mistake. He'd been so wrapped up in the events of the night he hadn't paid attention to the time. He checked his watch. Four twenty-two a.m. No one would be here at this hour.

On the other hand, if SA Adalet was involved with Gavin, then she must be in a panic right now. She had seen him at the station the same as Flannery had. She knew that the FBI had Weather in custody. If things were as Flannery suspected, she may very well be in her office even at this odd hour of the morning.

He stepped out of the elevator and made his way past the

unattended reception desk and down the dark hallway to its left. There was door after door of empty offices with glass walls and floor space just big enough for a desk and a chair for visitors. halfway down the aisle he saw light spilling out onto the pale beige carpet. Either there was someone still here or else someone had carelessly left their office lights on. Flannery suspected it was the former.

He was right. Inside the glass box midway down the corridor was a young woman sitting at her desk flipping through documents in a manilla file folder and typing data into her desktop computer. She was young and attractive, early thirties with auburn hair and thick horn-rimmed glasses. Flannery stuck his head through the open door of her office.

"Uh, hello" said Flannery, shaking his head apologetically. "I'm Special Agent Flannery with the FBI, I'm looking for SA Adalet."

"Oh," she said with surprise, both at being interrupted at this time of day and at the request itself. "Well, you found her."

Flannery frowned. He remembered Adalet from the police station and this wasn't her. He pulled his head out from the office to look for a name plate but found there wasn't one.

"Not me," she said. "But this is her office, well, the floor is her office. She's not in at this time of day."

"Oh, I see," he said.

"Did you say FBI?" she asked.

Flannery looked down at his notebook still in his hand, then back up. The woman had a slight grin on her face.

"Uh, yeah. Yeah, I did. FBI" he said, pulling out his badge and showing it to her.

"Well, I've known Maureen for a long time. Since before she was the high and mighty State's Attorney. Since she was a lowly Assistant SA like me. Maybe there's something I can help you with. I'd be happy to answer any questions I can."

She sounded eager.

Flannery looked back at the elevator, then down at his watch, then back up into the sparkling eyes of the excited woman.

"Uh, yeah. Yeah sure," he said. "That would be great Ms.?"

"Faraday. Autumn Faraday," she said. "Please, step into my office Agent Flannery."

Flannery scribbled furiously in his notebook as ASA Faraday described her career alongside SA Adalet.

"She used to be really sweet actually," she started. "She was a tough cookie for sure, but nice and even a little fun. She had a good record in the courtroom, but nothing extraordinary. It was that one murder case, that kid at UIC that really got her the attention. It was fairly high profile, at least here in the city. Lots of newspaper coverage."

"Why was that?" he asked.

"Well, I mean, it wasn't typical. It wasn't gang or drug related and everyone likes a good sex scandal. Also, the girl, the girlfriend, she was cute, and she wouldn't talk which of course led to lots of speculation. Speculation is a journalist's favorite pastime."

"Sure," Flannery said.

"Also, the perp was a young, good looking, white suburbanite engineering student. I mean, it was a Lifetime movie waiting to happen."

"I see," said Flannery. "So that was the case that made her career? The Gavin Gayle prosecution?"

"Oh, right, yeah. That was the kid's name. Gavin Gayle. Yeah, that got her the press. Put her name in people's heads. She won the State's Attorney race the very next year."

"And that's when she got all..." he trailed off.

Autumn took a sip of coffee from a mug on her desk that said #1 cuz I'm NOT a mom and shook her head.

"Oh no, no it wasn't the job. She loved the job, and she was a good boss at first. Fair, friendly, and appreciative of our time and work. No, it wasn't the job that turned her into a 'see you next Tuesday'."

Flannery looked surprised at her use of the ugly acronym.

"So?" he said.

"It was the thing with her daughter."

"What thing was that?" Flannery prodded.

"Right, so her daughter was drugged and raped by her boyfriend on a playground something like a hundred feet from her best friend's backyard. He left her for dead in the sand by the swings."

"Holy shit," Flannery said.

"Yeah," Faraday agreed. "The worst part is that someone videotaped the assault on a cell phone, but we only found out because another kid beat the shit out of the kid that did it and stole the phone to bring to us."

Flannery sighed and sat back in his chair. "Shit," he said in a tone that expressed that he knew what was coming next.

"Yeah," she said. "Inadmissible. The kid walked."

Flannery sighed, "and that..."

"Yeah," Faraday nodded. "That's when the bitch came out. It was our fault that the kid got off. Everything came down to us."

"That's unfortunate," Flannery said.

"Well, it used to be worse. The first year or so after the trial were really hard. After that she mellowed out a bit."

Flannery scribbled in his notebook.

"And what was that date?" he asked.

"Oh God. I can't remember exactly. Call it summer of 2012."

Flannery scribbled again.

"Actually," she paused and gazed off at nothing in particular. "I can remember. It was June of 2012. I remember because it was when he died," she looked back at Flannery with a sense of satisfaction. "Which, ya know, makes sense.

Flannery looked up.

"Who? Who died?"

"Kevin Dobson, the kid that raped her daughter. They found him shot in the face in an alley just a few blocks from his apartment."

"Are you serious?" he said, shocked.

"That'd be a pretty fucked up thing to joke about don't you think?"

"Yeah, yeah I suppose I do," he agreed. "Who did it?"

"Don't know. They never found the guy. Crime scene was cleaned up and there were never any leads. It looked professional, so they questioned everyone. Everyone involved in the rape trial, including Maureen, but ultimately nothing came of it."

"I see, and that was sometime in June of 2012?"

"June 14," she said.

Flannery stopped writing.

"Say that again."

She frowned.

"It was June 14, 2012. Why? Is that significant?"

Flannery flipped back through his notebook. He stopped, stared, then looked back at Faraday.

"You're sure about that date?"

She sighed and sat back in her chair.

"Agent, I may not be the State's Attorney yet, but I'm not dumb. Graduated top of my class at Northwestern Law. Yeah, I'm sure of the date."

Flannery stood up.

"Thank you, Ms. Faraday, you have been very helpful."

She smiled.

"Please, call me Autumn."

"Thank you, Autumn."

"Is she in trouble?" Faraday asked, trying to hide her hopefulness.

Flannery looked at her cautiously.

"Yes. Yeah, she's in trouble. I'm not sure what kind yet, but she's got something to be worried about."

He stepped out of the office and walked back towards the elevator processing the information that he had just received from ASA Faraday. SA Adalet's daughter had been raped much the way Gavin claimed Weather had, the difference of course being that Adalet had put Gavin away for killing the person he claimed had been committing the assault, while her daughter's attacker had walked free due to poorly obtained video evidence. The irony there being that Gavin had always claimed there was video evidence of his version of the story, but it never surfaced.

Then almost a full year after the case ends in an acquittal the kid that attacked Adalet's daughter is murdered in a back alley near his apartment in a professional looking hit, and that day is the same day that Gavin ends up in Stroger Hospital with a gunshot wound and is treated and then the treatment is covered up with a city slush fund account, all of which is just days after Gavin is reported killed in custody in prison and his records sealed.

Flannery paused.

It seemed clear, but the leap was just a bit too long to take to his bosses. Additionally, it didn't explain the current matter at hand which was what any of this had to do with Grayson and Weather. He scratched his head, looked back down the hall, looked back at the elevator and sighed. He turned back and walked down the hall and stuck his head inside ASA Faraday's office.

"Agent?" she said. "Was there something else I could do for you?"

Flannery smiled in a charming way.

"Maybe," he said. "Would you mind if I took a quick look in her office?"

"Agent," Faraday said, scolding him. "Do you have a warrant to search the private office of the State's Attorney for Cook County?"

"No Ma'am, nothing formal, I just wanted a little peak."

Faraday shook her head.

"You know that I can't authorize that. Anything you found would be inadmissible."

"Autumn," he said coyly. "I'm not looking for anything admissible. I just want to know you're not going to tell on me."

Faraday blushed a little and smiled.

"Tell on who? Who are you?"

Flannery smiled and nodded his head and backed out of her office.

He stepped into the spacious office through large glass doors. It was easily eight hundred square feet, carpeted in muted, sophisticated colors, with floor to ceiling windows on two walls. There was a wide desk on one side of the room facing two elegant but new wooden chairs that were nice to look at, but Flannery suspected, not very comfortable to sit in.

Across from the desk was a large flat screen TV hung on the wall over a long bureau covered in various media players and flanked on either side by tall wooden bookshelves, the left of which was full of dusty old law books, and the right of which was full top to bottom with labeled cases for matching kinds of media. There were VHS cases, DVD and Blu Ray cases. Old audio cassettes, CD jewel boxes. Small cases for Mini-Disc and Micro cassettes as well as old 8mm Camcorder tapes. Every box had a case name and number on the spine. They were all different, but they all started 'State of IL v. ...'

Flannery ran his finger along the spines, casually glancing at case names, then turned his attention to the desk on the opposite wall. He walked over and looked at the surface, well kept and organized. He walked around the back and found much the same except for a single drawer on the top right side that was open with a small brass key sticking out of the front.

He looked up at the glass doors to the office then back at the drawer. What he could see at first glance was an overstuffed manila envelope sitting under an open box of large caliber, brass jacketed bullets. The box was about half full, with a few loose rounds laying outside the box on the envelope.

Flannery looked again at the office doors and back again at the drawer. He sat down in Maureen's chair and lifted the box of shells out of the drawer and set them on the desk to the side. He carefully lifted each of the loose rounds out and put them back in the box. Then he removed the envelope and laid it on the desk in front of him and opened it.

* * *

4:59 A.M.

FBI Assistant Director Stacy DeBruin sat across from SAI.C. Colin Michaels and looked at him with steely gray eyes and a frustrated bite of the lower lip.

"Right now, we have a strong suspect in custody," Michaels said. "She was found at the scene in arms reach of the murder weapon and covered in A.U.SA Grayson's blood."

AD DeBruin nodded her head.

"And do we have any idea why she was at Grayson's apartment in the first place?"

"Right now, she isn't saying much of anything, at least not anything useful, but she was found in her underwear and her clothes were scattered by the bed. It's our theory that they were having an affair and had a lover's quarrel and she shot him."

Assistant Director DeBruin frowned and leaned forward in her chair. Her long legs were crossed in a way that made it hard for Agent Michaels to concentrate. She wrinkled her nose and looked directly into his eyes.

"Was the gun registered to the suspect?"

Michaels frowned.

"No. Would you expect it to be?"

"No, I suppose not."

"Her fingerprints were on it." Michaels pointed out.

"Of course, they were." DeBruin said in a dismissive tone.

Agent Michaels wasn't sure if DeBruin agreed with him and was testing his case, or if she didn't buy it and was grilling him. He wasn't sure, but he had the feeling that she didn't buy it. He felt like he was being interrogated.

"Why would she use an unregistered gun if she was just going to stick around and wait for the cops to show up?" She asked.

"Well," said Michaels, starting to show a touch of frustration. "Well the most likely answer to that is that it's just the gun she had. I'm not suggesting this was premeditated. Either way it isn't my theory that she planned on sticking around. She has a laceration on the neck consistent with a bullet graze, which works with the slug we pulled out of the wall opposite the altercation. It matches Grayson's weapon which evidence suggests he fired at some point. When the CPD arrived on the scene Miss Rose was lying on the ground appearing to have been unconscious."

AD DeBruin cocked her head questioningly.

"I believe," continued Michaels, "that she was knocked unconscious during an altercation and didn't have time to flee."

DeBruin shifted in her seat.

"It appears that there was a struggle, Miss Rose was rather badly beaten."

"Right!" The director came back. "There's that to consider too. Are we suggesting that A.U.SA Grayson beat this woman?"

"Director, I'm not suggesting that it was some kind of domestic abuse. I'm not trying to tarnish the A.U.SA in any way. I'm assuming it was defensive."

"What was she wearing?"

Now Michaels shifted in his seat, visibly uncomfortable with the question.

"I'm sorry, what?"

"What was she wearing? The suspect. What was she wearing on her body when she arrived at the A.U.SA's apartment? What kind of clothes?"

Michaels leaned forward and pulled a gray file folder off his desk. He opened it and leafed through the papers inside.

"Um, well, it looks like she was in jeans, a white t-shirt with a print on it, a light hooded sweatshirt, and tennis shoes. If you don't mind me asking AD DeBruin, what difference does it make what she was wearing."

"And you know this because these are the clothes that you found on the floor next to the bed."

"Yes."

"And was the bed made?"

"Sorry?"

DeBruin shook her head in frustration that was bordering on anger. She stood up and began pacing in front of Michaels' desk.

"The bed, was it made? Tidy? Or was it messed up?"

"It was messed up."

"So, the assumption was that they were having sex there?"

"Yes."

"Before she shot him?"

"Well, yeah, presumably."

"So, she came in, they had their pleasantries, they got naked, and they had sex. Then they got in a fight. She attacked him, and in response he beat her so violently that he broke her nose. Then he shot her, or tried, he shot at her. Then she shot him in the chest and head, and then she fell down unconscious and the police came and arrested her."

Michaels let out a sigh and shrugged.

"Yeah, that's how it looks."

"Where did she get the gun?"

"Um," Michaels opened the folder back up again. He flipped a couple pages and looked back up at the Director. "Well, we don't know yet. As I said, it's not registered so we will have to see if it can be traced back to another crime or a gun show or..."

DeBruin cut him off.

"No SAI.C. Michaels, not where did she buy the gun. Where did she get the gun? That night. Just before she shot him. The very moment before she shot him. From where did she produce the weapon?"

SAI.C. Michaels just stared at Assistant Director DeBruin.

"I honestly couldn't tell you. We are still investigating, but we have her in custody and Agent Flannery has already started interrogating her."

AD DeBruin looked startled.

"He's questioning her now?"

"No," Michaels shook his head. "No, he talked to her at the CPD precinct before we transported her.

She nodded. "Well, I'd very much like to talk to this Agent Flannery. Is he here now?"

Michaels gave a quiet sigh. "No, he hasn't gotten back yet."

"Well, where is he exactly," the Assistant Director demanded.

"I'm not really sure," he answered sheepishly.

"Well, SAI.C. Michaels, I suggest you find out, and get him in here now."

Chapter Eighteen

October 6, 2019 5:11 A.M.

Flannery was flying down Lake Shore Drive, the thin red needle of the speedometer creeping up moment by moment past notches and numbers, shaking slightly as if it were, itself, nervous of the clip at which he was pushing the SUV. Next to him was a splintered lidless wooden box with a brass handle and keyhole at one end. It held files and folders, envelopes and a box of bullets. Flannery had yanked the whole thing right out of the desk and darted out of Adalet's office.

The ASA, Autumn Faraday had seen him running down the hallway with the drawer in hand and tried to stop him.

"Agent!" she had shouted. "What are you doing? You can't take that! You're going to get me fired!"

He hadn't even looked back at her. Once in his car he had fired the engine and peeled out of the parking spot, rocketing out of the underground garage like a ballistic missile exiting its silo. Out on the street the police scanner that he had kept tuned to the CPD channel since the start of his corruption investigation crackled back to life in the middle of an all-points bulletin.

"...considered armed and dangerous. Use of force authorized. Vehicle is an early model black Chrysler 300, license plate..."

Flannery slammed on his breaks stopping the SUV in the middle of the street and stared at the radio.

"...known locations include 10550 Torrence Ave. Enter with caution. This is a high priority suspect, all officers, be on the lookout..."

The message repeated twice more. Gavin, they were looking for Gavin. Looking to bring him into their custody, their control, or more likely looking to kill him. The APB was pretty clear even while attempting subtlety. It was true, Gavin was the key. The lynchpin that if pulled on could unravel everything and bring down the tower of corruption that had plagued this city almost since its inception.

Flannery stared at the broken drawer next to him. This was all too much. Too much happening too quickly. Twelve hours ago, his pet theory about Gavin Gayle was just that. An unlikely hunch that his boss had rejected. The fact that he'd continued pursuing it at all was more of a reflection of his boredom with his assignment than a real belief that there was anything to it. Now that his boss was dead, apparently at the hands of Gavin Gayle's former girlfriend. Gavin was presenting himself in public and the State's Attorney for Cook County, who had been the one that convicted him in the first place, seemed to be behind the whole thing. Was she behind the murder of Grayson too?

He had a flash of rational clarity and decided he needed to bring in the rest of the team. It was irresponsible and unprofessional to go barreling into this himself. They needed to do things by the book; collect evidence, interview witnesses, make everything legit. He'd already fucked up by stealing the drawer from the SA's office without a warrant. It was time to slow this down and stop the bleeding.

He grabbed his phone to call the office and it rang in his hand. The caller ID was startling. SAIC Michaels-Office. He took a breath, composed himself and swiped the screen to answer.

"Michaels," he started.

"Where the fuck are you Kyle?"

The use of his first name by the Agent in Charge was as striking as the profanity.

"I was just getting ready to call you. We have a huge and really explosive situa-"

"I've been trying to reach you for hours. I've got AD DeBruin in my office and she's furious about this whole thing obviously, but mostly that you aren't here!"

Flannery frowned.

"Who," he asked.

"Assistant Director Stacy DeBruin. She's in from Washington about Grayson and wants to know exactly where you are."

Flannery felt a shiver. He recognized that name, but he wasn't sure why. He supposed it must be from some internal document or memo, but that didn't feel right. Also, a question popped into his head. How did Washington get an Assistant Director out to Chicago so fast? He felt his skin crawl and suddenly wasn't sure how much he wanted to share.

"Sir, I don't really want to do this over the phone, but we have a situation with Gavin Gayle and the State's Attorney."

"Who?" came from the Agent at the same time as another voice.

"Gavin?" was an exclamation as much as a question from a female voice in the background.

"Sir, this is extremely urgent. I'll be right in, but I need to go get Gavin first. I think this is pertinent to Grayson."

"No, just-" there was a rattle and click like a phone handset being lifted from the cradle.

"Agent, Flannery? This is FBI Assistant Director Stacy DeBruin. Listen to me very closely. You go and you get Gavin and you ratchet on the hardest cuffs you have as tight as you can make them and you drag him in here and you do it right fucking now or by God I'll have you charged with Grayson's murder."

There was a heavy click and the call went dead.

Flannery was breathing hard. That hadn't gone the way he expected. SAIC Michaels seemed genuinely rattled and this DeBruin, whoever she was, seemed very eager to see Gavin brought in despite the fact that he hadn't given them even the most basic groundwork on who he even was.

Something was going on and all of it seemed to center around Gavin. He didn't trust this AD but he agreed with her assessment. It was time to bring Gavin in. Flannery grabbed the thickest of the folders from the battered drawer next to him and flipped through the pages inside until he found what he was looking for, then he picked up his phone again and dialed.

* * *

5:15 A.M.

The five hours was a gift, and I knew she knew it. I didn't have anything. Nothing to pack, no one to contact and tie up loose ends with. If I had wanted to, I could have just got in my car and driven out of the city, or out of the state. Leaving the country would have been more difficult. I didn't have a passport, and with no identity getting one that would work at the border would be tough.

I had some savings. Money set aside from my weekly allowance that I stuffed in the safe I had acquired from Mr. Simons. To my mind I had about ten-grand stacked in there. That would get me pretty far living off the grid, but it would be a drop in the bucket if I wanted a real identity.

I'm not going to lie, I considered it. Had I been given the option the previous day I'd have already been halfway to New Orleans, but things were different now. Weather was in trouble and no one except for me was even interested in helping her. I couldn't leave her. I couldn't just let her die, which is exactly what would happen if she went down for the murder. It wasn't even a legitimate choice. Maureen knew that part too. She knew I wouldn't walk away. She had given me just enough rope to hang myself with.

It was five a.m. or thereabout, I had just under four hours left before I would be the target of every law enforcement officer in Chicago. Four early morning hours to come up with a plan and start making it happen, but not the whole four hours because there was something I had to do first. First, I had to clear out of The Club.

When you live somewhere, you accumulate things. Eight years living in that brick box twenty feet underground should have been enough to require a moving truck or two, but it hadn't been. I had almost no physical possessions and those I did have mostly were things I carried on my body.

I went back to my room and threw a black canvas duffle bag on my bed. I tossed in a few shirts and an extra pair of slacks. Socks and underwear, and my toothbrush. I threw my soap in the sink and ran hot water over it to melt it down. Anything else that might have my DNA on it went in a plastic trash bag and I poured bleach down the toilet and all the drains.

I had a small file cabinet next to the desk that contained letters I had been delivered over the years. They were from anonymous senders and addressed to no one in particular, but all expressed gratitude for the wrongs that they felt had been righted. They made me feel ambivalent. I didn't see any right in what I had been doing the past eight years, not anymore, but they reminded me that there was a reason for it and made me feel less like the monster I really was.

I took the stack of papers out of the metal drawer and laid them flat on top of my clothes in the bag. Then I opened the safe at the foot of the bed. Inside the small black box was the money, neatly stacked and bound in rubber bands; two cartons of my Treasurer Black cigarettes, and extra ammunition.

The money and smokes went in the bag, then I filled two spare clips. I put the extra clips in the bag and stuffed the gun in the holster under my left arm. I filled my lighter from the bottle on my desk, then took to wiping down all the surfaces with a clean undershirt. When all was said and done, I zipped up the bag, left the key on the desk and walked out of the room that had been my home for the past eight years for the last time.

By that time, it was 5:45. I was down to just over three hours and I still wasn't sure what I was going to do. One thing I knew was, I needed to find out exactly what Weather was doing with Grayson in the first place. The easiest solution was to ask Weather herself, but that wasn't going to be possible. The FBI had already scooped her up and she was almost certainly being held in federal lockup by now.

The first and second rule of my life for nearly a decade had been, don't leave the city and don't contact anyone from my past. I had stuck to those conditions and followed the letter of the law, at least as far as it applied to me, but things were different now. I was out. Out of a home, out of a job, and out of protection. Every benefit that came with my conditions had been stripped away so, it seemed to me, the rules were moot. Adalet had said as much when she told me to disappear. If she was telling me to leave, then my tacit understanding was I could do whatever I wanted.

I needed information about Weather so I needed to see someone who would have some. I didn't know her friends or her co-workers, but I did know someone. I knew her mom, and she would know Weather. The only problems were that she lived an hour and a half away in McHenry, hadn't heard from me in thirteen years, and of course, thought that I was dead.

It was a plan with flaws, but at this point, a flawed plan was better than no plan, so I threw my duffel over my shoulder and headed out of The Club for, what I expected, was the last time. As I passed through the dining room something happened that had never happened before in the eight years that I had resided at The Club. As I neared the heavy timber door that led to the stairs out of The Club the phone rang.

I walked over to the host stand and stared at the dusty yellow push-button phone ringing on the counter. I was shocked to learn that it even worked. I had always assumed it was just decoration. An anachronism meant to add to the out-of-timeyness of The Club.

I stared at it for a long, long time. It rang and rang and rang and I thought about how phones don't do that anymore. People don't even use phones for talking and when they do four rings is all you get. After that you fall into the never-ending abyss of voicemail. But this phone, it just kept ringing. Finally, I reached down and took the phone off the receiver and said, "Hello."

"Gavin," Agent Flannery's voice was panicked and urgent and it startled me to hear it as much as the phone ringing in the first place had.

"Agent Flannery?" then, "Wait, how did you get this number?"

"Yeah, Gavin, SA Adalet's coming for you. She knows where you are and she's on her way right now."

My blood went cold and a chill ran down my spine.

"What are you talking about?"

"Gavin, I just left her office. She's got a file on you a mile long. I was- it doesn't matter. It was in a locked drawer in her desk."

I interrupted in disbelief.

"If it was locked..."

"She left it open. She- I don't know, key still in the keyhole. It's not important, the file has everything. Everything you've ever done for her, or anyone else. Everything you got for it, including those fancy cigarettes you smoke. It's got anywhere you might go, including your Uncle Kevin's in the suburbs and that basement club you live in. That's how I got this number."

I was starting to feel cold. There was a file. Of course, there was a file. It would be stupid for her not to keep one.

"Look, Agent, she was just-"

"Gavin, there was something else in the drawer. A box of .45s. An open, half full box of .45s, but Gavin, there was no gun. There were bullets in the drawer but no gun. And she called you in. My scanner just picked up an APB on you, your description, your car and the address of The Club and it was pretty clear what she wanted done. Gavin, I think you need to get out of there now."

"Agent, why are you telling me this? If you have what you say you have, then you should be-"

"Because Gavin, there was something else in the file. A videotape. Your videotape."

I lost my breath.

"Gavin, I know what you said is true. Adalet knew it too, all along. I watched the tape. It was exactly like you said. I'm telling you now for your safety, and the safety of your family, get out of there."

"She'll still find me," I whispered.

"I'll take care of that," Flannery said.

"How?"

"I'm on my way to you now, I'm almost there. You can come with me; you can see Weather. I can protect you. The FBI can protect you. AD DeBruin wants to talk to you too. We're going to-"

I choked on my own spit.

"Who?"

"What?"

"Who wants to talk to me?" I asked breathlessly.

"Oh, uh, one of our Assistant Directors. DeBruin, Stacy DeBruin."

I nodded to myself.

"I'm almost there Gavin, you can-"

"Yeah, yeah I have a place. Out in the burbs. In Glen Ellyn. Cabs. Cabs bistro. It's a little place on Duane and Main. Meet me there."

"What? No! Gavin you need to-"

"Okay," I said. "Oh, Flannery," I added. "Bring Weather! You can't leave her there at your office. I don't trust your boss and you shouldn't either. I can't explain it all right now, it's, it's all just a little bit of history repeating. I'll explain when you get there."

"Gavin, I cant-"

I hung up the phone.

Chapter Nineteen

October 6, 2019 5:51 A.M.

The sun was not quite breaking past the hard edge of the Earth when Hinde's car rolled into the intersection in front of The Club. Gavin was still in the building and the rest of the neighborhood was utterly deserted. Hinde tapped the breaks and the car came to a stop in the middle of the intersection.

She slid the gear selector into park and popped open the door, stepping out of the car and leaving the engine running. There was a nervous feeling spreading through her body, creeping up her back and turning somersaults in her belly. She paused, staring at The Club then reached down and popped the trunk of her car where she retrieved and put on the heavy black Kevlar vest the department had issued her. Carefully she walked over to Gavin's 300, circling the car once to peek in all the windows then approaching the driver's door and opening it.

Hinde wasn't surprised it was unlocked. In this neighborhood Gavin was better known than the mayor, and arguably more respected. In an area of the city where violent crime was a day to day reality, the eight blocks that surrounded The Club were among the safest in the city, and no one that lived here had any doubt that it was because of Gavin.

The detective climbed into the driver's seat and took in the car. She smelled in the air, a strong tobacco scent, but the interior was immaculately clean. She put her hands on the wheel and leaned back in the seat, stretching her legs out, rolling her shoulders in the leather and staring out the windshield at the green door of The Club. It swung open.

* * *

Years of living in the shadow of the law had given me a sort of intuition about when a situation wasn't right. I hardly needed that since Flannery had told me that the buffer time I'd been given was a scam. Placate me long enough to let my guard down and then drop the hammer. Maureen was playing clean up. Getting rid of me before I could do any more damage to her or her system.

Still, as soon as my palm hit the door, I knew there was trouble. I felt that sour burn in my chest and tasted chalky acid in my mouth. I pushed the door open and let it swing until the hinges caught and it bounced back and closed again. In that short moment I sensed movement. Nothing I could identify, but something. Movement. Someone in my car.

I pulled the snub-nosed pistol from under my left arm and snapped the safety off. I held it low, against my thigh then slowly pushed the door open again and stepped through the doorway leading with my left shoulder, concealing the gun against my right leg.

* * *

Agent Flannery's SUV skidded to a stop a dozen yards or so from the address listed in the file. The neighborhood was old, tired and worn out. The street was littered with broken glass and potholes and there were as many shuttered storefronts as active ones. Sunlight was beginning to wash the sky in pale gray, but the sun hadn't broken the horizon yet and the street swam in civil twilight.

There was an unmarked police cruiser parked catawampus in the middle of the road, its engine still running but with the driver's seat vacant. He scanned the area and saw a thin figure moving in a boxy black car parked on the side of the street. He recognized it immediately. Gavin's car. The same Chrysler 300 he had seen tearing away from the police station late last night, but the figure in the car wasn't Gavin, it was the detective from the station. Hinde, he thought he remembered. What was she doing in his car? Was it an ambush?

Flannery saw the door to The Club swing open wide and slow until it met the extent of its flexibility and bounced back slamming shut. The cop saw it too. Flannery saw her glance up at the door and step out of Gavin's car. She drew her sidearm, aimed it at the door of The Club and pulled the hammer back, Flannery could hear it click into place from inside his Suburban.

The cop started moving slowly around the car, keeping her gun trained on the chipping green paint of the door, two handed, calm, collected, precise. She moved in small steps, foot over foot, sideways along the side of the car, then paused when she reached the front bumper. She was directly in line with the door, still standing on the street, maybe twenty-five feet from the building.

Flannery watched the door open again, slower this time, more deliberate. He saw Gavin step out slowly, cautiously. He was turned sideways with a duffle bag hanging off his forward shoulder giving the cop a smaller target with less vital organs to aim at. He had his left palm stretched out. It looked like he was pleading with the cop not to shoot.

The door swung closed behind Gavin. Flannery watched the two of them stand there, looking at each other. They were talking to each other, but Flannery couldn't hear what they were saying.

* * *

Detective Hinde was calm. On the outside she was calm. She was standing in the street aiming her weapon at a man who she knew for a fact had killed many people. Yes, he had done it at her request, and Maureen's and a few other members of city government, but he had done it and at the end of the day, when this intersection was filled with cops, other cops, cops that didn't know the details of everything that connected her to Gavin, they would know that he had killed those people. They would know that Gavin was a criminal and that Hinde had been justified in shooting him, and there would be no further investigation. Maureen would make sure of that. So, she was calm, on the outside.

Inside she was a mess. She knew every moment that had led up to this one. She could see all the chances there had been to avoid this day, this hour, this second. She knew that she had been selfish, wanting revenge more than justice. At the time she had thought it was justice. She reasoned that the system had failed so many people so many times that they; that she needed to get justice without the system. Now though, at that moment, aiming her Glock at a man for doing nothing more than what he had been asked; no not asked, told to do. What he had been demanded to do, she knew that punishment without the system wasn't justice, it was revenge. As Gavin spoke to her across the empty air that swam between them, she couldn't hear what he was saying, all she could hear was her own voice telling her "Just one more. Just this one more time and it will all be over. It will all just go away."

She took a step forward.

* * *

I stood on the sidewalk exposed. The door had shut behind me, no going back. The red awning hung overhead, the bare bulb hanging from the wire a couple feet in front of me. I had my gun pressed tight against my right thigh, safety off, hammer back. I was turned sideways towards Detective Hinde, which helped mask the fact that I was holding a weapon, but also had the added benefit of giving the detective less to shoot at.

Hinde was standing in the street directly in front of me pointing her nine-millimeter at my chest. The hammer was back, and her hands were steady, but she didn't look well. Her eyes were red and wet and there were tears visibly running down her face.

"Hey there, Detective," I said in a cautious but friendly voice.

Hinde just stood still, pointing her gun at me.

"What's going on? Is there something wrong Megan?"

Again, she just stood there.

"Listen, Megan, I'm a little late for an appointment. Would it be alright with you if I got in my car over there?"

Silence.

I tried a new tactic, changed my voice, made it serious, grim, soft.

"Listen Megan, it doesn't have to go down like this. You know I'm never going to say anything to anyone. Not about you. Not about Maureen. None of it. I just need to get Weather and we will disappear. Gone for good. Never see us again. Absolutely no one else needs to get hurt here."

Hinde just stood there.

"Okay, Detective," I said with the voice of a broken heart.

I moved as fast as I could. I side stepped, a short step, a half step, it was movement, but mostly it was shifting my weight onto the ball of my left foot.

Hinde stepped forward.

I spun on my left foot, stepped forward on my right, lifted my right arm, and pulled the trigger on my gun.

* * *

Flannery saw the muzzle flash on Gavin's gun and gasped. He saw the cop fall backwards and slap her head on the pavement. Not like in the movies, she wasn't thrown off her feet, just knocked backwards like someone had shoved her and she hadn't seen it coming.

Flannery hadn't seen it coming. He was shocked. He knew that Gavin was mixed up in something pretty bad, but he never would have expected to see him shoot down a cop in the street in cold blood.

Blood.

Wait.

There was no blood, cold or otherwise. He jumped out of his SUV and ran around the front of it, towards the cop.

"Gavin!" He shouted.

Gavin was already kneeling by the cop. Flannery saw him rip open the Velcro straps that held her bullet proof vest snug against her chest. Gavin flipped her over and pulled the vest off.

Flannery pulled his piece and shouted. "Freeze, Gavin, stay right fucking there."

Gavin looked up at Flannery and bounced. He jumped so

fast it appeared to Flannery as though, in one fell swoop, he leapt over the body of the detective the hood of his car and maybe the grand-fucking-canyon. Before Flannery had time to lift his gun Gavin was in his car with the detective's vest and the door closed. The tires on the 300 spun on the gravel of the pavement for almost a second before the car jutted forward and took off.

Flannery turned and aimed. He let off three rounds hitting the back bumper twice and shattering the rear window with the third, but the car was gone, and the cop was lying in the road at Flannery's feet.

* * *

6:23 A.M.

AD DeBruin stood up with a huff.

"Where the fuck is your guy Michaels?" she said with more anger than irritation.

"Yeah, okay, you're right, this is getting a little frustrating. I'll call him again."

Michaels dug in his suit coat pocket and pulled out his phone. He pressed and swiped until he found Flannery's number, then put the phone to his ear. After a couple seconds of ringing he spoke.

"Kyle, it's Michaels. Where are you man? You were supposed to be back here by now. Assistant Director DeBruin is getting," Michaels paused and glanced over at DeBruin. She shot back with a scowl. "Impatient," he said cautiously. "Hurry up and get back here with your suspect, and call and let us know where you are when you get this."

Michaels hung up the phone and set it face down on the desk. DeBruin paced back to the chair and dropped into it.

"What the fuck Michaels?"

"Sorry Director, Honestly it's totally out of character for him."

"I wouldn't say that," said DeBruin.

Michaels frowned.

"What's that supposed to mean?" he said.

DeBruin looked at him with annoyance.

"Well, from what you've told me," she said, "both you and Grayson gave him explicit instructions to stop his investigation into Mr. Gayle, yet it doesn't seem like he followed that particular order?"

Michaels sighed.

"No, you're not wrong, but turns out it's a good thing he kept at it huh? I mean it looks like that information is going to prove valuable."

DeBruin rolled her eyes and let out a sigh.

"Yeah, good for us," she said under her breath.

She slumped back in her chair and they sat in silence for a moment.

"Ya know what, ping him," she said.

"What?" Michaels said, confused.

DeBruin sat up straight and focused her gaze on him.

"Ping his car," she said. "He drives a government vehicle. Ping the GPS unit and tell me where the fuck he is."

"Well, I can't just, I mean I don't directly have access to..."

DeBruin cut him off.

"Michaels, I don't care if it's you, your secretary, or your fucking sister. Pick up the Goddamn phone and find out where he fucking is."

Michaels stared at her for a moment.

"Now!" she shouted.

He dove across his desk and picked up the handset on his phone. He punched four numbers and stood up with the handset to his ear, the long, coiled cord knocking over a tin cup full of pens in the process.

He barked orders for the on-call quartermaster to ping the GPS unit on Flannery's SUV and tell them where he was. Then he leaned back over the desk and hung up the phone.

"Was that so fucking hard?" DeBruin asked.

"They'll call back when they find him."

Michaels sighed and looked at his watch. He looked up at DeBruin, then turned and walked over to the bureau on the other side of the office.

"Mind if I have a drink?" he said, pulling a crystal decanter of bourbon out of the cabinet.

"Whatever, you're pretty much fired already anyway," DeBruin said flatly.

Michaels set the decanter and glass down on the bureau with a thud and turned back to DeBruin.

"What?" he said.

She raised her eyebrows and gave a condescending grin.

"Why don't you make me one too," she said.

Michaels looked at her dumbfounded.

She widened her eyes and gestured at the bottle on the bureau.

He sighed and shook his head, turned towards the bourbon and the phone on his desk rang. DeBruin didn't wait for him, she leaned forward and answered the phone.

"Assistant Director DeBruin."

Pause.

"No, that's fine, you can give the information to me, thank you."

Pause.

"Well, I'm the fucking Assistant Director, so you can give it to me, or you can go home and see what unemployment feels like."

Pause.

"Thank you."

DeBruin hung up the phone.

"You're pretty much a bitch," Michaels said.

"I'm thirty-two years old and an assistant director at the FBI. Do you think that that happens by being nice?"

"No," Michaels said. "In fact, that's not how I think that happened."

"Well fuck you too," she said.

"Nah, I'm just an S.A.I.C." he said.

"Not anymore you're not," she stabbed.

"Well then, I guess I'll be going home," he swallowed his glass of bourbon. "It was most definitely not nice knowing you."

"Hold on," DeBruin held up a hand.

Michaels paused.

"You can keep your job."

He looked at her skeptically.

"Dot dot dot," he said.

"They've got his location at Torrence and 106th. Where is that?"

"Wow, that's deep south side, not a great neighborhood. Not sure what he'd be doing down there."

DeBruin stood up. She grabbed her coat and purse and headed for the door.

"Wait, what's going on?" Michaels asked.

"What's going on?" she shot back rhetorically. "I changed my mind. You are fucking fired," she walked out and slammed the door behind her.

Chapter Twenty

October 6, 2019 6:37 A.M.

Flannery put his index and middle fingers firmly against the cop's carotid artery. There was a strong pulse tapping against his fingers. He patted her down and pulled her leather wallet from her waist band and inspected it.

'Detective Meghan Hinde'

Flannery pulled his small black notebook from his jacket and jotted down the detective's name and badge number. He dragged the woman from the middle of the street and up onto the sidewalk, then pulled his phone from his pocket and dialed 911. When the operator answered the line, he told her that he had witnessed an officer involved shooting and there was an officer down. When the operator asked for his name he hung up.

There were more missed calls and texts from SAIC Michaels, but he wasn't going to return them. Things were unraveling even faster than before and now there was a new piece to the puzzle, a new player in the game. This DeBruin. It made Flannery uncomfortable that Gavin recognized the name.

He had had a twinge of familiarity with it as well that he didn't think he could write off as innocent. For Gavin to know her, and for him to be so adamant about her being untrustworthy, that made Flannery nervous.

Gavin was gone, there was no trail of breadcrumbs, no bloody footprints or deep tire tracks to follow, not for the police and not for the FBI, but Flannery knew where he was headed, Gavin had told him. Did that mean Gavin was starting to trust him or was it a setup. He decided to assume it was the former, why else would Gavin have asked him to retrieve Weather?

Flannery climbed back into his SUV, spun the wheel, pointed the truck north, and stepped on the gas.

* * *

6:36 A.M.

Driving with a blown out rear windshield isn't like driving with the windows down. The air swoops over the car and creates a vortex sucking every drop of air out the back. It causes pressure on your ears and pulls at your clothes and the hairs on the back of your neck. It's an intensely uncomfortable sensation that gets worse and worse as you drive faster and faster. I was driving very fast.

I was wearing the Kevlar vest I'd taken off Detective Hinde. The huge .45 caliber round I'd fired was still lodged in the material that hung over my right ribs. She was alive, but probably hurting pretty bad with a couple broken ribs where the Kevlar had absorbed the energy of the bullet and dissipated it into her chest. She certainly had a concussion from slamming her head on the pavement. She was going to be an unhappy woman when she woke up.

I was hurting too. My head pounded and throbbed and I

squinted my eyes against the pain. I was speeding west down the Eisenhower expressway. I290 was the main artery into and out of the city, funneling directly into the heart of the loop. West was the suburbs, west was Glen Ellyn, Glen Ellyn was where I was going. It was where my uncle lived, it was where my grandfather had lived, it was the closest thing to home I had now. It was the closest thing to safety I could think of.

I wove in and out of traffic picking up speed as I got further and further from the city. At Harlem Ave. the expressway cleared to a wide-open ribbon of asphalt. The sun was starting to peak up above the ground now giving the skyline behind me red and purple edges.

I put my foot down hard and felt the seat reach forward and press against my back, it was sore. The bullet that had taken out his rear window had also blown through the back of the seat and embedded itself in the fabric of the vest I was wearing. It was a long shot and a smaller caliber than the one I had fired at Hinde, so nothing had been broken, but it was sore and sharp. Between that and the wound in my ribs from the night before there was enough pain to keep me awake and alert.

Five miles later the Eisenhower dumped off on Roosevelt Rd. in Hillside. I immediately felt better just being off the Interstate. I was in the suburbs now, and while my flashy car with a blown out rear window was more conspicuous here, the cops were lazy and disinterested. I drove west on Roosevelt through little suburbs consisting mostly of strip malls and closed up car dealerships; three gas stations on every corner and a McDonald's every half mile or so. Chain restaurants that all served the same over cooked hamburger and the same deep-fried onion, just with different names, lined the road offering 'kids eat free'. I felt a dual sense of disgust and nostalgia, a lot like the feeling one gets seeing old pictures of themselves on their parent's walls at the holidays. This was the environment I had grown up in, but it was also what I had grown out of and being back made my skin crawl.

I drove past the old chiropractic college my grandfather had taught at, past the grocery store that used to be a K-Mart ironically situated next to a Cadillac dealership and dipped under I355, and up Baker Hill to the to the little side street that wound down into the residential neighborhoods of Glen Ellyn. This was my father's hometown. It's where he went when he and my mom split up. It's where my Grandfather and Grandmother had lived and where my aunt and uncle still lived. It crossed my mind to go there, to ring the bell and beg for understanding and help, but it was an obvious choice and one that Maureen would quickly think of. It wouldn't buy me any time and it would put my family in danger. I allowed myself to slow down as I passed their house, staring in the windows at the lights coming on for breakfast, but I didn't stop. I rolled past the house and up the street heading to the address I'd given Agent Flannery earlier.

* * *

7:30 A.M.

Maureen got the call late. Hinde had been unconscious for almost twenty minutes, and by the time she came to, the scene was crawling with cops. Hinde had been groggy for another ten minutes or so, so by the time she knew where she was and what was going on, she was under siege by officers, detectives, IAD, paramedics, and even the department's lawyers trying to get her story, make sure she was okay, and make sure she wasn't looking to sue anyone. By the time she was able to find enough privacy to call Maureen more than an hour had passed.

"What the fuck is going on down there Hinde?" she whisper-shouted into her burner cell from the sofa in her office. "This was supposed to be quick and easy!"

She was shaking. Out of anger sure, but also fear. That quiet gut-wrenching fear that builds over long periods of time. The kind that keeps you awake at night and distracts you while you should be thinking of other things. The shaking wasn't violent, it was under the skin. Small creepy crawly muscle spasms in her arms and legs and shoulders. This was it, this was the worst case scenario. This is what she always prayed would never happen. Gavin was loose. He was rogue. He was off book, doing what he wanted to do, not what she wanted.

She had always known that something would have to be done. This little game, this arrangement couldn't go on forever. She knew that eventually she'd have to have him put down. She also knew that if it came to that crossroads that he'd be smart enough to see it coming. She knew that the only way to do it would be out of the blue. To just send someone down one night and do it, but she kept putting it off. The system had been working too well. She kept telling herself, one more job, one more time. Just get this last bad guy off the streets and then I'll get rid of the dangerous dog. You can't keep a dangerous animal forever, eventually it's going to bite you.

Now here she was. The dog was off its leash and out of the yard. Sure, it didn't have tags, but it wouldn't take anyone that was looking that long to figure out whose house it had come from, and now people were looking. A cop had been shot, and it had been reported (who the fuck had done that). IAD was investigating, the department lawyers were all over it. Plus, the FBI was sniffing around Gavin, that connection would be made soon enough.

"Sorry," Hinde said. "I honestly didn't think he'd shoot me."

"Why the fuck not?" She screamed. "He's fucking shot

everyone else! That's what he fucking does you asshole! God fucking dammit!"

She threw the phone across the office and it hit the wall and fell on the floor.

"Fuck!" She screamed again.

She stopped, put her palms on her knees and breathed deeply. She stood up and walked to her desk and dug through her purse. She dug deeper and deeper, starting to curse more under her breath. Finally, she remembered when she saw the gun. She'd left the key in the drawer. She stepped around the desk and looked down in horror.

She was seeing red and not thinking at all anymore. She had one thing to do and it didn't involve thought. It involved ending this before it got any worse, and now, at this point, she was the only one who could do it. She was the only one who knew who she was after. The cops didn't know who Gavin was yet, and Hinde was at least fucking smart enough to keep her mouth shut about that. The FBI was looking for Gavin, but they didn't know him, not like she did.

She didn't know where he'd go, but she knew one thing. She fucking knew how he'd get there. She pulled out her personal phone having destroyed the burner in her office and called Hinde. When she'd delivered the car to him, a gratuity from the family of one of his jobs, she'd installed a LoJack device on it; a simple GPS tracker that gave the vehicle's location. She wasn't stupid enough to give him a car she couldn't trace. She asked Hinde for the GPS location on the tracker and eighteen seconds later she hung up the phone, climbed into her Audi and entered Glen Ellyn into the navigation system.

* * *

7:34 A.M.

Flannery exploded into SAIC Michaels' office already talking a mile a minute. Michaels was sitting behind his desk with his jacket off and his tie loosened, gulping from a glass of scotch who's bottle sat half empty on his desk.

"I need to take Weath..."

He trailed off and stood silent for a moment looking around the room.

"What the hell is going on here?" Flannery said.

"That bitch is crazy," Michaels slurred.

"What bitch?"

"The Director. No, no! The Assistant Director. She's not even a real director. She's a fucking assistant!"

"What happened?" Flannery repeated.

"She went all crazy. We couldn't find you, which, where the fuck were you by the way? I called like ten times. Why weren't you answering your phone?"

"Yeah, sorry about that," Flannery said in an apologetic tone. "I was in the middle of something important."

"Of course, you were!" Michaels shouted. "Down south in the slums."

Flannery's forehead curled.

"How'd you know-?"

Michaels let out a long, exasperated sigh through closed lips.

"Your GPS dumbass. Piece of advice, if you are trying to hide from the FBI, don't do it in one of our cars!"

"Fuck," said Flannery.

"Fuck indeed," said Michaels. "So, what were you doing there anyway? Why'd it piss off the Assistant Director so much?"

Flannery dropped the file from Maureen's desk in front of

SAIC Michaels. He looked at it skeptically then picked it up and leafed through it.

"That's it?"

Flannery looked confused.

"That's what you were getting? I thought you were arresting this Gavin guy. I thought you were going to show us the mystery man."

Flannery frowned.

"What? No. This isn't- I got this at SA Adalet's office. This is her secret file on Gavin Gayle. Turns out everything he said when he was arrested, everything he said at trial, all of it was true. She had a videotape that showed him beating the kid to death, but it also showed that he was defending Weather. Adalet hid the tape to lock down the conviction."

Michaels stared at Flannery bleary eyed.

Flannery sighed, exasperated.

"Look, I need Weather."

"What," Michaels laughed.

"I'm going to see Gavin, and I need Weather. We have a problem. Adalet's has been using Gavin as some kind of enforcer here in Chicago. It's bad for Gavin, but it's all been under duress. But now that his cover's blown, she's going after him. Sounds like AD DeBruin is somehow involved too, so I don't have a lot of time."

Michaels leaned back in his chair, finished off the scotch in his glass and set the glass on his desk.

"Look Flannery, I have no idea what you're talking about. You and your cockamamie conspiracy theories, but ya know what? I'm drunk, and besides that, the ASSISTANT fired me, so I really just don't give a fuck. Do whatever you want, it's your ass."

Flannery stared stunned.

Michaels waved his hand with a flourish that said, 'go away

now'. Flannery didn't move. Michaels reached into his desk and pulled out a printed sheet and scribbled in some blank spaces, then signed it and threw it at Flannery.

Flannery grabbed the sheet from the floor. It was a prisoner transfer order giving Flannery the authority to move Weather.

"Now get out of here before I fucking change my mind."

*** * ***

7:47 A.M.

Another steel door swung open and Weather reflexively stood up. The man who stepped in was familiar. He had been in the other dreary beige room at the police station with her.

"Good evening Weather." The man said.

"It's got to be morning by now Agent." Weather yawned with a tone of ambivalence.

The agent pulled out the chair across from her and sat down.

"Alright, good morning, if you prefer."

Weather sighed and leaned back in her chair. "I don't really have a preference, I'm just saying that I've been sitting here, alone, for quite some time now. So long in fact, that I imagine it must be morning."

He chuckled. "I can see the connection," he said.

"Connection?" She was trying to act disinterested.

"Yes, the connection. The attraction. Between you and Gavin."

Weather looked up at him.

"You both have the same personality. The same animus for figures of authority. The same sardonic wit and elusive conversation style."

"I'm not really sure what you're talking about."

"See!" Agent Flannery pointed at her. "Right there, that's what I'm saying, elusive conversation style. You do know what I'm talking about. I'm talking about your boyfriend. I'm talking about Gavin Gayle. The guy that made you jump out of your chair when he walked past the interrogation room at the CPD station. The guy I spent an hour with tonight, an hour discussing you."

Weather shifted in her seat and brushed her hair out of her face. She scooted her chair closer to him and leaned in over the table.

"I think I jumped up when you walked in the room too, Agent. I was handcuffed and chained to a table. I was just told that the police believe I murdered a man and at that point I couldn't even remember where I'd been or how I'd gotten there. I'd say I had a right to be a little jumpy, or are you suggesting I'm sleeping with you as well?"

Agent Flannery didn't flinch, he just smiled and kept staring at her.

Finally, she acquiesced, dropped her shoulders and lolled her head to one side. "What did he say?" she asked with a defeated tone.

Flannery tilted his head to match hers and leaned back in his chair.

"He said you didn't do it."

Weather dropped her head and closed her eyes. She sat silently for almost a full minute, breathing deeply and fixing her eyes on an invisible spot on the wall. After a minute she looked up at Flannery. Her eyes were red and wet.

"He also said he hasn't seen or spoken to you in over a decade."

Weather sniffled.

"So, my question was, if he hasn't seen or spoken to you in so long, how does he know you didn't do it?"

Weather allowed a look of curiosity to wash across her features.

"What do you think Weather? Why is he so sure?"

Then the look of wonder hardened like a pool of water when the temperature suddenly reaches freezing. In a flash her face went pale and blank and her eyes turned to steel.

"Do you want to know my theory?"

"I did it."

The voice was so soft it was almost inaudible.

"I'm sorry?" Flannery said, an icy shiver running through his shoulders and down his back.

Weather cleared her throat, and with a gravelly voice, said again, "I did it. I killed him. It was me."

Flannery shot forward in his seat. He leaned far across the table and looked Weather straight in the eyes and shouted in a whisper.

"Weather, stop talking right now."

She shook her head and repeated, "No, I did it, I killed the guy. It was all me. I don't know who that person you were talking to is. I've never seen him before, but whoever it was, he's wrong. I killed that guy tonight. All me. All by myself."

"Don't be stupid Weather." Flannery said in a tone more pleading than confrontational. "Don't make a mistake that can't be unmade. I know about you and Gavin. I know everything now, things you probably don't. He didn't go to prison for killing the guy you were sleeping with. He went for killing the guy that was trying to rape you. I saw the tape and I have his file from the State's Attorney's office. I know she got him out somehow and I know it's all a big secret. I also suspect that if he says you didn't do this, then you didn't do this."

Flannery stood up and began pacing the interrogation room.

"Look. Clearly something is going on here. I don't see any satisfactory connection between you and Grayson. I don't believe you were having an affair with him. I knew him pretty well, and I never had any sense that he was in any kind of relationship at all.

"I don't believe that you killed him to protect Gavin because Grayson wasn't even interested in Gavin and had ordered me to stop investigating him. As far as I can tell, you had never even met him before last night. I honestly can't figure out why you were in his apartment in the first place, but it clearly has something to do with your boyfriend, and that's what I want to know.

"I want to know exactly how Adalet got him out of prison, who else is involved, why you got brought into the whole thing, and mostly I want to know what he had to do with my friend's murder."

Weather stared at Flannery. Her face was a mess to begin with, and now her eyes were red and swollen and damp, but she was not crying, and her jaw was set in a defiant angle.

"Agent..." She paused, not finishing the thought.

"Flannery," He said.

Weather felt the world spinning around her. She didn't know what was right anymore. She didn't know who she was or who Gavin had become. She didn't know what was going to happen to them, but she did know something. She knew why she'd been at that apartment and she decided that if this agent was going to put his cards on the table, she would do the same. Maybe he really was there to help, so she told him everything.

She told him that his boss hadn't dismissed his ideas so blanketly. That he'd been hounding her for information on Gavin. She told him that she'd agreed to meet him. She told him that when she'd called his assistant had answered and that she'd given her the address of the apartment.

Flannery frowned.

"What?" Weather said with annoyance.

"Well Weather, that's interesting because Grayson's assistant isn't a woman."

She felt confused and closed her eyes trying to remember the call.

"It's time to go," he said to her. "We have an appointment."

"Who am I going to meet now?" she said. "Is it the NSA's turn with me?"

Flannery spat out a stutter of a laugh. "No," he said. "Now, now we're going to see Gavin."

Chapter Twenty-One

October 6, 2019 7:50 A.M.

I parked the Chrysler with the blown out back window and the bullet hole in the driver's seat in the public parking lot on Main Street, just south of the railroad crossing, fed four quarters into the parking meter and walked the dozen or so paces north to the lavender purple door of Cab's Bistro.

I'd spent considerable time there growing up. Mom and dad would bring me on Sunday nights for dessert after dinner at Papa's down the street. As I got older, high school, after I'd gotten my driver's license, I would bring Weather up there. It impressed her, I thought, that I knew the owners and we seemed to get special attention from the wait staff.

I hoped that the same people still owned it, and that they would remember me all these years later. Though even if they did, I figured, I would probably wear out that hospitality today.

That morning would be my last in Chicago, or for that matter the state of Illinois, no matter how it all played out. Best case scenario I'd square things with Flannery, hopefully get him to provide some sort of mercy, say goodbye to Weather and get out of town before Maureen or her goons got to me. The tough part would be starting over. I didn't have an identity. Not a usable one anyway. No searchable name, no credit or job history. No driver's license or valid social security number.

It hadn't been an issue in the city. Maureen took care of that. She took care of money, a place to stay, took care of food, and even, as distasteful as it was, activities that kept me busy, occupied, mentally engaged.

Now I'd have none of that, and that was assuming I was able to wrap this up quickly and get away in the first place. It was equally likely that the FBI would arrest me on the spot. Part of me liked it better when I was still a mystery to Flannery. Sure, it felt good to know that someone knew I'd been telling the truth about Weather, but the one who knew, he also knew everything that came after that. Coercion or not, I'd still been a hired gun, and I didn't really think that was something that the FBI was going to just gloss over. If I was going to get out of town, it likely would involve giving Flannery the slip, after I'd had my words with Weather; assuming Flannery was bringing her in the first place.

Even that plan operated on the premise that Flannery got here before Maureen figured out where I was. If she got there first, which was honestly the most likely scenario, then it would be a very short conversation. Just me and her, and her very loud lead goodbye.

The door was locked of course. It wasn't even eight a.m., but I knew someone would be there. It takes all day to prep a from scratch kitchen. My only concern was, would it be someone I knew. I knocked hard and waited. Seconds later a rush of relief washed over me as I saw Dave, the senior bartender, walk towards the door.

I made pleasantries and a suitably convincing story as to where I'd been when he let me in. I gave the owners hugs and apologized for not having been by in so long. We caught up a bit, then I laid it on them. I asked in as conciliatory a tone as I could, if I could have a short meeting with an associate in the upstairs section.

They were kind and accommodating, allowing for my early morning meeting, but apologized and admitted that the room upstairs wasn't set up for guests. I nodded understandingly, but gently insisted, noting that I only needed one table and three chairs and that I was very sorry to be a bother. In the end they agreed and asked simply that they have time to clean up the space.

After a short drink at the bar that Dave served against his better judgment, my table was ready, and I climbed the steep wooden stairs to the small second floor space normally reserved for private parties. I sat at the table situated in the far corner of the space and selected the seat facing the stairs. I ordered another rye and bourbon blend on the rocks and a severe pinot noir with three glasses. I also asked for a buffalo carpaccio and a baked brie wedge in apricot chutney.

When I was done, I checked the load on my gun and the spare clips. My piece was down one round. The spares fully loaded. I set my weapon down on the table to my right side and covered it with a white linen napkin. Then pulled out my cigarette case and drew out a Treasurer Black and laid the case on the table to my left. I snapped open the gold Zippo and spun up the flame, bringing it to my face. A flick of my wrist and it closed. I leaned back in my chair to smoke.

* * *

8:00 A.M.

Flannery put Weather in the back seat of his SUV and closed the door. Once he was in the driver's seat he turned around and uncuffed her.

"Obviously you won't be needing these," he said.

Weather looked confused.

"It's okay," he said. "A lot has happened in the last twenty-four hours. We're getting out of here now, we're going to see Gavin, but I'm going to need some information from you on the way."

Weather just stared at him.

"I'm telling you Weather. You can trust me."

Weather opened her mouth, but nothing came out.

"Alright, I'll give you a few to get yourself together, but I am going to need you to be able to talk to me before we get there. Do you think you'll be able to do that for me?"

Weather nodded.

"Good. Now we need to get going. We're running late already."

Flannery turned forward and started the car, threw it in reverse and backed out of his spot, then dropped it into drive and sped out of the garage.

* * *

Maureen wasn't stupid, but she knew people thought she was. She had one good case, one big media trial and that gave her the name recognition to get elected. They said things like that when they thought she wasn't listening. She was a one hit wonder that didn't have the brains or talent to make it on merit alone. In all of that there was the thinnest sliver of truth. But that truth, she thought, only proved that she was smarter than all of them.

She had had one big case, and she had known how important that case was from the beginning. The local news was covering it wall to wall from the moment Gavin had been arrested. Cute white kid at a good school murders his girlfriend's lover with his bare hands in a jealous rage. It was media gold. She knew immediately that it was a career case for whoever it was assigned to. Either make it or break it; win or lose.

When the calendar came up and she drew the prosecution she was more nervous than excited. She knew that it could be the case that took her to the top, but if she lost it her career would be over.

At first the case seemed like a slam dunk. Lots of witnesses, the girlfriend wouldn't back up his story, and the mysterious evidence that Gavin kept going on about didn't seem to exist anywhere. She was going to drive this case straight to the top job. This would get her elected State's Attorney.

Then the envelope came. The brown paper envelope delivered through standard U.S. Mail. The envelope with the tape. The tape simply labeled 'Justice'. The tape that proved that everything Gavin had said was true.

She must have watched that tape a hundred times. Sitting alone in her cramped ASA office watching on a ten-year-old television strapped to a communal audio visual cart. Over and over again. Seeing the girl attacked and beaten. Watching that boy tear her clothes and touch her skin. Then seeing the camera swing and focus on Gavin. Watching as the camera fell to the floor. Hearing the crash as the attacker was thrown to the floor. Hearing the thuds of Gavin's fists slowly drove the life out of that scumbag.

She laid awake for nights thinking. If she accepted the tape, acknowledged it, made it public; she would have to drop the charges. Gavin would go free. The media would let out a collective anticlimactic sigh and she would be forgotten.

She waited days, watching the news for signs that copies had been sent to the media. Nothing. Finally, she decided. She went to her tiny office, put the tape in the bottom drawer of her Ikea desk and locked the drawer. No one else would ever know the tape existed.

She was smart. She knew what the tape meant. She knew what the case meant. She knew what she had to do to win it.

She also knew what she was doing when she let Gavin out. She knew what she was doing when she gave him a gun, and she knew what she was doing when she gave him a car. She knew precisely.

Her phone rang.

"Adalet here."

"Hello, SA Adalet, this is Sergeant Bradford. You asked for updates on the LoJack tag 5732981."

"Yes Sergeant, what do you have?"

"Ma'am, the car has moved. It's now parked at the corner of Duane Street and Main Street."

"Still in Glen Ellyn though?" she asked.

"Yes ma'am."

"Thank you, Sergeant. Please let me know if it moves again."

"Will do ma'am."

So, Gavin hadn't gone to his uncle's house, but he wasn't far. Main Street sounded like downtown. Public place. Had he been tipped off that she was coming? She couldn't see how, but best to be prepared for anything. That's what a smart person would do.

She reached forward and punched the new address into her GPS.

The car spoke back at her.

"Rerouting."

* * *

Weather pressed her shoulder awkwardly against the ceiling of Flannery's SUV as she climbed into the front seat. They had just left the city limits and Flannery said it was safe to be seen.

"I think it'll feel less like an interrogation if you're up here with me," he said.

So, Weather negotiated her way through the moving vehicle to the front seat rather gracelessly.

"Where are we going?" she asked.

"A place Gavin knows," Flannery said. "Someplace downtown Glen Ellyn."

"Cab's?"

"Uh, yeah. That's it," Flannery nodded and glanced at her with a smile.

"Agent Flannery," Weather said with an audible edge in her tone. "I don't want to sound ungrateful, but, well, if we're trying to stay under the radar, I really can't walk into a restaurant dressed like this."

Flannery glanced at her again. Still bruised, still blotchy with patches of rusty dried blood, still in orange prison clothes.

"Shit, you're right."

"Can't we meet him somewhere else?" she asked.

"No, not really," he said. "Gavin chose this place for a reason. He needs a public place, but a place he can trust. Someplace he feels in control, and a place where we can talk. Plus, Maureen's on her way too, and she's got a head start."

"Maureen who?" Weather asked, sounding like she was losing her grip.

"Adalet. SA Maureen Adalet."

Weather stared at Flannery confounded.

"Her? Why is she on her way? Is she coming to arrest him

again? Which, by the way, how is he out? And actually, Agent Flannery, what the fuck is going on?"

Flannery pulled off the interstate at Roosevelt Road and slowed to a stop at a red light. He looked over at Weather with a grim face.

"Actually Weather, that's what I was hoping you could tell me."

* * *

Stacy hung up the phone having told the FBI quartermaster to keep an eye on Flannery's GPS tag and to push updates of its location to her cell. As of this moment it was heading west on Roosevelt Road through the western suburbs.

Gavin was at home, she thought. At his uncle's place. The closest thing he had to home anyway. That must be where Flannery was headed. She wondered if he was going to arrest him or help him.

Stacy had been as surprised as anyone to find out that Gavin was alive and out of prison. She had felt bad when he was arrested for the murder of that loser at the party, but she also felt a little like he had it coming. He had been such an idiot, leaving her for that slut Weather. She had just wanted him to see that. That's why she'd sent the boy at the party to pick her up, why she'd given him the camera.

Josh had been obsessed with her. He said he loved her, but she knew the truth, he just wanted to get in her pants. They all did. Boys were amazing in their single-minded stupidity. The fact that they thought girls couldn't see through it just made it more egregious. As soon as Gavin had tried to break up with her Josh had been all over her. He told her he would treat her better, love her better, give her everything she wanted. He didn't seem to get it, what she wanted was Gavin.

She'd known Gavin was at the party with his little whore, she'd seen them walk in together arm in arm. It was how she used to walk with him. It's where she belonged. Josh had been standing with her trying to convince her to go back to his room on the second floor. When they saw Gavin and Weather come in, he'd said, "I hope she cheats on him and he finds out. He deserves it."

That's when the idea had come to her. She'd given him the drugs and the camera. Told him to get her in bed and get it on tape. Told him if he did that for her, she'd go out with him, but the coked-up jock wannabe had been a little more aggressive than she had expected. But that didn't change the fact that Weather was a slut and Gavin needed to know it.

She honestly didn't expect Gavin to walk in on them. She figured that a day or so after the party the tape would find its way to Gavin, he'd see her cheating on him, and finally dump her like the skank she was. The fact that he found them and freaked out the way he did complicated things a little bit beyond her control. She had tried her best to help him out of it. She had grabbed the camera from the room and sent the tape of the incident to the SA's office, but they didn't seem to think anything of it because it never showed up at the trial.

She was surprised when the jury came back with a guilty verdict. Surprised, but stuck. She couldn't get involved. She didn't need a mark like that on her record, didn't need to be a named individual in a murder investigation. She had big plans. Goals. She had a future ahead of her, and something like this would only make those goals more difficult, maybe even impossible to achieve.

She did keep track of Gavin of course. She knew where he was serving his time, knew when his parole opportunities would come up. She always knew when she'd be able to see him again, and she knew that when he got out, he'd be so sorry that he ever made the mistake of leaving her. She knew he'd come back to her and beg her to take him back, and they'd be together again, forever this time.

Then she got the news that he'd been killed. She'd heard that he was stabbed in prison during some kind of argument. She was so angry at him for that. So angry that he let that happen, that he had once again taken away their chance to be together.

She had tried to get past him. She enrolled at Quantico for FBI training. She had a series of affairs with other cadets and then professors. Men and women. When those affairs didn't go anywhere, she would break them off in angry and often public scenes forcing faculty to distance themselves from her by removing her from their classes with high marks. She ultimately graduated at the top of her class and got a prestigious post right out of the gate.

She enjoyed her job and was excellent at it, but she always seemed to find her way into bed with her superiors. When the affairs would inevitably fail, she would be promoted and transferred away to a new assignment. Eventually she found herself being promoted to Assistant Director under an old prudish nasty woman who seemed to dislike her as much as the feeling was mutual.

She pulled her weight in her new role, but she began to once again feel the weight of loneliness. That was, until she met Grayson.

She encountered him in a meeting just before he left for his assignment in Chicago. It was a staffing meeting; they were discussing the human resources to be assigned to him for his corruption task force. He was good looking and successful. He was neither a superior, nor a direct report of hers, and she found that lack of a power differential both new, and exciting.

She took him home that night and fucked him three times.

They were both made of jelly when the sun came up in the morning. She knew that she had found the right man. The man that would be able to replace Gavin in her heart.

Their courtship was sporadic. Grayson was living in Chicago on his assignment, and she was in Washington D.C. She did her best to find frequent, and often ludicrous reasons to make trips to Chicago to see him, and he came to D.C. monthly for his assignment reports to the Director's office. Whenever they were together, they fucked like crazy people. Hours long sessions followed by short meal breaks and then more sex. She could tell they were getting closer, becoming more and more dependent on each other. She knew it was going somewhere important.

It was at one of his debriefs that he first mentioned Gavin. It was a side note about a possible disciplinary issue he was having with one of his agents. The agent was continuing to spend time and agency resources on a lead that Grayson thought was probably a no go, despite being told directly to drop it and find another avenue to pursue.

When asked to elaborate on the lead, Grayson explained that it was a Chicago urban legend about a guy named Gavin Gayle who records showed died in prison, but whom many believed was actually out acting as a vigilante arm of the Chicago P.D.

Stacy hadn't heard much past Gavin's name. She couldn't believe that he was alive. She couldn't believe that he was out. But mostly, she couldn't believe that he hadn't come to find her. That he hadn't come to apologize for his mistake. Hadn't come to beg her to forgive him and take him back.

She left the meeting without Grayson and went back to her apartment to do some research off of the FBI network. Maybe it was because she was from Chicago and knew how that city thought, or maybe it was because she really was a better investigator, either way, she was able to track down Gavin's story much faster than Agent Flannery.

She figured out the connection to Adalet immediately. All it took was looking at crime reports occurring in the three months prior to Gavin's supposed death. Cross reference that with names of people who would have the resources, not only to fake his death and get him out of prison, but to then cover it up in official documents. Adalet stood out like a sore thumb.

Add to that the seemingly similar circumstances of her daughter's attack with Gavin's story about Weather and it was an obvious connection. That had been easy, but with a little more work she had been able to suss out even more.

She knew who owned The Club that Adalet had dumped Gavin at. She knew that before she knew he was even there. She had done some digging into Adalet and discovered that squeaky clean Maureen had a half-brother that was doing time for trafficking drugs through an underground club he owned. This brother's name was Jake Hartwell, the same man that the paperwork said had killed Gavin in prison. She pulled his documents and found that his will named Adalet, and some guy called Simons as the beneficiaries of The Club's deed should he die while in prison. A short one-night stakeout confirmed that Gavin had set up shop out of The Club.

She followed him around for a few days. She saw that he drove a car with fake DMV registration data. It was registered to Leroy Brown, like from the song.

She dug up the medical records from the GSW trip to Stroger, found out about the jobs Adalet had him do and the little gifts he got after each job was finished. She knew all of it. She knew, and she thought, and she decided to let him go. To let him be.

She let him go because she had Grayson now. Never mind Gavin. Never mind his mistakes and his slut girlfriend Weather.

She had Grayson now, Grayson had her. She had Grayson and she didn't need Gavin anymore.

* * *

8:15 A.M.

"I have no idea who she is," Weather said defensively.

Flannery sighed.

"I promise, this isn't a setup. Somehow she's important to this whole situation."

Weather pulled her lips back and shrugged.

"Sorry, I don't know any DeBruin."

"Okay," Flannery said. "Maybe you don't, but what about Gavin? What about back in school? Do you remember him knowing anyone back then?"

Weather looked helpless and shook her head.

"Gavin didn't really know anyone. He was kind of a loner. Not in the messed-up school shooter kind of way, he just didn't have a lot of friends."

Flannery sighed and turned right onto Baker Hill Drive, winding behind the school for the blind and then turning right onto Route 53 before jumping onto Bryant Avenue.

"Where are we going?" questioned Weather. "This isn't the way to Cab's"

"Well," Flannery sighed. "Like you said, you can't very well walk into a restaurant looking like that, and I can't exactly walk you into a department store either. Not out here. So, I guess we're going to have to depend on the kindness of others."

Weather looked out the windshield, then jerked her head towards Flannery.

"Oh no. No no no no no. No, that's a bad idea."

"I don't think we have a choice," Flannery said.

270

"They'll never help me! They might just call the cops right there on the spot."

"I'll be with you. Don't worry. It'll be fine. I'm sure it won't be as bad as you think."

Weather stared at him in horror, and then, white as a ghost, looked out her passenger window as Flannery pulled his SUV up in front of Gavin's uncle's house.

Flannery and Weather stood on the green porch in front of Kevin Gayle as he inspected them up and down.

"Sorry to intrude on you at this time of the morning Mr. Gayle," Flannery said.

Weather stared at her toes.

"Mm hmm," Kevin said. "A little surprised to see you," Kevin said in a soft voice.

Weather looked up into his eyes, then back at the ground.

"Yes sir," she said.

"Did you do it?" Kevin asked her.

"I'm sorry, what?" she asked, a little shocked. "Did I do what?"

"Come on Weather. I watch the news. Did you kill that man?" he said flatly.

Weather looked at Flannery for help.

"She did not, Sir," he offered. "She hasn't done anything wrong."

Kevin raised his eyebrows.

"Oh, hasn't she? You let my nephew go to prison, didn't you? You did do that."

She looked at Gavin's uncle and ran her fingers through her sticky hair.

"Look Sir, lots of people have made mistakes, and right now we're trying to fix a big one, but Weather needs to clean up a bit.

She could use a shower and some clean clothes, and we're in a bit of a hurry."

Kevin stared at them hard, motionlessly, like a stone wall. Weather shrunk slightly and moved to turn around, but Flannery grabbed her by the shoulder and held her in place. The standoff created an air pressure that made Weather's ears pop.

Silence.

Then.

"Yeah, okay," Kevin said like he, himself, was coming up for air. "Do you remember where the master bathroom is?"

Weather nodded.

"I'll have Kristen pull some clothes for you."

Kevin stepped aside and Weather slunk into the house and disappeared across the living room.

"Is he going to be okay?" Kevin asked with just a tinge of worry in his voice.

Flannery looked up in confusion.

"I'm sorry, is who going to be okay?"

"Gavin," Kevin said. "I don't need the details; I just need to know he's going to be okay."

Flannery felt a flush of shock wash across his face then pushed it back down.

"Sir-" he started but didn't have time to finish.

"I'm not stupid Agent," Kevin said. "I don't know what's going on, but I have an idea it's been going on for a while. I notice things and I'm smart enough to put two and two together, like when Gavin supposedly died in prison. There was too much information released. The prison isn't going to give us the level of details they did. I'd expect to be notified, maybe, but the circumstances, no. No way, they'd be setting themselves up for a lawsuit."

Flannery nodded, mouth half open.

"Okay, so..."

"So, he's into something. They tell me he's dead, and now I have a Fed at my doorstep toting along Weather, all bloody and beaten and in prison scrubs. I don't know what's been going on, but I'm the only family that boy has, and I want to know that he's going to be okay."

Flannery gave a long sigh.

"That, sir, is very much still in the air," he admitted. "There are some powerful people who would be better off if he was out of the picture, and we still have a few pieces of the puzzle left to put together."

Kevin's shoulders fell and he took on a look of genuine worry.

"Well, we won't tell my wife that, okay?"

Flannery nodded.

"Is there any way I can help?" Kevin asked.

Flannery looked at him with a frown, then suddenly raised his eyebrows.

"Actually," he said. "Did Gavin ever mention anyone named Stacy DeBruin to you?"

Kevin looked at Flannery and laughed out loud.

*   *   *

Weather dried herself with the soft oversized towel that Kristen had laid out for her in the bathroom. She wrapped it around herself and stepped out of the bathroom into the large master bedroom. Kristen was sitting on the bed in the middle of the room waiting for her.

"I have some makeup for you if you'd like to do something about that eye."

Weather smiled weakly.

"Thanks."

Kristen stood up.

I pulled out this dress, it should fit you pretty closely and it'll work without underwear since, I assume, you'd rather not borrow that."

Another weak smile.

Kristen looked at her with sad eyes.

"It's not true right?" she said. "What the court said about Gavin. He didn't just kill that boy. He really was protecting you right?"

Water pooled at the corner of Weather's eyes and she quickly wiped it away. She nodded.

"Why didn't you say something?" Kristen asked. "How could you let that happen to him?"

The water pooled faster now, and she couldn't wipe it fast enough. It began running down her cheeks.

"There has to be a reason Weather, if he was helping you why wouldn't you help him?"

"I," she sobbed. "I don't know."

The door to the bedroom burst open and Flannery fell into the room.

"Weather, we gotta go!" he ordered.

Weather clutched the towel wrapped around her.

"What is it?"

"I have a feeling we're not the only ones who know where Gavin is."

Flannery darted out of the room and Weather turned back to Kristen who was standing with her arms stretched straight out holding a long black dress and a makeup bag.

Chapter Twenty-Two

October 6, 2019 8:46 A.M.

"She was his college girlfriend," Flannery said, putting the SUV in drive and peeling away from the curb in front of the big yellow house on Duane.

"What?" Weather said in shocked disbelief. "That can't be right, he didn't have-" she cut herself off. A cold shiver of remembrance climbed up her back and dug its fingers into her neck. "Oh-" she gasped.

"It wasn't long," Flannery said as if apologizing for Gavin. "According to his uncle it was a short fling right after he got to school."

Weather nodded.

"Yeah," she said. "The boy, Josh Miller, the one who drugged me and tried to-" she gagged on a sob. "The one Gavin- who he," she couldn't get the words out. "He told me. He said Gavin had been with someone else. It's how he got me to take the..." she trailed off.

"You knew he's been seeing someone else?"

She shook her head.

"No, not at first. He never told me. Then the boy at the party said-" her breath quivered, and she sobbed. "I asked Gavin after. That first day when he was in lockup. He didn't say anything, but I could tell from his face it was true. It was the last thing I ever said to him."

"Weather it's-"

"No Agent Flannery, it's not. He did nothing wrong. I told him to see other people while we were apart. I was the one who broke us up before he went to college. I insisted, but deep down I didn't think he would. I knew he loved me, real love, and it was more than I was ready for, so I made him promise. It was really to get myself off the hook, so I could have fun and enjoy my last semester at high school. The irony is," she took a moment to wipe tears from her eyes. "I never did. I didn't get together with anyone that semester, and he-" another choke.

Flannery took his eyes off the road for a moment to look at her. He put his hand on her shoulder as he turned back to the road.

"Weather, he loved you a lot, and I think he still does. And ya know what else, I think you love him too."

She nodded silently.

"So, we're going to go get him now, okay? We're going to get him and go somewhere safe because right now we're far from it."

Weather pointed across the dashboard and out the windshield.

"There it is, Agent. That's Cab's"

Flannery looked at the small black storefront with the purple door. It looked quiet and plainly elegant. He turned the wheel and the SUV took a wide left turn onto Main Street. He pulled up to the curb and cut the engine.

"Okay Weather, are you ready for this?"

"It doesn't really matter," she said. "It's time. It's been time for thirteen years."

* * *

I heard the voices before I saw her face. His was stern and official sounding, hers was light and delicate like a wounded bird. Dave directed them upstairs. Then footsteps, across the dining room and up the steep staircase. Flannery appeared first but said nothing. He simply gave me a kind smile and stepped aside revealing Weather behind him.

She was a woman now. Her body grew out of the floor and swayed elegantly in a long translucent black cocktail dress that clung to her in all the places you'd want it to. Her body didn't contain a single straight line and her hair glowed softly, falling elegantly past her shoulders and bouncing gently as she moved. Her fingers were long and delicate with fire red nails and perfect rounded tips. Her eyes were whirlpools of deep brown that gleamed in the morning light of the space.

I tried to hold it together, but my shell fractured and fell apart almost immediately. I felt my face shrivel and tears push their way from the corners of my eyes. My heart stopped and I felt a giant ache build in my chest. She was perfect, exactly as she had always been. Clean and smooth and delicate with the strongest will I'd ever seen in a person. She stood slender, backlit by the sun streaming through the restaurant's windows below; it made her look like Audrey Hepburn in Breakfast at Tiffany's.

"Hello Gavin," she said sweetly with the slightest quiver in her voice.

I burst into sobs. Tears cascading from my eyes like an overful bathtub. My body shook and I struggled for breath. I tried to say something, to apologize for everything, to make her understand what had happened but all that came out were childlike wails.

She walked across the tiny room and slid gracefully into the seat next to me. She put her arms around me and squeezed with the gentleness that comes from pure love. She squeezed me and rubbed small soft circles on my back with her hand. She held me like that until I could breathe again, then she took my chin in her hand and lifted my eyes to hers.

"I'm sorry," she said, and I felt my body wrack with guilt. My bloody aching ribs were crushed under the weight of my own shame and I felt the avalanche of tears crest over my eyelids again. She was apologizing to me. I was the only one who had done anything wrong. And I'd done so much wrong, over and over and over again, and here was an angel holding me in her arms and apologizing to me.

Flannery sat down across from us and poured cold water on the reunion. "Sorry to have to do this, but we're going to have to make this part fast"

* * *

8:59 A.M.

Maureen turned off of Roosevelt Road onto Main Street in Glen Ellyn and headed north. The LoJack on Gavin's car was just about a mile ahead of her now and she was ready to get this over with. There would be considerable clean up after it was over. She had to put her dog down and she didn't have the luxury of doing it in her own house. Trying to clean up a murder outside her jurisdiction was going to be a problem, but she didn't have time to worry about that now. She would figure out the clean up after the task was done. Something would come to her, something always did.

She passed block after block of nice suburban homes. Some large, some not so much, but all clean and well kept. She thought for a moment how nice it might be to live in a quiet community like this, outside the city, outside the crime and abuse. All the little things that asked you, demanded you to bend your morals just a little bit. Each little bend adding and compounding until you didn't even recognize yourself in the mirror.

She passed a community center and then crossed into a quaint and charming downtown. The streets were quiet and clean, and the shops were all spotless and inviting. There was a corner drug store, a wide locally owned hardware store, a huge shoe store that wasn't part of any chain she'd ever heard of and at least half a dozen little restaurants. Gavin's car was here somewhere, on this little street that she doubted had ever seen any real trouble. The question was which of these shops was Gavin hiding in. It didn't take her long to figure it out.

At the end of the block in front of a small French bistro was the large unmistakable presence of a government issued GMC Suburban. It guarded the door to the place called Cab's like a steel Centurion. Clearly that's where Gavin was, the problem was he apparently wasn't alone. Cleaning up his execution outside the safety of her city was one thing. Making that happen with a Federal Agent as a witness or, almost certainly worse, another victim was another thing altogether. Another thing that might just be outside of her capabilities.

She parked her car and stepped out making sure she had the loaded revolver in her purse, then she crossed the street and stepped up onto the pristine smooth sidewalk.

"Nice town," she said to herself, and walked down to the front door of the restaurant.

* * *

9:03 A.M.

Stacy was surprised when she saw that the address the GPS was taking her to was in the commercial rather than residential neighborhood. She had expected Gavin would retreat to family, to someplace he felt safe. Visiting a store didn't seem like the logical choice. On the other hand, if he thought someone was coming for him, then maybe it made total sense. She parked on the street in front of Soukup's Hardware, a large local hardware store displaying snowblowers in the front windows.

She took a deep breath. There was a lot to think about, but thinking wasn't something she was in the mood to do. Everything had gone to shit and all she wanted to do was fix it and get her life back. Gavin had been hers and then that bitch Weather took him. Then she had Grayson, and boom, somehow, she shows up and steals him too! How the fuck had that happened. Now it was time to make things right again. Walk in there and get Gavin back. Just tell him it was all a mistake and they could still be together.

The tables had turned. Weather was in prison and Gavin was free. No Weather, no Grayson, just the two of them and the chance for the happiness they should have had all along. A chance to start over. She felt the excitement wash over her as she stepped from her car and headed to the restaurant to get back her man and the life she deserved.

* * *

"Your ex is on her way I think," Flannery said.

I looked at Weather, she gave me a sad smile.

"I-"

"It's okay," she said softly. "Gavin, it's okay. It was a long time ago."

The tears started working at the corners of my eyes again, trying desperately to break free.

"Guys, we need to move this conversation to the"

"Jesus Gavin, how many exes do you have?"

The voice was tinny and hollow. We all looked up as one unit. Maureen stood at the top of the stairs shaking with a manic anger I had never seen in her before. She raised her right arm and pointed a gleaming nickel-plated revolver at my chest and pulled back the hammer.

"Maureen," I gasped.

"SA Adalet?" Flannery was startled and confused.

"Yeah, sorry you had to be here for this part, Agent. Really. No one wants to have to do the laundry in front of strangers, but I have this rabid dog I have to put down and sadly, it has to be now."

Weather's face was ghost white and I could feel her trembling next to me. My hand left hers and moved onto the napkin covering my piece. Maureen wasn't having any of it. Her gun shook and she poked the air between us with it.

"No no no no no," she said. "Give it here. Don't even or I'll put down your little girlfriend first.

I froze.

"Give it give it give it give it give it," she spat. "Leave the napkin on top and push the whole thing off the table."

I did as I was told.

"Maureen," Flannery whispered. "What are you doing? Think about this. You have a family, a daughter. You can't do this and walk away. I'm a federal agent. If you do this your life is over-"

* * *

October 6, 2019 9:10 A.M.

The sound was like thunder indoors. It echoed off the walls and made my ears ring and my head pound. Maureen's throat exploded and blood sprayed across my face and Weather's. Maureen's body leaped forward and collapsed on the table; her gun sliding across the surface at us before finding the ledge and disappearing to the floor. Her body cracked the table in half before sliding back and falling to a lifeless heap on the ground. There was screaming downstairs and the sound of dishes breaking and silverware spilling on the floor, then doors opening, and slamming shut. Stacy stood at the top of the stairs with a satisfied smirk.

Flannery was on his feet, weapon drawn and aimed at his boss. Weather was alternately screaming and sobbing. Her hands were covering her face, smearing blood into her skin while her body shook like a Harley Davidson idling in neutral. I was calm, calm on the outside. Inside my heart was beating at a hundred miles an hour and my brain was trying to calculate my odds of retrieving my gun before that bitch could do anymore damage. They were small.

"Well look at this," Stacy said. "The three of us right back where we started."

I was dumbfounded. Of all the scenarios I had ever pictured for the end, of all the people I imagined I would end up facing in my final moments, this had never entered my mind. I stared at my ex-lover and tried to piece together the path that got me there.

"Stacy," I said softly. "I think you have some things confused."

She looked back at me with genuine befuddlement.

"Not at all," she said. "Look, you're back with that little slut, which what the fuck by the way," she addressed Flannery. "She was in custody. What the hell Agent. Grayson had such a high opinion of you, how did you manage to fuck this up so badly?"

Flannery took a breath, but Stacy didn't let him respond.

"And now I'm back here pointing out what a little slut she is, someone is dead, and sadly, Gavin, it looks like you're going to go back to prison."

Flannery was struggling to process what was happening. He looked at me and gave an expression of confusion, then back at his boss.

"AD DeBruin, I don't think you have a grasp of what's going on right now. We're damn near across the street from the police station, and all those folks that just ran out of here are sure to be calling 911 right now," Flannery pleaded for her understanding.

"Well that's a relief," Stacy mocked. "This here is a very dangerous man."

Flannery cringed.

"Do you have any idea, Agent, how many people he's killed in the last thirteen years?"

Weather jerked her head and looked at me in stunned horror. It sent cold shivers down my spine and I had a sick feeling beginning to grow in my belly. I glanced at her with an expression of I'll explain later, then back to Stacy.

"Stacy," I said as softly and calmly as I could. "I get it, breakups are hard, but college was a long time ago. I mean really, a long time ago. How about this," I slowly slid myself out of the booth as I spoke. "How about we just let Weather go. She didn't do anything. Let's le-"

Stacy let out a laugh like a jackal. She began swinging her gun in wide wild arcs between the three of us that still had a heartbeat.

"Didn't do anything?" She pointed the gun at Weather and shook it aggressively. "She did everything! I don't know what I ever did to her, but she's made it her life's mission to fuck with me."

I looked at Weather who was pale with bewilderment. She sat shaking and wiping at her blood splattered face and hands. Her eyes darted around the room in manic jerks and her teeth chattered like it was twenty below. She rocked back and forth in her seat and tried, it seemed, to hold her gaze on Stacy.

"Fuck with you? You crazy bitch I don't even know who you are. The only thing I even know about you is that you just killed someone, and I've got her esophagus all over my fucking lips. I never did anything to you, you, you psycho fucking cunt."

Before Stacy could process the tirade, I stepped around the table and put myself between her and Weather. The gun was pointed at my chest now and it was shaking pretty bad in her hands. Her eyes were red and glossy, and her chest rose and fell erratically. Flannery tried to pipe in.

"Director," her eyes swung over to him then back to me. "Stacy-"

Her eyes stayed fixed on mine, but her right arm swung ninety degrees to her right. The muzzle flare made my eyes squeeze shut just before the call of the weapon split my ears. I didn't hear the thud of Flannery's body hitting the wall behind him, or that of him collapsing on the floor, but when I opened my eyes they knew where to find him.

Weather screamed and I spun around just in time to see her hide herself under the table. I jerked back to Stacy who was swaying manically back and forth trying to keep the gun steady. I took a tentative step forward and she stilled, finding balance and aim.

"Stacy, I don't understand. What happened? This can't be about us. That was so long ago."

Tears drowned out her eyes and poured down her cheeks. She began heaving, trying to hold back her sobs. "It's not about us Gavin, it's about her! It's about how she's always taking everything away from me."

I shook my head. "No Stacy, she didn't take me away from you. You never had me. We had a fling. Maybe it was a mistake, but I've always loved Weather. Always, since I was a child."

Her eyes drooped and her cheeks and lips pulled tight in horror, like she was seeing a creature emerge from my face.

"A fling?" she screamed. "I was a fling? What the fuck is it with you men? You have love, and adoration. You have everything and you piss on it like it's nothing. A fling. You say that, but we could have been happy if it wasn't for her. She came and ruined everything."

"No," I said. "That's not what happened."

"Of course, it is, and then when you needed her she just discarded you like garbage. She just let you go. I tried to help you. I sent the tape to that bitch," she pointed her gun at Maureen's corpse on the floor. "I tried to do what that dumb bitch Weather wouldn't, but it didn't work, and then..." she paused trying to breathe. "And then you died. YOU DIED! And I mourned for you. Not her, me.

"And then I met Grayson. And he was wonderful and loving and kind and we were going to be together."

I took a step and she pulled the hammer back on her gun. I stopped.

"We were in love, and then SHE showed up again! That same fucking bitch from thirteen years ago. We were talking about marriage and she calls him in the middle of our conversation and suddenly I'm a fling! Again!" she screamed. "I'm not a fucking fling Gavin, I'm not some little slut that just gets used and thrown away! I'm not. She made it all fall apart again. She needed to suffer, and Grayson needed to see that I wasn't that kind of girl. And now, now all of you are going to see it. She made me kill Brandon, she made me kill his stooge over there, and now she's going to kill-"

The remaining half of the table behind me shattered into a million pieces as round after round exploded through it tearing Stacy into red and white ribbons of flesh. Her body crumpled to the ground and the detonations were replaced with a slow steady click, click, clicking.

Shaking, I turned and saw Weather balled up under the demolished table aiming Maureen's revolver at the space where Stacy had been standing, still pulling the trigger over and over and over. I wiped my face and stepped to her. She cringed and pulled away, but I knelt down and slowly took her in my arms and pulled the gun from her hands.

We sat like that, quietly weeping together on the floor for some time, I couldn't tell you how long. At some point there was a rustle and we both looked over to see Agent Flannery roll on his side, open his eyes with a moan, and sit up. There was no blood on his shirt, just a black hole where the bullet had burnt through the white fabric and embedded in the Kevlar of his vest.

"Oh my God," Weather gasped.

"Shit, I thought I'd lost you there, Agent," I concurred.

"Guys, no lie, we've got to get you out of here," Flannery wheezed.

The three of us got up, leaving everything behind but our clothes and climbed down the stairs. We headed out the back door and into the back alley of the restaurant.

"I've got to stay here to clean this up with the cops. The Feds, State Police, and Glen Ellyn PD, and probably the Chicago PD will be here soon, and they'll want answers."

"What are you going to tell them?" Weather asked.

Flannery looked defeated. He was tired and in physical pain. His shoulders hung low and his pupils were pulling in and out of focus. "I don't know," he said. "But whatever it is, you weren't here. You need to get out of here now."

I put my arm around Weather.

"Where am I going to go?"

Flannery smiled.

"Well, for starters, why don't you go see your uncle. He's been waiting thirteen years to know that you're alright."

Weather and I left the car and walked the long way back to the house on Duane. As we approached the wide yellow residence with its large white porch, I felt the familiar dread form in my stomach and the tension creep up my spine. Then, for the first time in thirteen years, I felt the soft hand of Weather find its way up my back and start to rub small circles between my shoulders. The tension melted away, and suddenly everything was fine.

Epilogue

One Month Later

Flannery called that morning around ten. The internal investigation at the Justice Department was ongoing, and would be for some time, but the cops in Glen Ellyn had washed their hands of it, preferring to reassure their citizens that the FBI was on the case. CPD was trying to sweep everything under the rug and therefore was not putting any effort into an investigation and the State Police had been ordered by the Governor to let the Feds do their job.

Weather and I had been staying with my Aunt and Uncle and keeping out of the way. We talked a lot about the events leading up to the party and about my time in prison, but we shied away from discussing the eight years since I'd been out. There was a lot to unpack there and it seemed best to let it all go. I didn't want to talk about it, or even think about it and Weather seemed fine to let it lie.

We were quick to slip back into a life together. Sometimes there are people who are like that. You can go years, or even lifetimes without seeing them, and then when you do, it's like no time has passed at all. I still loved her, even more than I did before perhaps. She said she loved me too, and I was fine believing it.

When Flannery called, he said he needed to talk to us about something important, so he was coming out to Glen Ellyn. It was less than an hour later that he arrived. He pulled up in a long sleek black Cadillac with vanity plates reading MESS RND. Weather and I looked at each other and shrugged. The agent stepped out in street clothes, jeans and a blue polo shirt that were far from his traditional garb.

"Did they fire you?" Weather asked.

Flannery frowned, then understood and laughed as genuinely as I'd ever seen anyone laugh.

"No, not yet," he said. "But things are starting to get sticky. Congress is talking about appointing a special prosecutor to look into what happened here and I think it's time for the two of you to get gone."

I shifted my weight on my feet and felt Weather grip my hand.

"Are we in danger?" she asked.

"I don't think so," he said. "But I'd rather not have you available for questioning if someone started looking in that direction. I got you papers and some starter cash, just don't tell me where you're going. I honestly don't want to know."

He held out an envelope, just like the ones Maureen used to have my orders sent over in. I cringed and looked away. Weather let go of my hand and took it. Inside were two Illinois Birth Certificates, State ID and something I hadn't had in over a decade, a driver's license. She handed mine to me and I looked at it. It was my picture, but next to it, it said Jim Walker.

"You're very funny," I groaned.

"Sorry," he said with a smile. "Apparently Leroy Brown was already taken."

"Is the car for us?" Weather asked.

Flannery smiled, "Do you think your uncle will give me a ride back to the city?"

"That won't be a problem," came the gruff voice of Uncle Kevin behind us.

We had dinner as a family that night, then Weather and I packed what little we had into the back of the 1971 Cadillac Eldorado. It was hard saying goodbye to my family, but at least this time I had the chance. Then Weather and I climbed into the car, started the engine and pointed ourselves south, unsure of where we'd end up, but sure that wherever it was, we'd be together.

The End

Acknowledgments

This book has been a long time coming, a really long time. Over the years so many people have helped me in big and small ways, and there is no way to properly thank everyone. If I've forgotten you here, know that I have not forgotten you in my heart.

Thank you to my kids: Cole, Gavin, Reilly, Coraline, Noak and Josette. You bring me joy and humility every single day. Thank you to my father for always supporting my dreams and encouraging me to keep at it even when I thought I wanted to quit. Thank you to my brother Kyle for being there for me any time with any problem writing related or not and giving this book it's final proofread.

Thank you to my teachers and mentors throughout my life, especially Deborah Barber, Sharon Kociak, Mark Ketzer, Randal Hendee, and David Rice. Without you I would not be the creative person I am.

Thank you to my friends on Twitter who've motivated me and kept me going. Special thanks to Autumn Faraday who has been a rock for me in all my creative endeavors. Mica Scotti Kole is my writing god.

Thank you to my partner Blair for her unflinching support, unencumbered criticism, and creative input. You make me a better writer, a better artist, and a better man. Thank you to Harlow and Isla for your special creative energy and for helping me laugh at myself.

Thank you to author Michael Kelso for helping me reach

past my self imposed limitations of style and genre, and for finding all the mistakes I left in the original printing of this book.

Finally, a special thank you to the two women who I consider the most influential people in my entire creative life. My mother, Linda Christiansen who gave me a love of theatre, music, and literature and my director, Alison Vesely who taught me everything, but especially how to be a professional. These amazing women are no longer with us, but I think of them both every single day.

About the Author

 Neil Christiansen is an author with a unique blend of experiences in the world of theater and audio visual production management. His journey from the stage to the world of literature is a testament to his creativity and versatility.

Neil pursued a degree in theater. This academic background instilled in him a deep appreciation for storytelling and the arts, which would later find expression in his writing.

Neil is a proud parent of six children. For Neil, family is not just a word; it's the cornerstone of his life, shaping his values and driving his creative endeavors.

"Dark White" is a reflection of Neil's passion for storytelling. Dive into the world he has crafted, and you'll discover the heart and soul of an author who knows the true power of words and the depth of human connection.

9 789898 991580 4